The Charteris Mystery

A Chief Inspector Pointer Mystery

By A. E. Fielding

Originally published in 1925

The Charteris Mystery

www.ResurrectedPress.com

Published by Resurrected Press

ISBN 13: 978-1-937022-81-5

Printed in the United States of America

Other Resurrected Press Books in *The Chief Inspector Pointer Mystery* Series

Death of John Tait
Murder at the Nook
Mystery at the Rectory
Scarecrow
The Case of the Two Pearl Necklaces
The Charteris Mystery
The Eames-Erskine Case
The Footsteps that Stopped
The Clifford Affair
The Cluny Problem
The Craig Poisoning Mystery
The Net Around Joan Ingilby
The Tall House Mystery
The Wedding-Chest Mystery
The Westwood Mystery
Tragedy at Beechcroft

RESURRECTED PRESS CLASSIC MYSTERY CATALOGUE

Journeys into Mystery
Travel and Mystery in a More Elegant Time

The Edwardian Detectives
Literary Sleuths of the Edwardian Era

Gems of Mystery
Lost Jewels from a More Elegant Age

Anne Austin
One Drop of Blood
The Black Pigeon
Murder at Bridge

E. C. Bentley
Trent's Last Case: The Woman in Black

Ernest Bramah
Max Carrados Resurrected:
The Detective Stories of Max Carrados

Agatha Christie
The Secret Adversary
The Mysterious Affair at Styles

Octavus Roy Cohen
Midnight

Freeman Wills Croft
The Ponson Case
The Pit Prop Syndicate

J. S. Fletcher
The Herapath Property
The Rayner-Slade Amalgamation
The Chestermarke Instinct
The Paradise Mystery
Dead Men's Money
The Middle of Things
Ravensdene Court
Scarhaven Keep
The Orange-Yellow Diamond
The Middle Temple Murder
The Tallyrand Maxim
The Borough Treasurer
In the Mayor's Parlour
The Saftey Pin

R. Austin Freeman
The Mystery of 31 New Inn from the Dr. Thorndyke Series
John Thorndyke's Cases from the Dr. Thorndyke Series
The Red Thumb Mark from The Dr. Thorndyke Series
The Eye of Osiris from The Dr. Thorndyke Series
A Silent Witness from the Dr. John Thorndyke Series
The Cat's Eye from the Dr. John Thorndyke Series
Helen Vardon's Confession: A Dr. John Thorndyke Story
As a Thief in the Night: A Dr. John Thorndyke Story
Mr. Pottermack's Oversight: A Dr. John Thorndyke Story
Dr. Thorndyke Intervenes: A Dr. John Thorndyke Story
The Singing Bone: The Adventures of Dr. Thorndyke
The Stoneware Monkey: A Dr. John Thorndyke Story
The Great Portrait Mystery, and Other Stories: A Collection of Dr. John Thorndyke and Other Stories
The Penrose Mystery: A Dr. John Thorndyke Story

The Uttermost Farthing: A Savant's Vendetta

Arthur Griffiths
The Passenger From Calais
The Rome Express

Fergus Hume
The Mystery of a Hansom Cab
The Green Mummy
The Silent House
The Secret Passage

Edgar Jepson
The Loudwater Mystery

A. E. W. Mason
At the Villa Rose

A. A. Milne
The Red House Mystery

Baroness Emma Orczy
The Old Man in the Corner

Edgar Allan Poe
The Detective Stories of Edgar Allan Poe

Arthur J. Rees
The Hampstead Mystery
The Shrieking Pit
The Hand In The Dark
The Moon Rock
The Mystery of the Downs

Mary Roberts Rinehart
Sight Unseen and The Confession

Dorothy L. Sayers

Whose Body?

Sir William Magnay
The Hunt Ball Mystery

Mabel and Paul Thorne
The Sheridan Road Mystery

Louis Tracy
The Strange Case of Mortimer Fenley
The Albert Gate Mystery
The Bartlett Mystery
The Postmaster's Daughter
The House of Peril
The Sandling Case: What Would You Have Done?

Charles Edmonds Walk
The Paternoster Ruby

John R. Watson
The Mystery of the Downs
The Hampstead Mystery

Edgar Wallace
The Daffodil Mystery
The Crimson Circle

Carolyn Wells
Vicky Van
The Man Who Fell Through the Earth
In the Onyx Lobby
Raspberry Jam
The Clue
The Room with the Tassels
The Vanishing of Betty Varian
The Mystery Girl
The White Alley
The Curved Blades

Anybody but Anne
The Bride of a Moment
Faulkner's Folly
The Diamond Pin
The Gold Bag
The Mystery of the Sycamore
The Come Back

Raoul Whitfield
Death in a Bowl

FOREWORD

The period between the First and Second World Wars has rightly been called the "Golden Age of British Mysteries." It was during this period that Agatha Christie, Dorothy L. Sayers, and Margery Allingham first turned their pens to crime. On the male side, the era saw such writers as Anthony Berkeley, John Dickson Carr, and Freeman Wills Crofts join the ranks of writers of detective fiction. The genre was immensely popular at the time on both sides of the Atlantic, and by the end of the 1930's one out of every four novels published in Britain was a mystery.

While Agatha Christie and a few of her peers have remained popular and in print to this day, the same cannot be said of all the authors of this period. With so many mysteries published in the period, it is inevitable that many of them would become obscure or worse, forgotten, often with no justification than changing public tastes. The case of Archibald Fielding is one such, an author, who though popular enough to have a career spanning two decades and more than two dozen mysteries has become such a cipher that his, or as seems more likely, her real identity has become as much a mystery as the books themselves.

While the identity of the author may forever remain an unsolved puzzle, there are some facts that may be inferred from the texts. It is likely that the author had an upbringing and education typical of the British upper middle class in the period before the Great War with all that implies; a familiarity with the classics, the arts, and music, a working knowledge of French and Italian, an appreciation of the finer things in life. The author has also traveled abroad, primarily in the south of France, but probably to Belgium, Spain, and Italy as well, as portions of several of the books are set in those locales.

The books attributed to Archibald Fielding, A. E. Fielding, or Archibald E. Fielding, are quintessential Golden Age British mysteries. They include all the attributes, the country houses, the tangled webs of relationships, the somewhat feckless cast of characters who seem to have nothing better to do with themselves than to murder or be murdered. Their focus is on a middle class and upper class struggling to find themselves in the new realities of the post war era while still trying to live the lifestyle of the Edwardian era. Things are never as they seem, red herrings are distributed liberally throughout the pages as are the clues that will ultimately lead to the solution of "the puzzle," for the British mysteries of this period are centered on the puzzle element which both the reader and the detective must solve before the last page.

A majority of the Fielding mysteries involve the character of Chief Inspector Pointer. Unlike the eccentric Belgian Hercule Poirot, the flamboyant Lord Peter Wimsey, or the somewhat mysterious Albert Campion, Pointer is merely a competent, sometimes clever, occasionally intuitive policeman. And unlike, as with Inspector French in the stories of Freeman Wills Croft, the emphasis is on the mystery itself, not the process of detection.

Pointer is nearly as much of a mystery as the author. Very little of his personal life is revealed in the books. He is described as being vaguely of Scottish ancestry. He is well read and educated, though his duties at Scotland Yard prevent him from enjoying those pursuits. In *The Charteris* Mystery it is revealed that he spends a week or two each year climbing mountains, his only apparent recreation. His success as a detective depends on his willingness to "suspect everyone" and to not being tied to any one theory. He is fluent in French and familiar with that country. He is, at least in the first two books, unmarried, and sharing lodgings with a bookbinder named O'Connor, in much the manner of Holmes and Watson.

One intriguing feature of the Pointer mysteries is that they all involve an unexpected twist at the end, wherein the mystery finally solved is not the mystery invoked at the beginning of the book. I leave it to the reader to judge whether Fielding is "playing by the rules" in this, but it does keep the books interesting up to the last chapter.

The Charteris Mystery is the second mystery in the series involving Chief Inspector Pointer. In it, Fielding was still developing her style and the book is centered around the activities of Pointer while the characters surrounding the mystery are not as fully developed as they are in the later mysteries. Interestingly, O'Connor, who in addition to being a book-binder is a former secret service agent takes an active role in the story, though he disappears completely in subsequent novels. As with many of Fielding's early mysteries the current political situation plays a part in the story, in this instance in the form of Italian Fascists and Bulgarian Bolsheviks.

In *The Charteris Mystery*, Pointer finds himself investigating the death of a young woman whose body is found at the bottom of a sand pit. He quickly determines that her death is not an accident from certain discrepancies in the evidence. There are the usual cast of relatives, fiancés and mysterious strangers to complicate the plot and Pointer's subsequent investigations will take him to Italy and back again before ultimately solving the mystery surrounding the death.

Despite their obscurity, the mysteries of Archibald Fielding, whoever he or she might have been, are well written, well crafted examples of the form, worthy of the interest of the fans of the genre. It is with pleasure, then, that Resurrected Press presents this new edition of *The Charteris Mystery* and others in the series to its readers.

About the Author

The identity of the author is as much a mystery as the plots of the novels. Two dozen novels were published from 1924 to 1944 as by Archibald Fielding, A. E. Fielding, or Archibald E. Fielding, yet the only clue as to the real author is a comment by the American publishers, H.C. Kinsey Co. that A. E. Fielding was in reality a "middle-aged English woman by the name of Dorothy Feilding whose peacetime address is Sheffield Terrace, Kensington, London, and who enjoys gardening." Research on the part of John Herrington has uncovered a person by that name living at 2 Sheffield Terrace from 1932-1936. She appears to have moved to Islington in 1937 after which she disappears. To complicate things, some have attributed the authorship to Lady Dorothy Mary Evelyn Moore nee Feilding (1889-1935), however, a grandson of Lady Dorothy denied any family knowledge of such authorship. The archivist at Collins, the British publisher, reports that any records of A. Fielding were presumably lost during WWII. Birthdates have been given variously as 1884, 1889, and 1900. Unless new information comes to light, it would appear that the real authorship must remain a mystery.

Greg Fowlkes
Editor-In-Chief
Resurrected Press
www.ResurrectedPress.com

CHAPTER ONE

The conversation, judging by what he heard of it as he sauntered up to the east lounge, did not threaten any great demands on his brains.

"All I know is that cricket's jolly good for the liver," Arthur Bond was saying earnestly.

"It is really," echoed Cockburn.

"Isn't it!" agreed Rose absent-mindedly, as, with an apology, she cut open a letter that had just come for her.

"And it doesn't have to be first-rate cricket, either," Bond ruminated. He was a pretty boy, with a girlish face that amused his friends, and misled his acquaintances.

"Not a bit," chimed in Cockburn, the elder of the friends by ten years. The Honourable John Cockburn could not by any stretch of affection be called handsome, but he had a pleasant, freckled face, lit by a pair of eyes which were very steady and observant, though their colour might be indeterminate.

Sibella gave her throaty laugh.

"Hush—h! If you say such brilliant things, Mr. Thornton'll crib them for his book."

"I wasn't saying anything brilliant," protested Bond ingenuously. Then, after he had shaken hands with Thornton, he turned to their host.

"I really ought to've phoned you before blowing in like this, but the Chief was so sure the professor would still be here—"

"My brother-in-law's a will of the wisp. Quite a respectable variety, of course, but as uncertain."

"He's dancing around Genoa just now," Sibella announced idly, "to keep to your simile, dad."

"Milan, my dear, Milan!" corrected her father shortly.

"In this note father speaks of having been in Genoa." Rose replaced a half-sheet in a long envelope, drew out a sealed enclosure, glanced at the address, doubled it up in her little handbag, and turned again to the table.

Cockburn thought that the colonel looked vexed. An old scar on his forehead blazed a bar of crimson. A sign of anger. Yet he could hardly be annoyed with the girls for knowing where the professor was. But already the colonel had puzzled him on the courts. Generally a fine player—to-day! Cockburn eyed him as he cut a cigar unevenly, and decided that something was up. It was not Colonel Scarlett's habit to chip a Corona like that. Nor to hold it so tightly that it leaked. Nor to smoke it at a pace which would turn it into an overheated cabbage stalk.

"Of course you'll stay the night," Rose said hospitably. She was pouring out tea. "Oh, I insist." Professor Charteris had one wing of Stillwater House, and Rose had a free hand in it. The two young men, however, glanced at the colonel. His eyes were on his cigar.

"Sorry," Cockburn said at once, "next time we'll be delighted"

"Well, you must stay for dinner," she insisted, "and for bridge afterwards."

They thought they might venture thus far, uncle or no uncle.

Again the bar of red showed in the colonel's face. He, who was supposed to be one of the most hospitable of men! He said with seeming, heartiness, however, "Your bridge'll be a perfect godsend. I never can understand how a clever chap like Thornton can call a hand as he does. He'd go three no-trumps on one guarded knave."

"Not I!" Thornton protested "I don't say what I might not do, if, like most people, I weren't restrained by the fear of what comes after. You, Colonel, are the 'what comes after' at cards."

"Do you think fear is a deterrent?" di Monti asked suddenly.

Thornton maintained that in many cases it was the only one.

"Well, perhaps with you here in England. With us in Italy—no! If a man wants to commit a crime, does he care that he endangers his own life? Not a bit. What he wants is revenge. Revenge!" The word rang out. "And he takes it!"

"With our poachers it's only fear of us J.P.'s that keeps them under." The colonel spoke as though trying to turn a distasteful subject.

"Especially as in their case there's no difficulty about the disposal of the—what shall we call it—body or booty?" Thornton put in idly. The colonel got up suddenly.

"Mind if I open the window a little?" he asked, and stepped on through it, stepped so hastily that Rose looked after him wonderingly.

Thornton found no chance of speaking to di Monti till tea was over. He solved the problem by drawing a chair up close to the gate that opened into the drive. Presently the purr of a large car caught his ear. It was the count driving away in his Alfa Romeo. He was due at a meeting of the London Facista.

Thornton stepped out down the drive and opened the gates. Mrs. Bennet could be heard in the lodge trying to hand out impartial, but hasty, justice to a couple of squabbling children.

Di Monti got out for a light, and they stood discussing the car's points. Then the conversation drifted around to the professor.

"His departure so unexpected is annoying," di Monti said crossly; "it delays the announcement of my engagement to Miss Charteris."

"My most hearty congratulations. Has it got so far as that?"

Di Monti stared at him. "Well, I suppose!"

"I'd no idea. With us, girls have so much freedom nowadays," Thornton replied easily.

"It is not a question of freedom," the Italian said haughtily, and Thornton thought how cold his eyes were, in spite of the slumbering fires deep within them. "It is merely a question of announcing the engagement."

"Always supposing the young lady doesn't change her mind meanwhile." Thornton spoke casually. "Such things do happen."

Di Monti made no reply. Thornton glanced at him, and then glanced again. He made no mistake. He was looking into the face of what could be a most dangerous man.

"Such a thing does not happen to a di Monti" Cangrande spoke slowly, very slowly. "I possibly do not understand your meaning aright."

"I have none, beyond a general one that it's so easy for foreigners to think an English girl means more than she does. Or shall we say that her words and actions mean less than he might think. I have seen some awkward incidents."

"And you will certainly see one more, if—but I must not detain you. The evening is too fine to waste in generalities which do not apply to what we are discussing."

Di Monti had his voice under control, but the car leapt at his touch, and Mrs. Bennet, who had come out to do her duties, ever after maintained that the Italian had deliberately tried to murder her.

Thornton took up his book again, feeling that he had done all he could to prepare the man for the blow which was to come. He began to understand a little of Rose's feeling. She, and possibly—yes, quite possibly—her father, might be in for a very unpleasant time. However, Rose could be trusted to choose the easiest going.

He sauntered down to the hard courts later.

"I did my best with your kinsman," he said half ruefully, sitting down beside Rose.

"Don't call him, that!" she begged with some warmth. "He's no kin of mine! Of Sib.'s, yes. She's quite Italian, but I'm not."

"No, you're Greek. You're Circe's daughter." He shook his head at her.

"How old would that make me?" She looked at him under the long lashes, straight and golden, which framed her eyes like the rays of a star. "Do you think two thousand years would be about right?"

"The professor's lovely daughter carries off the prize," he announced with a bow. She laughed with him, then her face clouded.

"Unfortunately, Cangrande won't turn into anything so simple—and so useful—as a mere pig. And he's sure to think that father—or some one else—" With a little nip of her perfect mouth that made her look years older, Rose turned away in answer to a call.

Wilkins, the chauffeur, was surprised that Miss Scarlett decided to drive herself, in her own little two-seater, to the concert. As a rule, she was nervous of night driving. If Mrs. Lane wondered at the car, and the whim, she made no comment.

When they were nearly into Medchester, Sibella turned to her.

"You asked me to put you down at Jephsons' for some book or other, didn't you? Do you mind if I don't wait for you? It's only a step from there to the town hall, and I've a visit to pay before the concert. I may be a bit late. If so, I shan't trouble to join you in front, but I'll find a seat farther back. We can meet in the lobby afterwards, if not before."

Sibella stopped the car. Mrs. Lane, got out and shut the door. She went on into the shop, looking as though the arrangement suited her too excellently. Sibella waited a moment, then turned the car, and pressed the accelerator. Like a bird she darted away through the evening light. The concert was from nine to eleven o'clock. It was over when Mrs. Lane, waiting in the little portico, saw Sibella again. She was coming out with an elder woman, who was laughing at something that the girl was saying.

"Wasn't it splendid" Sibella turned away to Mrs. Lane. "But I thought they took that Third Movement much too fast. It's a mistake to try and copy Kussevitsky's tempo."

They were out on the steps now. Their car was parked to one side. As they walked to it, a lad ran up

"Miss Scarlett! Miss Scarlett!"

Sibella turned.

"Oh, it's our newspaper boy. Well, Tommy?"

"Your handkerchief, miss. You dropped it just now when you ran into the hall." He held out a wisp of lawn.

"Thank you. But hardly just now,'" Sibella said in a laughing aside to her companion.

Mrs. Lane gave her one of her thoughtful, considering looks.

It almost seemed to her that the girl was rouged. And that her eyes shone like fire-flies in the dark of the night, but again she made no comment.

Bond looked up from his cards to say heartily, "This is better than a stuffy concert hall, what?"

He, Cockburn, and Colonel Scarlett were playing bridge with Thornton in the latter's cottage.

Suddenly there came an interruption. Cockburn, who was dummy, and like every other dummy, took a turn through the gardens while the hand was being played, stuck his head hurriedly through one of the long, open windows.

"I say! I heard a rifle shot over in the lane. Come on, you fellows! Let's see what's wrong."

The interruption was most welcome to Thornton, who had allowed himself to be goaded into calling four hearts, and had been left to rustle for them with the help of a Yarborough. He happened to glance at the colonel as he jumped up. So did Cockburn. Both men saw a look of fear leap into Scarlett's eyes, and saw him crush it down as he might have a dangerous spark as he, too, made for the door.

"Where did it come from?" asked Bond, hard on his friend's heels.

"Somewhere over the other side of the orchard. I—" Cockburn fell sprawling into a flower bed—"shouldn't wonder if it's a row between some poachers and a keeper."

As he picked himself up, he turned towards the colonel, whose feelings about poachers were well known.

"Or Mrs. Viney's pug burst at last," Bond called back, as the colonel made no reply. "She lives across there."

They found the lane deserted, but Cockburn insisted on searching every foot of road and hedge, till they worked around to the main gates of Stillwater again.

"There's nothing to catch here except a wetting. A downpour is coming." The colonel seemed to have suddenly regained his good humour.

In the face of such matter-of-factness the excitement simmered down, and after a few more unanswered shouts, and the first heavy drops of rain, some one suggested a rush to the garage close by, and a general clean-up.

Wilkins was out, but the pump, a towel, and a little petrol repaired all damages, and chaffing the cause of the disturbance, the men returned to finish the rubber, which lasted so late that Thornton insisted on putting "Bond and Co." up for the night, since the colonel still had no suggestions to make.

CHAPTER TWO

The day after the concert was one of those wonderful spring mornings, when even the dullest man feels his kinship with the fields, and the birds, and the play of shine and shadow.

Across the grass of Medchester Common, which stretched in a sheet of clearest green, for its leopard skin of daisy and buttercup was still to come, ran Bond, with Cockburn several yards behind him. Both men were in running kit. Once, the man in the rear stopped, and called out something. But as he regularly recorded some injury every hundred yards or so, which necessitated a halt, Bond only laughed and ran on.

This time, however, an exclamation followed which made Bond wheel. The other was staring with bulging eyes and dropped jaw into a sand-pit just off the path. The look on his face made his friend come sprinting back.

"What's wrong? What's up?"

Cockburn only pointed, and Bond, following the direction of his hand, felt his own muscles slacken.

"Good God!" he breathed. Then, with a "Here! There must be a way down!" he ran around the pit, and together they slithered to the bottom, where lay the body of Rose Charteris.

She was quite dead. Her face, serene and beautiful, upturned to the periwinkle deeps above her. And compared with the utter stillness of it, the sky seemed a turmoil, the clouds a fighting army.

It was unmarred by any injury, but it lay appallingly far over one shoulder. Only a broken neck could take that position.

Cockburn picked up one little clenched hand. His reverent manner told again what both men knew.

"She's quite dead."

Bond touched it too. It was as stiff as a piece of ivory.

"I'll fetch a doctor." He bounded off as though time still had a meaning for that which lay behind him.

Cockburn took up the watch beside the shell of Rose. The sound of steps walking slowly along the road reached him. He clambered out of the pit and saw Thornton coming around a bend.

The neighbourhood seemed to keep exemplary hours. As a rule, "Bond and Co." had their morning dips and runs to themselves.

"What's the time?" Cockburn called. Then coming nearer as Thornton replied, "Six," he went on, "Miss Charteris has fallen down the sand-pit here. She's quite dead. Bond and I've just come upon her. Frightful to see her lying there."

"Dead! Miss Charteris dead!"

Glancing at him, Cockburn noticed how gray his face had grown.

Bond came running back.

"Medico's coming along at once."

A raucous horn sounded, and a two-seater stopped beside a clump of trees some yards from the path. "Morning everybody! Surely there's some mistake. Miss Charteris—" The doctor had looked into the pit. He left his sentence unfinished. Turning, he replaced his little black bag with a shake of his head, and made his way down.

"Shocking thing to've happened." He got up from beside the dead girl "She's been dead for hours. It's criminal to leave places like this unfenced. Well, I suppose we shall get our railings—now! She must have stepped off the path right over the edge. I'd better be getting along to Stillwater House to break the news. Poor—"

"Morning, gentlemen!" said a brisk voice, with a hint of breathlessness in it. The Medchester superintendent of police was not as young as he had been. "I met a young gentleman down the road—oh, there you are, sir!" This to Bond. "Ay, that's our Miss Charteris right enough. Not much chance of mistaking her for any one else" His eye took in professionally but sympathetically the still young figure and the oddly bent head "What a terrible thing to've happened. No need to ask if she's dead."

"Neck's broken. She must have gone too near the edge and fallen over."

"When do you think it happened, sir?"

But the doctor was too young a man to set an hour by the old-fashioned clock of *rigor mortis*, or temperature. He shook his head.

"Some hours ago evidently. Apparently on an early sketching expedition She's got her little outfit with her." He picked up the japanned box as he spoke.

"Has she now?" The superintendent looked more shocked than ever. "Ah, here's Briggs. Blest if he hasn't brought the broken stretcher. I'd best go back with him."

"We'll leave you to come on with the body, superintendent. But how about my car? She only holds two."

"Bond and Co." at once offered to wait for the stretcher.

"Then shall I give you a lift, Mr. Thornton? This has been a great shock even to me, and a doctor's used to death."

Thornton thanked him, and after arranging with the two friends to breakfast at Red Gates, got in.

"Sad case!" The doctor, a fair, chubby young man, started the engine at last. "Going to be married to that Italian staying down at the Medchester Arms, I understand. Though I seem to remember something about her having been as good as engaged to Bellairs, the artist, and that it was only the count's huge fortune that tipped the scale. But if one believed all one hears!"

Thornton gave his usual, non-committal nod.

"Her father's against the marriage with the count. Quite right, too," the doctor went on. "Very clever man,

Professor Charteris. He was talking to me about a synthetic-emerald company which he's going to start, on the links the other day. I mean, he was talking on the links, not going to start making 'em there." The doctor checked his laugh. "This will be a terrible blow to him. And to the ladies up at Stillwater. At least—I dunno. She and Miss Sibella weren't supposed to get on over well together lately. But you know how wide of the mark idle chatter of that kind often is. I really hope for once, though, that there may be something in it. It'll break this blow, a bit."

"I had no idea there had been any ill-feeling between the two girls," Thornton murmured truthfully. He felt like a man, rather proud of his sight, who tries on a stranger's eyeglasses, and finds his field of vision trebled.

"Of course, I don't know anything about it—I never pay attention to gossip, but they're said to've been at daggers drawn for some time past. Some say over the legacy, and some over the way Miss Charteris turned down young Bellairs before it was known how his mother was going to leave her money—after she married again, you know. I think it was over the legacy myself. Well, Miss Scarlett'll have it all now. She little thought it would come to her so quickly. But of course, if what people hint is true, and it's to do with the count! Both the girls had that hot Italian blood in them, you know. Old blood. Too old. Give me a nice English girl or woman—like Mrs. Lane, now. There's a woman for you! Nerves of steel."

"Indeed!" Thornton said politely, looking bored.

"Lots more in her than you'd think. Wonderfully taking young woman, too. I had to set a sprained wrist for her once. The rumour runs that she only has to lift her little finger to be Mrs. Scarlett the second, for all she's young enough to be the colonel's daughter. But I make a point of never listening to tittle-tattle."

"Oh?"

"Can't as a medical man, you know. Quite impossible."

There followed a little break in the impossible.

"Do you know when the professor's coming back?" Thornton thought that amid such a flood of information that item might well be washed up.

"I? Not the faintest notion! How should I have? But there's an idea about that he's off for Verona to see if a law-suit can't be avoided by a friendly settlement out of court. If you ask me, I should say that he's much more likely to see if the engagement, or whatever it is, can't be stopped. As for expecting any family, however rich, to hand over land, that's always rather a pill, isn't it? And so's my breaking the news here."

The doctor's car clanked noisily up the drive. Thornton saw one of the curtains on an upper floor twitched a little to one side. Nothing was visible of the face looking out except a pair of eyes. They were so nearly level with the window ledge that their owner must be stooping or kneeling. The strange thing was the expression in them.

Thornton called his companion's attention to something on the other side of the gardens, as they stopped with a grinding clash that would have disturbed the driver of a donkey-engine, but which left the doctor unruffled.

He himself walked on past the house. He took quite a turn in the grounds, before returning to his cottage. Mrs. Bennet, she of last night's narrow escape, was setting the breakfast table. One glance at her and he saw that she knew of the accident.

"Oh, sir, the poor young lady's just arrived! The poor young thing! To think that I warned her only last week about that path. 'Miss Rose,' I said, 'don't you believe Miss Sibella that it's so much shorter, or, if it is, it's dangerouser.' But there!"

A light knock interrupted her. It was Bond and Co.," and a very quiet breakfast followed. Mrs. Bennet's cooking conduced to silent meals, but it was not the reason this time. When the three men had lit their pipes, they strolled out into the garden. Another silence fell. Each seemed deep in thoughts that he was in no hurry to share. As usual, it was Bond who took the lead.

"You know, I'm not quite easy in my mind," he said at last in a low tone, "not at all easy! No, I'm dashed if I am!"

"Easy about what?" Thornton asked after a pause

Bond jerked his head towards the house. "Frightful end to come to a lovely girl like that, and Heaven knows I don't want to make bad worse. Yet—well, I'm not easy in my mind. There was something about the way she lay in that sand-pit. I can't put a name to it, but there was. Look here, I'm going to have another inspection of that place, and round about. Care to come, either of you?"

Thornton nodded. It was a favourite way with him of carrying on a conversation. Cockburn had already turned.

They started to walk back by the footpath. Suddenly Cockburn stopped.

"By Jove! I believe those are her very footprints before us!"

All three saw the marks of a small shoe with a low heel, just such a shoe as Rose wore, in fact, clearly marked in the damp earth. Walking carefully on the grass, they traced them until they stopped at the spot where the sand-pit ran in close to the path

"Then here's where we ought to examine a bit more closely." Bond's voice was very low.

All around them the common stretched. Close beside them on the right lay the sand-pit. Some distance to the left a copse straggled untidily. Just the usual brambles, spindly aspens, and twisted nondescripts On one of the branches a willow warbler was pouring out a little song, as perfect and as finished as his own green-and-white feathered coat. A cuckoo called from far away—melancholy, mysterious. Such sounds might have been the last that Rose Charteris's ears had ever heard.

Suddenly Bond pounced on something lying just beneath the singer. Something that glittered like a drop of belated dew. It was an amethyst bead of a beautiful full purple. Cockburn picked up a second. As he turned his find over on his palm it left a red stain.

A little thing, this bead, he thought, to possibly hang a man.

"Blood," Bond nodded to himself. "Yes—well, I felt sure that something was wrong. And here again on this little clover patch, here's blood again."

No one spoke for a tense second, then he went on.

"I don't think we ought to track up the place any more, or paw things over. I think we ought to go at once to the police."

"Surely to Colonel Scarlett first, and let him call in the police," Thornton objected.

"Every moment's of value," Bond pointed out briefly. "I don't think this is a time to stay for mere politeness."

"It's a question of common decency," Thornton spoke with warmth. "We ought to go to him first, and tell him about the beads. Not spring the police on him before the stretcher carrying his niece has more than reached the house."

Cockburn looked as though there were something to be said for this point of view. But Bond thrust out that slight, rather retreating jaw of his.

"Sorry, I don't see it that way. We might waste half the morning in talk. Look here, the superintendent seems a decent chap; let's lay the affair before him, and he can see to it that no one's feelings are unnecessarily shocked. Or why not you go back to Stillwater, and let the colonel know, while Co. and I go on to the police station?"

Thornton did not seem to care for this suggestion.

"No. I'll go on with you, since you insist on doing it this way."

The three walked to the nearby police station. And, a moment later, to the accompaniment of whiffs of kippers, the police officer they had met at the sand pit hurried into the room. He was a stout, florid man, who owed his position to the pluck with which he had stopped three bank robbers after they had killed the manager.

Now he himself was due to retire very shortly. He had done very well. He was an honest, fair-minded, kindly man. Popular, in spite of his strictness, even with the tramps that passed that way.

He listened attentively to what his three visitors had to say, looking, thoughtfully at the two beads and the tuft of clover laid in front of him. Then he turned to the telephone and rang up the doctor. There followed a quick interchange of questions and answers. Then the receiver was laid down, and Superintendent Harris turned with a smile.

"You heard, gentlemen? Doctor's perfectly satisfied that death was due to a fall from the path above into that sand-pit. I must say I share that opinion. Very likely the beads broke as she was walking along. She may have stopped to knot the string together in that copse. As for the blood, just the remains of a bunny-and-stoat tragedy, I fancy, such as you can find a-plenty among the lanes. Were the beads valuable?"

All three looked to Thornton.

"Not compared with the crown jewels, but the amethysts were of a rare colour. And the pendant, besides being an unusually fine piece of Persian lapis lazuli, well veined with gold and silver, had belonged to Cosimo de Medici. That, of course, might enormously increase its value to a collector."

"I see"—the superintendent, at any rate, tried to—"but it's not like—say, a fine diamond brooch, I mean the whole lot?"

Thornton agreed that that was so.

"Well, gentlemen," Superintendent Harris said after another pause,, "I really don't see any need to distress the family. Though I'm sure I'm much obliged to you for coming to me so promptly." And he bowed them out.

Each of the three was very distrait as they parted at the garage of Stillwater House, where "Bond and Co" got out their car. As for Thornton, he went on up the drive and rang the bell.

It was Paul, the general man-servant, who opened the door. Paul was a gentle, garrulous soul. He looked very subdued and mournful.

"Come in, Mr. Thornton, sir. I see you've heard the news. Oh, sir, what a tragedy. What a blow for the family, and especially for the professor, he being away on his holiday so to speak." Paul shut the door as though it were a coffin lid. "The colonel's not in, sir. He's just gone up to town with Mrs. Lane to see about getting into touch with the poor gentleman I'm sure I don't realise our loss yet, sir. None of us do. But having been born on the estate"—Paul always referred to Stillwater's few acres as though it were Balmoral—"finds it doubly hard."

He could not say when the colonel would be back, nor where he could be reached, and Thornton was let out again with the same solemnity. He walked slowly to his cottage, looking like a man weighing something very important, and by no means certain on which side the scales will ultimately dip. Yet evidently extremely unwilling to do—whatever he thought of doing—until he had reasoned out where the most weight should ultimately lie.

Finally he picked up a telephone book and hunted up a number. It was the number of New Scotland Yard. He asked for Detective Chief Inspector Carman. Now, as it happened, that police officer was out on a case. But scribbling a note for him in his room was a tall man in worn tweeds, with a spare, athletic figure, and a certain look of quiet competency on his sunburnt, good-looking face. A very resolute face it was, only saved from being a hard face by the kindly, wide-apart, well-opened, gray eyes. It was he who took down the receiver.

"Detective Chief-Inspector Carman? I'm afraid he's out. Friend of his, may I ask? Oh, just read of him in the morning paper; I see."

"Hullo, Pointer!" a brisk voice hailed him from another room, "I thought your leave wasn't up till day after tomorrow!"

"Busman's holiday. I had to come up for a visit to the dentist." The man at the telephone turned to the tube again.

"Are you there? Can I give Chief-Inspector Carman a message? I can't say... he may he out all day... it's Detective Chief-Inspector Pointer speaking."

There was a pause at the other end, then he heard Thornton say very slowly:

"A young lady has been found dead. I was one of those who found her. The doctor says it's an accident; the superintendent at the police station says the same; but—" Here followed an account of the beads and the tuft of grass. Then he continued, "And since thinking it over, I have an impression that there may be something wrong, and that's not a pleasant impression to have in such a case."

"Certainly not. Who is speaking? The name will be quite confidential. Thornton? Mr. Thornton of the 'Athencum' and the 'Saville'? Quite so. And the young lady? I see. Well... " There followed a pause. "Of course, as you're no doubt aware, sir, New Scotland Yard can't take a hand in any investigation unless asked by the chief constable of the county. But there are ways, of course... " Followed another pause. "Are you there, sir? I'll tell you what I'll do. Have you a car?. Good! Drive it yourself? Excellent! If you'll meet me half-an-hour from now, that's nine-thirty exactly, at—" Pointer had opened an ordnance map of Hertfordshire. He indicated a spot very close to Stillwater House. "I'll come down myself unofficially. I'm on leave and, of course, where I choose to spend it is my own affair. You write, I believe, Sir?"

The clubs mentioned made this a likely shot. Thornton said that he did, on Eastern art chiefly.

"Just so. Illustrated? Good. Then I'll come down as a draughtsman sent by your publishers to take your instructions about some new plates in your coming work."

"A most unlikely story to any one who knows publishers," objected Thornton, "but the point is to get the case cleared up. The girl's father is abroad. Her uncle's un-get-at-able in town. And one always understands that to be early on the spot is half the battle for an investigator."

Pointer agreed heartily and hung up the receiver. He proceeded to have a car sent around. He was very particular about its appearance. Just as particular as he was about his own, though Thornton did not suspect the care in either case when a battered, dirty, noisy little two-seater coughed its way around the bend at the hour set by his Scotland Yard ally. Its looks certainly suited the man who lumbered out into the road. A big depressed-looking figure, round-shouldered and shabbily dressed, with spectacles on his drooping, slightly-reddened nose.

"Mr. Thornton?" His voice suggested ill-health "I'm Brown, the man you were talking to on the 'phone just now." He coughed wheezily. "From the printers', sir. May I get in?"

"Tumble in," said Thornton, and Brown obeyed him literally, giving him a meek glance as he did so. The detective officer saw a man of about thirty-six, medium-build, dark, good looking but for an air of weariness, spiritual rather than physical. Life bored Mr. Thornton, and life is apt to resent that attitude. He had a satirical smile, and a veiled, non-committal eye.

"Keep the car away from the hedges, please," suggested the man beside him, undercover of a none too clean handkerchief, "and as you take me to the lane behind your cottage perhaps you would give me an idea of how the rooms lie in Stillwater House, especially Miss Charteris's room."

Thornton did so.

"One thing more," his companion continued, "when we get there, will you kindly make your way to outside her room and wait there on guard till I come out. If any one passes her door, just strike a match. I see you smoke. If they make as though to enter, strike a second. When I'm done with the room, I shall join you at the place where you stop your car. Of course, should I be noticed in the house, I should be simply sent by the undertakers."

Once arrived at Red Gates, the man slipped out and disappeared up a side path as though he knew the grounds by heart.

Thornton met no one as he climbed the broad staircase in the dim light of drawn blinds, and sat down on the landing: He heard no sound from within the room where they had carried Rose.

Yet the man from Scotland Yard was inside it. He was just lifting the sheet which lay over the dead girl. Her head had been straightened on the pillow, and her wrists loosely crossed, otherwise she lay very much as she had been found.

Pointer parted the beautiful hair gently. The cut on top was not deep. From his bag he took a tiny phial. Fastened to the inside of its screw top was a wire with a pad of sterilised wool at the end. He carefully swabbed the cut, going only a little way along it, so as to leave a possible trail for others. He looked, at the swab closely.

It showed what seemed like earth, and a few tiny specks of what his magnifying glass told him were bits of flower-pot ware, or possibly red tiling. He re-screwed the phial, labelled it, and dropped it into his bag. Then he rapidly examined the girl's face and dress The shoes detained him some minutes The soles at the heels showed traces of having walked in damp, sandy earth Some country lane, he guessed The bows had both been tied very carelessly, and both very much off to one side The same side. He took a small dot of the mud from. one heel and labelled its envelope. Then he cut two patterns of the soles out of paper, and put them away in his pocket.

There was a small bruise on one arm. It told nothing as to its origin, except that he did not think that it had been caused by any encircling pressure such as a grip Under both her hands, which had opened since she had been laid on the bed, for *rigor mortis* was passing off, he found some withered twigs, and what looked like tea leaves, so shrivelled were they by the icy touch of death.

Out of the bag came an outfit that formed a small microscope when put together. The leaves showed now as crushed withered flower petals, almost like tiny white roses. Pointer was a Bideford man. He knew his plants and trees. This was from a sloe tree. This was blackthorn. He examined the dead girl's hands carefully with one of the glasses that he detached They were lightly scratched on outside and inside, but they showed no trace of sand. Neither did the nails.

On one sleeve was a tiny smear of green paint, very faint. He knew that the dead girl had had her painting box with her, but it held water-colours. This felt like oil paint of some kind. A few drops of turpentine from his bag settled it. It was oil paint. He turned the still figure gently over.

Across the back of her frock, a few inches above her waist, ran a broad tear. It looked at a glance, remembering where she had been found, as though the frock had caught, on an overhanging bough or pointed stone. But the glass showed that two threads of the knitting had been cut, quite definitely cut with scissors. Nor was the remainder of the dress pulled in any way, as it would have been had she hung from some projecting catch. He decided that a strip as long as his span, and as broad as his hand, had been taken from the back, and the silk 'teased' to look as though torn.

He turned to the things which had been found with her. They were lying on the table. There was the tin box with a sketch of some ruins in the lid. Pointer felt the picture. It was dry. So were the brushes. So were the little china pans of paint. They had not been dampened for a week past, he felt sure. Next he picked up her hat of silver gray felt, soft as a kid glove. At the mere feel of it he gave an inward jump. It was quite dry. All the rest of Rose, even to the hair which had clung in cold tendrils around his fingers, was wringing wet. As he examined the hat his features stiffened. The inside was badly stained with blood from the cut, but the outside was unmarked in any way. There was no trace of blow or fall. The hat had been put on after the injury was inflicted. Must have been. After all her clothes were soaked through. After she was dead, or unconscious, in other words

The case had some unusual features already. It was speedily to acquire more. Pointer, in his guise of Brown, slipped out of the room, locking the door again on the outside as he had found it. Without a glance at the waiting Thornton, he drifted down some back stairs.

Thornton went out to his car. A minute later Brown joined him.

"Sand-pit. As near as possible without our being seen, please."

Then, when they were well under way, he asked whether Miss Charteris had been wearing a hat when her body was found.

"Yes. A gray felt. The doctor took it off to see the extent of the head injury. He brought it home with him in the car along with her painting outfit."

Close to the pit, Brown stumbled out again, and Thornton waited. Disguise there might be, but he felt certain that many halts, and much missing of the path, would mark the progress of this hound of the law.

The man from Scotland Yard walked back a little way along the short-cut, examining the shoe-prints carefully. Then he clambered down into the pit. There was no water there. Then he scrutinised the nearby copse. He saw no blackthorn tree amongst them As for the pit, neither in it, not at its edge, was there green of any kind but grass. He returned to the car.

"Well," Thornton asked tensely, "have I got you down here on a wild-goose chase?"

The voice that answered him was the one that up till now he had only heard over the telephone. A quiet voice, but resonant, and full of character.

"I think not, sir."

Thornton was surprised at the change in the eyes looking into his. The make-up was still there. The reddened lids, the watery effect, but there was in them now the look of the captain on the bridge taking over command when dirty weather is expected.

And Thornton's face, too, though he was unaware of the fact, had altered. There was a hint of pallor in it of stress around the mobile mouth that was carefully noted. It was not more than might have been expected under the circumstances, but it was not less.

"I suppose you couldn't tell me if you have found anything that looks like foul play?" Thornton's eyes were more veiled than usual as he put the question.

Apparently the man beside him could not.

"What *did* kill her?" Thornton asked after a futile wait.

"A fall."

"You think she was flung into that sand pit, then?"

"Well, she was found there, wasn't she?" Thornton thought that it would be hard to imagine a more inane reply.

"Now, sir, I shall walk back along this short cut," Brown went on in a whisper. "May I ask you a few more questions at your cottage presently?"

"Certainly. I am quite at your service. Of course you must let me put you up."

Brown thanked him, and then shambled slowly back beside the marks of Rose's shoes. His eyes were now on them, now searching the trees in sight. Here and there he saw patches of snowy blackthorn, but the trees were never where they could have played a part in the mysterious death that he was studying. Yet Rose

Charteris's hands had grasped their leaves as she fell. Fell whence? Fell where?

Back at Stillwater he turned into the grounds and walked slowly through them. He came to a halt not far from Thornton's cottage, facing the lake that gave the house its name, and which now marked one boundary of Colonel Scarlett's grounds. An Italian summer house stood at one end, so surrounded by evergreens that it was hidden alike from house and cottages. Its two stories ended in a waist-high railing which marked out half the flat roof into a square, with high corner posts crowned with flowers. The railing was green. So was an outside stair that ran from the ground to the little Lookout, as Pointer learnt later that the roof was called.

Around the summer house ran a row of flower-pots set on a broad band of red tiles. There were four doors, each marked by a tree. On the side farthest from the house lay a pile of cut boughs beside one of these little sentinels.

The tree, a blackthorn, had been lopped back almost to a pole.

Pointer hurriedly lifted the snowy branches one by one. Those underneath had been badly broken, as though by some heavy object falling through them. He ran up the outside stairs. The railing was being repainted, and repainted green. The same coloured green as the faint smear that he had just seen on Rose Charteris's sleeve. It was still tacky. On one side, the side above the cut boughs, were three dull smudges. A broad smudge the length of his span, and two smaller ones, well to one side. All three showed a sort of turning movement.

He looked very closely at them. The two smaller ones he took to be hand grips, though they showed no definite fingerprints. The turning movements of whoever had gripped the rail to look down on the flagging below had been too strong for that.

All three marks had been made before last night's rain, and judging by their looks at about the same time.

The balustrade was still bordered with a fringe of tiny drops.

The broad one corresponded in length and height from the flat roof top, with the missing strip on the back of the dead girl's frock. The balustrade was not a broad one, but Pointer thought that the greater width of the cut-out oblong had been caused by a rotary movement on the paint.

That would mean that she had been flung over backwards. And those hand-grips—they might well be those of the murderer peering down at the lifeless body of his victim. They were not made by Rose, and he thought not made by any woman, Rose had exceptionally slender hands.

He knew now where Rose Charteris had met her death. He believed that he was standing on the very spot.

The line of clues had been so straight that he hoped for a short, clear case which would be over in a couple of days. It had begun like that, but a few minutes later he saw that it was not going on like that. Not at all. Pointer always considered the Rose Charteris murder as puzzling a problem as any that he had ever tackled.

He made his way through a gate close by to the short cut again, and traced those shoe-prints, that corresponded exactly to the two outlines which he had in his pocket, back to the sand-pit.

The marks were deep and clear. They must have been made when the sandy path before him was soft and yielding, but not sloppy after the rain. Their edges were far too sharp and definite for them to have been washed by such a flood as that of last night.

But Rose Charteris's dress, her hair, her shoes—but not her hat—were wringing wet. There was no water in the sand-pit; its sides had been too deep to let the very slanting downpour strike in hard. Nor would any pool there have explained the fact that though her clothes and hair were soaked through on top, they were merely damp beneath her. No. Rose must have lain out in that hard rain from start to finish. Lain in all likelihood where she struck the flagging. That meant that these shoe-prints were made some hours after Rose herself had taken her last steps.

Pointer remembered the hasty bows on the shoes. Both tied to the same side. The rain, as he had ascertained from the meteorological expert at the Yard, had come down in this part of England at half-past ten, almost to the second, and lasted just twenty minutes.

That being so, he decided that the prints before him had been made somewhere around one o'clock in the morning.

He took some casts with stearine powder and some careful photographs with his tiny camera, that photographed vertically downwards.

The steps were those of a woman light in weight walking slowly, and balancing herself very strangely. At one moment her weight was on her right foot. At the next it would be on her left." Sometimes a step backwards had been taken, sometimes the forward step checked halfway. She was a young woman with a springy gait. He judged, though, that the shoes were too big for her. Now Rose had small feet for her height, so whoever had taken her place would be shorter than she, or much smaller-boned, slighter built. But the gait! The strange, halting, pressing gait! Lurching at times... the word was the key he needed. On the instant he guessed the reason, for this was no drunken woman's purposeless perambulation. The woman who wore the shoes of the dead girl was not carrying a load, but she was steadying one.

Pointer studied the ground like a bushman. He found a mark such as he was looking for, first on one side of the path, and then—in one other place—on the other side. Such a mark as a hard-tyred bicycle would make But it did not cross the path He made quite sure of that He deduced something like two hard-tyred bicycles with a space between. Possibly a plank had been lashed to them, the body of the dead girl placed on this, and wheeled to the pit.

But this did not explain the fact that though some of the prints showed the woman as steadying she was never pushing a weight. She was keeping something true, but she was not using force. Evidently some one else had done the pushing or drawing, her task merely being to see that no wheel ran on the sandy path where Rose Charteris's were to be the only marks left behind. All other footprints had come much later, when the path was far dryer, or else had been pounded flat by the rain previously.

Under the trees in the copse, Pointer read some more of the cryptogram which every crime leaves behind it.

He saw now that it was not two bicycles lashed together which had been used, but a sort of trolley mounted on two hard-tyred wheels about three feet apart. He had never seen such a carrier, but, like some savant, reconstructing a prehistoric monster from a jaw-bone and an inch of fossil spine, he could by now have drawn it to scale.

Under the trees he found prints of Rose Charteris's shoes, of a man's boots, and of a woman's high heels, all in inextricable confusion, but the marks of Rose were nowhere on top.

Here, then, he thought, the woman had changed into her own footwear.

He did not think that the body of the dead girl had been flung into the pit. It might in that case have shown cuts which a doctor would know had been made after death. The Scotland Yard officer examined the pit minutely. There were no marks detectable as those of the sinister couple who had walked from one of the farther gates of Stillwater House to the pit last night with a corpse between them. He decided that Bond, Cockburn, and Thornton, the doctor, and the men with the stretcher had obliterated them. There was only one easy way down, to the bottom.

Pointer walked rapidly to the police station, but Superintendent Harris was up in town, the chief constable was down with influenza, and Briggs, the constable in charge, looked to Pointer a better judge of beer than crime.

He returned to Red Gates, where he found Thornton doing a good five miles an hour in front of his fireplace.

"I want to ask you a question or two about the doctor who was fetched when Miss Charteris was found dead. Is he the sensible, family doctor type?" Pointer asked

"More of the leaky-sieve type, though doubtless the soul of good nature. Why?" Thornton wheeled sharply about.

"I'm thinking about that death certificate that he's going to fill out. You see, it's not so easy opening people's eyes when you're not supposed to exist—officially. You don't happen to know at what hospital he studied? Though we can easily find that out."

"My dear Mr. Brown, I've met the man at least three times! I doubt very much if there's one fact of his past, or present life therefore with which I'm not on nodding terms. Give me a moment for reflection, and I can doubtless supply you with the name of the patent food on which he was reared. As for your question—he's a St. Thomas's man.

Pointer laughed outright. He had the laugh of a boy.

"Good. Yes, I think I can work that." But what it was that he proposed to manipulate he did not say. He turned away, but Thornton stopped him.

"A moment. Of course it's natural that I should be interested in this case." He paused, as though really waiting for an answer.

"Quite so, sir."

"Do you think it's going to be a simple affair, or a—well—complicated case?"

Pointer looked at him with an apparently absentminded eye.

"Simple cases," he said thoughtfully, "'there aren't many —presuppose a simple life, simple surroundings, simple conditions. Say it's murder. Well, life nowadays is often so complicated that when you take it—obviously, you take something exceedingly complex. At least, that's been my experience."

There followed a long pause.

"Then you think—here—that will prove to be the case? I mean, you think that it's murder, and that there's more than one person implicated, and so on?" Thornton spoke without turning round.

"It's hard to say," Pointer answered. And so exceedingly difficult did he appear to find it that he was evidently disinclined to attempt the feat as he slouched off to the summerhouse again.

CHAPTER THREE

POINTER found the summer house still quite deserted when he returned to it to continue his investigations.

Around where the boughs lay heaped, the flags looked darker than on the other side of the house. Examining them, he saw that this was due to the red tint of the mortar in this one place.

He pried a bit loose. From a phial he dropped a little ammonia on to it. The colour did not change. It was blood, and fresh blood. But such a rain as that of last night would have lashed the bloodmarks off wood, let alone cement. So these, too, must have been made after that short, fierce storm. Yet the tiles here were as clean as elsewhere. There was but one explanation. The tiles had been wiped, but in the deeper cracks of the mortar the blood had remained.

He pushed open an arched, ornamental door that had no lock. Behind it he found a mass of broken geraniums and pots.

The damage was recent, not more than twenty-four hours old.

All around the house, except on the side that interested him, the side below the smudged balustrade, were similar pots set close in against the walls and outlining the paths to the four doors.

Behind another door Pointer found a bag labelled Fertiliser, and some gardener's tools. Out of an iron stove in the middle he fished a piece of sacking that had been used as a floor-cloth. It was smeared with blood, and spots of what he first took to be earth, but which he found differed from the earth around. Then he guessed it, rightly, to be fertiliser spilled in the afternoon by the gardeners, a little of which had got blown against the house in between the pots, and so escaped the downpour.

Pointer stared at the sacking. It was soaked with blood. But whose blood?

Not Rose Charteris's. There was far too much here for that. Besides, this had taken place after the rain. Nothing is more misleading as to the amount of damage done than bloodstains. But even so, this must have been a formidable affair.

Besides the sacking, he found a mass of what might be the remains of six or seven more flower pots, but so ground to powder were they, so trampled the plants, that it was impossible to count them. They told one thing plainly. The paving outside had been washed. Not so these broken remnants. They were soaked with blood, trampled into it.

He cut away a corner of the sacking and dropped it into an indiarubber envelope. He added to his bag a couple of lengths of cord, very stout, and of a kind new to him in colour and texture.

He heard steps on the gravel path. He had replaced everything as he went along, and now lit his pipe and waited.

It was Bennet, the under-gardener, and a boy wheeling a barrow. They began to collect the branches.

"You prune so late?" Brown pointed to the almost stripped thorn.

"The master he thinks the trees at the doors want thinning. Done it before we got to work this morning." Bennet gave a wrathful sniff.

"Must have lost his head over that terrible accident," Brown mused aloud. "I'm staying with Mr. Thornton at his cottage. Colour-printing is my trade. His niece's death must have upset the old gentleman."

"It couldn't upset him beforehand," retorted the gardener. "Not beforehand! And I must say he made thorough job of it all right. Killed the old tree, thats what he's done. Murdered it! And then fell off the ladder on top of them pelargoniums. Collected them in a lump just on purpose, he says, so as not to damage 'em. And then went down bang on top of the lot. Nose bled; too, he says. I don't wonder. Next time he'll leave it to those as understands the job, let's hope"

"Fond of gardening, is he?" Brown struck in wheezily "That's like me. I like to do a bit that way myself."

"Fond? Not beyond seeing as there isn't a stray leaf, and that the flowers come up to time. They mustn't be late for parade, or he wants to know the reason why." Bennet began to help the boy to pick up the broken pots inside. "Just look at 'em". The gardener was almost in tears. "I think he's going dotty, lately, that's my opinion. I wouldn't stay on, not if he asked me."

"Leaving, eh? The colonel hard to please?"

Bennet straightened himself with some difficulty.

"I was fourth gardener at Welbeck," he said with dignity, "and I take it there's nothing in my work I aren't up to. No, he gave me notice out of temper. Pure bad temper."

"Because some of the flowers didn't come up to time?" Brown asked, with the tactlessness of the dull.

Bennet's eyes snapped.

"I've told you once already that I know my job, thank you. The colonel gave me notice because he lost a telegram, or a letter. He called it first one, then the other. Couldn't find it, and said it must have blown out of the window. I'm not a betting man. I'm not interested in tips. He would have it that I'd picked it up. I was marking out some plots in front of his study. Later on, next day it was, the thing turned up. Daresay he still was able to put his bit on. Anyway he was ashamed of himself. I will do him that justice. He apologised quite handsome. But I'm leaving at the end of the month. He's getting too peppery lately. There's no pleasing him. He'll order a thing one day and change it the next. Look at this place. Yet just before he drove off he says that he wants nothing more done here till further orders. Told me not to cart away the broken pots. But I knows him and his little ways by now. This time to-morrow he'll be raving because the rubbish has been left here."

"Mr. Thornton'll miss your good lady. When do you leave?"

"Four weeks from this last Wednesday. I don't say that if—"

Bennet was interrupted. He was wanted down on the grass courts immediately. The colonel had left an order that they were to be prepared for returfing, and it was a case of all hands on deck.

"There!" Bennet handed Brown back his tobacco pouch. "Thank 'ee. Those courts was new sown last week. Mr. Cutbush won't stand much more of this. *He'll* be leaving next."

Bennet hurried away.

Pointer mounted a short flight of stairs inside the house to the landing where two doors opened, one on either side. He found both to be prettily furnished bedrooms, and guessed them to be used at times as an overflow from Stillwater House.

The left room he only glanced at. The right room detained him longer. Some one had lain on the bed last night. There were the marks of dusty boots on the flowered coverlid, and still an impress in the crumpled pillows. He was a tall man and very light, Pointer decided. His walking had been done before the rain. "Before the rain" had come to mean to him by now "before the murder of Rose Charteris".

One of the lace blinds that covered half the window was on the floor. He found that it was liable to come off at a touch. The window looked out over that side of the tiled surround where Rose must have fallen. On testing it, the pear-shaped window latch gave a nearly perfect print of a thumb and first finger. A long, slender finger which had never been calloused by toil.

It was not Mr. Thornton's first finger and thumb. Pointer had prints of those already from the back of a prepared notebook that he had handed his host to hold for a second. He examined the ground around the summer house while apparently looking for a dropped pencil. He found no marks, except once that same hard-tyred wheel mark which he had seen before on the short cut.

He thought of Mr. Thornton's cottage, which lay quite close.

Opening the gate into the lane beside it, he looked around him. From that gate to where the lane turned into the high road to London, Pointer saw the marks where a light little car had run up and down many times about three this morning, judging by the depth of the half-dried earth. He decided that this case was going to be a shining example of how favoured detectives are in the British Isles in the matter of damp. Seldom indeed is the ground not able, and willing, to date some event for the investigator. He often maintained that the work of his confreres in really good climates must be much more arduous.

The little car had apparently been used as a shuttle. Four times it had run out to the main road and back to the gates close beside Mr. Thornton's cottage. It had been going light and had been driven very slowly. One might have thought that someone was waiting? But why not wait patiently? Why patrol that one little part of the lane, now as close as possible to the Stillwater hedges, now as close as possible to the other side?

Pointer, deep in thought, entered the grounds again, and decided to have a look at the two garages.

The colonel's chauffeur was busy at work, but Brown asked for a little petrol to take a stain out of his coat. He used his eyes while he sponged. Then he went on to Red Gates. Thornton's two-seater was out, but a big Bently saloon was there. Pointer lit one of the lamps, as well as the electric light, and began his examination.

The car had been lately and hastily cleaned. It certainly had been out very recently, and as certainly after, not in, or before, last night's storm. The wheel-discs still held marks of wet splashings, but the mud was of a fairly thick consistency. The door handles and steering wheel yielded no finger prints.

The criss-cross markings of the clutch showed sand, and a few particles of what, fished out with a pin on to white paper, showed under his magnifying glass as crushed flower-pot dust.

Caught in the clutch was a wisp of thin, black silk material. Pointer laid that away in an envelope. So a woman had driven the car!

The inside of the saloon had been swept out, also very hastily. He found more sand, and more flower-pot crumbs in the corners under the seats. There, too, far back, he found a pencil, not much used, with a protective metal tip. It was a French make.

He found the oddest thing last of all.

Two marks like little horse shoes, side by side, showed on the gray cloth upholstery. One pair at the top of the window, but a little to one side. One pair was overhead.

Pointer studied them They were reddish brown in colour. He decided that they had been made by a pair of men's boot heels. The stains showed under his magnifying glass to be of the same horrible blood and fertilise mixture which he had found on the sacking, and which he believed he had found on the swab taken from the cut on Rose's head.

The two marks were close together each time, all but touching. That told its own tale. The man's feet had been bound—lashed together. His hands must also have been tied, or those convulsive efforts to free himself, to kick open a window, or the carriage top, of which the marks told, would have been accompanied by some torn cushions. But their very cording was intact. Down by the door he found a few bloodstains, very small, but still damp. Judging by the height of the heel marks, a man of about the same size as the man who had lain on that bed in the summer house had been carried in this car last night.

Pointer felt his pulses quicken. His intelligence rose to meet the puzzle like a good horse at a stiff fence. But for the moment he reined it back. He thought of that to-and-fro driving of the little car in the lane outside. Suppose that a large car, such a car as this, had passed out first along the lane, and then suppose that the little car, such a car as he had seen in the Colonel's garage a few, minutes ago, and of which he had the particulars in his notebook—suppose this little car had taken up the work of destroying the marks made by the large car in the soft earth?

Yes. Pointer decided to suppose just that.

When Thornton drove back to Red Gates, he found that obvious failure in life, his colour-printer, waiting on his doorstep with a wilting bunch of primroses in his hand.

Pointer followed him into the cottage, and at the suggestion in the other's rheumy eyes, Thornton closed the window.

"Now, sir, there are many things I haven't had time to ask you yet. How did Miss Charteris come to be living with her uncle?"

Thornton explained that the colonel being poor, and the professor wealthy, the latter had taken over a wing of his brother-in-law's house, and helped materially with the expenses. That had been going on for some years now, and seemed to work excellently. He himself was a friend of the professor's, and had taken Red Gates because of that.

Pointer went back to yesterday, the last day of Rose's short life, and had Thornton run the events over to him as far as he knew them. The evening's alarm interested the detective-officer especially.

"Then, as I understand it, sir, all you four gentlemen were playing cards from nine to close on twelve?" Thornton nodded.

"Whist or bridge, I suppose?"

"Mahjong parts of the time, and bridge the rest of the evening."

"Could you give me an idea of how long the mahjong lasted. You see, I like to get even the smallest details clear in my mind, especially as far as time goes, then, when new facts come in, I can place them where they belong."'

Again Thornton nodded.

"Mahjong was over by a little before ten. It struck the hour as we got out the cards."

"And there were absolutely no other visitors except one lady at Stillwater House yesterday?"

"I don't see how there could have been, unless they, were fasting experts. I saw nobody at meal times.

"Has this Lady Maxwell been down here before?"

"To Stillwater House? Not as long as I've been here; that's nearly six months now."

"Do you know her at all?"

Thornton gave his rather sardonic smile.

"Oh lor', yes! She's a widow of some worthy baronet or other. Quite well known. Absolutely no good an object of suspicion, I should say, Chief Inspector."

Pointer looked hard at his boot-tips.

"Brown, if you please, sir. Even when the house is empty as now. I suppose you haven't noticed any change at Stillwater House lately—no one has seemed to act in any way differently from usual? Colonel Scarlett, for instance, to take him first?"

Thornton looked uneasy. He adjusted his glasses

"It's rather an unpleasant feeling, being asked anything so important as that I mean, a mistaken impression on my part might lead to such unforeseen consequences—"

"Not so bad as that," Pointer comforted him with some inward amusement. He never took any one's evidence quite so seriously as they did themselves. But that was a secret between himself and his Maker.

"And it's a most unpleasant thing to do. Report on a man who's a friend, in a way, and my host—in a way."

"There's only one thing to be done in an affair of this kind," Pointer said in his pleasant voice, "and that is to sink personal feelings altogether. Just act as a sort of gramophone disc. Just record the impressions made on you. In every walk in life one has to put one loyalty against another, hasn't one? Loyalty to justice seems to me to be high enough to serve, even at the cost of a great deal of discomfort."

"Then I should say that Colonel Scarlett has seemed to have something on his mind for about a month or more back—at least, that's my impression. The day before yesterday, Wednesday, he certainly got a letter that disturbed him greatly, though he tried not to show it."

"Exactly what happened?"

Again Thornton hesitated.

"You never know what trifle may not help," Pointe prompted, "and very often it throws a light on some other person or event, far away from the thing you're talking about."

"I suppose that's so. Well, a letter was brought in while we were in the lounge, just before lunch. The colonel gave a start as soon as he saw the envelope. went to the window, and tore it open. When he turned around again, he looked very odd. As a man might look who had learnt suddenly that something on which he confidently counted had gone all wrong."

"Did he speak about the letter at all?"

"Not when I was present. He excused himself, and didn't see him again till Thursday at lunch."

"He wasn't back to dinner, then? Were you alone with him in the lounge when the letter was brought him?"

Thornton said that he had been.

"He's a racing man, I believe. Heavy backer?"

"I believe so, but as I never backed a horse in my life he doesn't discuss those interests with me."

"Was it dark down here last Wednesday at noon? mean, was the lounge so gloomy that the colonel couldn't have read his letter where he sat?"

"It was a particularly bright day."

"Did you happen to notice the letter at all, or it's envelope?"

Thornton had not. It was only the results that had struck him.

"Now about Mr. Bond and Mr. Cockburn, they're friends of the colonel, I believe?"

Thornton nodded.

"Yet you put them up?"

"I was very much surprised. And so were they," he added with a faint smile. "As a rule, Stillwater House is a sort of hotel."

"Possibly this change in the colonel you noticed may have meant rather a pinch—money-pinch?"

"I shouldn't have thought," Thornton balanced a Persian tile on his finger, "I shouldn't have thought that Bond and Co. could have made much of a hole in his finances in one breakfast. An apple and a biscuit is their usual way of beginning the day, I believe. Always training for something or other."

"And the colonel on Thursday evening, did he seem like a man who had another engagement still ahead of him? Was it he who suggested stopping the cards?"

"No. I'm afraid my yawns did that."

"Do you think that shot in the lane surprised the colonel?" Pointer asked suddenly, and Thornton felt more respect for him. Possibly the man was not quite such a fool as he looked in his rigout. Possibly.

"I think it did," Thornton said, "but I had an idea—just a fancy—that he connected it with something in some way. I mean—it's hard to explain—I think it suggested something more to him than to the rest of us."

Pointer absorbed that for some seconds.

"I asked you just now about the other visitors at the house. But perhaps the colonel might arrange to put up some acquaintance in Medchester, or in one of his cottages? Say it was a business matter?"

Thornton nodded carelessly.

"Doubtless."

"How about that house by the lake? Some one came out of it just now."

"The Lookout, as it's called? As far as I know, it's empty. It's generally only used when Stillwater's full."

"Yet the colonel didn't suggest it for Mr. Cockburn or Mr. Bond," mused Pointer. "It's a trivial point doubtless. Is he on good terms with them both?"

"He doesn't know them well enough not to be." Thornton's smile was faintly ironical. "They're the merest club acquaintances of his. They came down to see the professor."

But Pointer was only using the two known guests as a stalking-horse for the unknown man. Unless Mr. Thornton was a good actor, he knew nothing of that visitor. But Mr. Thornton had been quite a star in the O.U.D.S fairly recently.

"You realise, of course, how important it is to make sure that no unchecked-off visitor, or stranger, was near Stillwater last night or early this morning?" Point explained.

Thornton's legs were crossed. The swinging foot gave a sharp jerk. He uncrossed them.

"Quite so," he said evenly. "I quite realise that."

"Now the ladies, were they on good terms with Miss Charteris, would you say?"

"Excellent" The reassuring word seemed to come out from force of habit. "I mean, as far as I know," Thornton ended lamely.

"Just so. What dresses were they wearing yesterday at dinner?"

"Surely you don't suspect any of them of being concerned in this ghastly affair?" Thornton asked, with one of his quickly-veiled glances.

Pointer did not reply.

"Mrs. Lane was all in pearl gray, as usual, a sort of misty, lacey frock. Lady Maxwell wore a navy dress. Miss Charteris was in peach colour, with silver bits on it here and there. Rather a gorgeous affair. Miss Scarlett was in something dark, brown or black, I forget which."

Pointer next asked whether Thornton could give him Lady Maxwell's home address. She had left Stillwater the first thing in the morning, so he had learnt from his couple of minutes' gossip with Wilkins the chauffeur.

Thornton told him that she practically lived at Batt's Hotel in London, and Pointer, thanking him, slouched off.

Once more he searched the lane, but he found nothing that could explain the shot heard last night. He had no time, however, to waste in hunting for what possibly did not concern the case at all, when the things that did concern it were so numerous and so baffling.

His first aim was, if possible, to stop valuable records from being lost. Nothing had been burnt in the iron stove of the summer house. Stillwater House had central heating, and gas stoves. Yet Pointer felt sure that the body of Rose Charteris must have been covered when it was trundled along in the dark. She was a tall girl. He looked to find something of about six feet in length A blanket, or a curtain possibly. Then, too, whoever had wiped those flags, might well have left some marks on their clothes. He had looked over the empty bedrooms of the lady housekeeper and the master of Stillwater. He had found nothing suspicious in either. Mrs. Lane's gray lace frock was immaculate. He decided to try once more, and see whether Sibella were still in her bedroom

As he passed up a back stair leading from the library he heard some one moving about in Rose's sitting-room. Cautiously, noiselessly, he set the door ajar.

It moved without a sound of latch or hinges, as he had already noted.

Pacing up and down was a girl with straight black hair drawn smoothly back from a pale, narrow face. He guessed her rightly to be Sibella Scarlett. Finally with a little resolute squaring of her shoulders, she walked towards the door that led into Rose's bedroom.

That bedroom, where, in the darkness, a girl's body lay waiting to be consigned to deeper darkness yet—never to see the light again. Had the living cousin part or knowledge of the dead cousin's fate? Was it through any act of hers that—terrible thought—the flowers heaped around the bed were fading merely because of what lay in their midst, were withered by one touch of that skin, so cold, so white, still so fair?

Sibella walked decisively enough towards the door, after that curious little shake of herself, but with her fingers on the knob she stopped abruptly. Had Pointer been a believer in apparitions, he would have thought that she stopped by something which she could see only too well invisible though it might be to him. For a second she struggled hard to throw off whatever banned her. She did not succeed. Turning, she almost ran to an arm chair and sank into it. She was out of Pointer's range of vision but after a few minutes he saw her again. Walking with a lagging step, a picture of something more than grief or depression, with compressed lips she passed on out and down the main stairs.

A minute later and Pointer came up from the staircase where he had retired and glanced over her bedroom. A black evening frock hung in her wardrobe. He ran it though his fingers. It was unstained. Then he bent over her shoes. From the buckle of a pair of black satin slippers he shook out quite a teaspoonful of soft garden mould. Dry mould. Not the dark fertiliser of the summer house. This was plain earth, but of a light kind. There were no stains on the soles and no particles of sand. He replaced them, and drove in his battered car to

Medchester station, where, as he expected, he found the most deserted telephone booth in the town. Over the wire he explained himself to Paul, and said that he had had an accident with a tablecloth of Mr. Thornton's. What was the name of the cleaners employed by Stillwater House? Paul gave him an address in the High Street. Pointer telephoned there at once. No. No parcel had been left from Stillwater this morning.

Next he got the number of New Scotland Yard, and was soon speaking to Detective-Inspector Watts. He directed that officer, in code, to have a look at any evening frocks of a Lady Maxwell, who was staying presumably at Batt's Hotel. He was particularly to notice a navy dress. Should any of them not be in perfect condition, Watts was to bring the garment in question down himself on a motor bicycle.

Pointer gave him the number of Red Gates, and went there to await the report.

He hunted up Thornton again on his return, and found that gifted author drawing Persian scrolls and leaves on his blotter, a pile of untouched paper beside him.

This time it was Medchester's evening entertainment that seemed to interest the detective.

So Miss Scarlett had driven Mrs. Lane off to the concert in the little two-seater that really belonged to Miss Charteris, but which either of the girls, or, at a pinch, Mrs. Lane, used.

"They can all drive, then?"

"Most women can nowadays," Thornton said easily.

"Yes, but how?" Pointer replied. "I don't suppose the colonel ever lets them take out that big car of his?"

There was no reply.

Pointer drifted out of the room again. He felt that Thornton was not a man in front of whom to drop a card and expect him to be unaware of its suit.

Half an hour later the telephone bell rang. Mr. Brown was wanted by a friend. The friend went on to say that he had found one of the books rather dog-eared, and was bringing it down for him to look at. He might, or might not, want it.

Pointer rang off and made his way to the handsome old inn in Medchester Main Street. Smoking in front of the entrance, he was hailed by a motor cyclist, who waved a kit-bag at him and followed his slow steps up to a bedroom that Brown had just engaged.

There Watts spread out a dark blue silk dress with velvet embossed flowers in high relief. It was one of those modern affairs that can be drawn through a napkin ring and looked rather as though some one had tried that experiment on it quite recently.

"Hotel sneak-thieves must get their living easy," Watts said, standing back. "Lady Maxwell was out, so was her maid. I found this in a package done up as though for the cleaners. I put something else in instead. What do you think of it, sir?"

Pointer was running the soft material through his fingers. He could find no stains, but he felt several stiff places. Turning up the electric light, they showed as purple splotches.

He dropped a little guaiacum solution, and then a few drops of peroxide on one place. Up rose at once a bead of a beautiful bright blue.

"The stiff places are blood right enough." Watts folded up the dress again.

"Humph!" Pointer said, and decided to keep the frock for the moment.

It was late in the afternoon when he drove up to a house in Bayswater, where he shared rooms with a bookbinder friend. O'Connor was his one real confidant, for the Irishman had done some first-class work as a secret service agent during the war, and Pointer could rely on his discretion. Just now he wanted to rely on more than that.

O'Connor had a collection of pencils and inks unrivalled even by Scotland Yard. The pencil that Pointer had found in Thornton's car puzzled him. It made only a thick, oily smear when tried on paper, yet it had evidently been used about one-third down.

O'Connor tried it on his thumb.

"It marks all right like that," Pointer said, "but it's a kind I've never met before."

"I have." O'Connor went to a Wellington cabinet. He turned the Chubb lock, and after a minute laid before his friend another pencil.

"Try that, and see if it isn't the same kind."

It behaved in exactly the same way. The name, *Cos* tallied.

"What sort of thing is it?" Pointer asked curiously.

"Writes on skin. French surgeons use them a good deal, I believe, to explain to their students just what they're going to do before they cut up a patient. I had a case during the war of a boy with a message written or his back with one of these. That's how I recognised it. And what's the meaning of your blowing in with this implement when you're on your leave?"

"If you care to come down with me in my car to a town called Medchester, I'll spin you a yarn. It's a hop, skip and jump affair, or I would wait and have supper here. Just let me send off some telephone messages first."

O'Connor doubled his long legs in beside his friend and Pointer drove off for the Barnet road.

He gave the other a brief summary of the facts as they sped along. When he got to the marks on the green balustrade of the summer house, O'Connor struck. "You think she was killed there? Flung off the top of that lookout?"

Pointer nodded "I do."

"Was she as lovely as the papers make out?" the Irish man asked irrelevantly,

Pointer slowed up for a second and handed him a photograph that he had annexed. O'Connor stared at it.

There is something infinitely touching in beauty, in spite of all that saw or tale may say of its deceitful quality, the heart knows better. Knows the contrary.

Knows that here before it is Truth, is Abiding Reality. Is a message faint and dim, which the soul has managed to get through to mind, or body, or character—rarely to all three—and of which we see but the blurred record.

O'Connor handed back the portrait without a comment. He looked moved.

"Glad it's you! You'll get him yet, or her! But what beats me is why was the body moved? Sure it was a perfectly good accident. She just overbalanced herself. I call it a capital murder. Why botch it by taking her off to the sand-pit? It looks inexplicable, it does that—so far as you've told me the story."

"And so far as I know the story. I found the carrier later on which she was moved. It's practically a shed door mounted on a pair of old-fashioned bicycle wheels. A man pushed it, a woman walked behind, steadying it."

"A woman! It must be a woman in a million to stand in with such a crime! And where's the motive?" demanded O'Connor, as though Pointer had it in his pocket. "Jealousy, of course," he assured himself, "though it's a bit carefully worked out for that. Yet that might depend on the man—" His voice faded off into thought.

"Now, Jim," Pointer said briskly, "that's the end of the links that fit together, even though poorly. Here comes a jumble of odd bits. And odd, they are!"

He told of the blood in between the wiped tiles of the broken flower-pots.

"A fearful struggle must have taken place on that same side of the summer house last night. But what sort of a struggle? The plants aren't trodden into the earth, except a few found stuffed into the stove. The rest were broken off horizontally. A lasso? It's a fantastic thought, but so's the nature of the damage done. You'd expect a powerful snake to leave traces like that, supposinig some one had tried to capture it."

O'Connor sat rigid.

"Another tragedy, or attempted tragedy?" he asked finally.

Pointer pursed his lips.

"You think it was the murderer and the girl herself?" O'connor asked under his breath. "Sure that would be a terrible thought! A lovely young thing like that, struggling for her life within a stone's throw of home, and help and then losing it."

"I don't believe it happened that way." Pointer looked far ahead of him. "Apart from anything else, I can't think her face would look as peaceful as it does, if death hadn't been instantaneous. The doctors will tell us that at the inquest for certain, of course, but I think she was looking up at the sky when the end came. I'm sure I hope so. For bear in mind that the girl hasn't a scratch on face or hands, except such as would be made by the branches of a tree on one wrist, nor her frock a crumple bar that cut-out place. But none the less, the fact remains that an awful tussle of some sort went on close to where she fell."

"Could the struggle have come first, and she got away, rushed up those outside stairs you spoke of, got to the top, and then been flung over by whoever was after her?" O'Connor was intensely interested.

"Then why didn't she cry out?" Pointer asked. "If it was some one else, why didn't they shout for help? The damage looks as though done by men. Footprints, as we mean the word, there are none, but still... Now, as I see it, this is a sort of side-show, for it took place after the murder, but it evidently occupies some vital place in the mystery, or why is nothing known about the man or his fate. To my mind, he is in all probability connected with a letter that the colonel received at lunch on Wednesday, and thought afterwards had blown out of his study window, and been picked up by the under-gardener. Thornton spoke of the colonel's marked discomposure when he read it. Suppose that letter, which so upset him, was to say that some one, some enemy likely, was coming on to see him. Perhaps it was a friend's warning. No post gets in at that time. I take it it was sent by hand, though I haven't been able to find out yet. Perhaps it was written by the man himself. At any rate, let's say that Scarlett expects him some evening soon, which is why he makes no move to put up any visitors, and, as I've learnt from Maud, Miss Charteris's maid, was exceedingly annoyed that Lady Maxwell was asked down by his niece for over the week-end. I think he expected some one. And those marks on the flagging rather suggest that he made his arrangements accordingly."

"Big man, I suppose, the colonel?" O'Connor asked.

"Fair. Bit overweighted, but quite powerful in an emergency. Now as to the unknown himself, the murderer or another victim, I can't see yet which he stands for. He lies down on the bed. Apparently till a certain time, or till a signal is given."

"Ah ha! That shot!" breathed O'Connor.

"Seems so. Still, that lying down is odd. As far as time goes, he could have been the murderer all right. But in that case—" Pointer gave a short impatient movement to his head, like a horse tossing his bit.

"The bits of cord you found pointed to binding," O'Connor said thoughtfully, "probably to gagging also. Was the man gagged immediately he stepped out of the summer house, was he bound, nearly got free from his bonds and fought on a losing battle, unable to call for help?"

"I doubt if any gagged man could have put up such fight. Besides, if he could have struggled like that, he could have loosened the gag. And then, what about the lateral break of so many of the plants. You asked why the girl was moved." Pointer drove on in silence for minute. "Well, there's only one easy guess, so doubt less it's the wrong one. But one might think that the murderer was seen by the man in the summer house. Knew that he had been seen. Moved the body of that poor child to the sandpit just in case—and carried off the man."

"How?" asked O'Connor.

"He was driven off in Thornton's large car."

"By Thornton?"

"Ah, if I knew that! But I don't, yet. All I know so far is that the man was taken away in that car of his bound, and presumably gagged."

"And how does the pencil come in?"

Pointer told him where he had found it. "I think it dropped from some medical man's pocket as he stooped to lift out the man, on his arrival."

"That's why you set your myrmidons on to investigating last night's arrivals at all the hospitals and nursing homes of London before we left?"

Pointer nodded.

"Why not try mortuaries?" O'Connor asked.

Pointer only shook his head.

"Unless he were already dead," mused the Irishman, "that cord looks as though the man was not to be killed outright. Why? Pity? Hardly. Something which he knew, and was to be made to tell?"

"Ah," Pointer nodded, "now you're making for the same place as I am. Something, possibly, for which he's to be nursed back to life in secret. And that's as far as I've got yet. And here's as far as you get, Jim. An up-train's due in ten minutes. So long." And Pointer unceremoniously dropped his friend, at Medchester railway station.

It was midnight when he slipped out of Red Gates and up to the big house again. He expected to find work enough there to last him till morning.

At first sight it would seem likely that Rose Charteris's murder was some act of mad jealousy. But the reason might be much more obscure. The motive might not have spent itself with her violent death. On the contrary, it might still be existing, still operating

He set to work on Colonel Scarlett's study. He had looked through Rose's papers earlier in the day. They had given, him no clue to her death. But they had brought out one strange fact. There was not, one scrap of her father's writing among them. Pointer found the same odd circumstance duplicated here. Yet Professor Charteris had been gone from the place some ten days now. From a *Sphere*, however, lying on an under-shelf of a wicket table in the hall, he shook out a registered envelope addressed to Miss Charteris in the same intricate hand which had marked some of the professor's books in the library with his name and comments.

The envelope, a long linen one, bore an Italian stamp, and the postmark Bolzano, Italy. The date was that of last Monday. On the back, in accordance with foreign regulations for registration, was the name of the sender A. Charteris, Hotel Laurin, Bolzano, Alto Adige. It had been sealed with red wax, and was empty, save for some dots, which proved to be black sealing-wax under his glass.

Apparently that envelope was the only communication from the professor that Stillwater contained.

That meant something.

Pointer was about to return to the study when he hear a slight clink on the gravel outside.

Some one was trying the windows. Now Pointer had left one ajar in case of need. He slipped behind a leather draught-curtain and watched.

Cautiously the window was opened, and a slim figure entered. Another followed.

"What do we do first?" whispered a voice nervously.

"Stub our toes," came in an aggrieved snap. "Flash the torch, Co., for a minute."

"Seems all right," the holder of the torch said again "I'll venture to turn on the light."

Pointer saw the first man move to the mantel-piece. "There's none here now," he said in a disappointed voice.

"Let me look, Bond." The other strode across. "There may be some in a drawer, but I'll reconnoitre before we start a hunt."

And Cockburn, with an acumen which Pointer grudged him, very sensibly decided to begin his investigations with the thick curtain on its leather rings.

Pointer immediately stepped out, an antiquated Colt in his wobbly hand.

"Not another step, either of you! I'm a peaceable man, I am, but not another step, if you please!"

Pointer's accents were those of a nervous man screwing himself up by sheer resolution.

"What in the name of—here! Dash it all! Leave that bell alone, whoever you are!" Bond called in a ringing whisper.

"I'm a peaceable man," quavered the voice, "but I intend to do my duty. Now, not a move from either of you, or I'll fire all six balls off at once."

"Good God!" Bond gave a half-amused, half angry snort, "are you the village constable making a night of it?"

"Never you mind who I am! I'm a respectable man, as I can prove."

A second time a reddened finger made for the bell, push, and just missed it.

"Take your hand away from that dashed bell!" Bond fairly hissed. "Look here! We're friends of the people in this house, but who are you?"

"I'm doing a bit of work for Mr. Thornton of Red Gates cottage," Brown jerked his head towards the library behind him, "but what I want to know, is—"

"Look here, Bond. Let's walk across to Thornton's cottage. If he vouches for us, will that content you?" Cockburn turned towards the blinking figure facing him. That worthy evidently considered the proposition from every point of view.

"Well, I'm sure I don't want to overstep my place. Seeing you two come in like that... but, of course, if Mr. Thornton O.K.'s you I've nothing more to say. But take hands, please, and walk straight in front of me. I'm a peaceable man, I am, but—"

"Oh, shut up!" Bond's patience snapped. "And for Heaven's sake don't let off those six bullets the first time you trip."

At Red Gates Mr. Brown made them precede him to the back of the house, where a light shone reflected on the hedge of holly. Mr. Thornton sat at his writing-table, but he seemed to be paying more attention to Scotch whisky than Persian art, for the moment.

"Look here, Thornton," Bond called in softly through the open window, "do you mind asking your blood-thirsty friend behind us not to shoot us at sight, as he's inclined to?"

"Just assure him that we're not professional burglars, there's a good chap," Cockburn added.

Thornton set his tumbler down hastily.

"Why, it's Mr. Bond and Mr. Cockburn, Chief Inspector. These gentlemen are from the Foreign Office they—"

"Chief Inspector? Where?" Bond turned swiftly and gazed past the awkward figure with the pistol in his hand. Seeing nothing, he stared hard at his captor.

"You mean—oh, good egg!"

"C.I.D.!" came from Cockburn in tones of rapture.

"Oh, Lord, that's torn it!" Thornton smote his breast as Pointer, gazing at him more in sorrow than in anger closed the window, and drew down the blinds.

"I apologise for the slip in forty different positions, but the surprise—"

"Amateurs will be amateurs, sir." Pointer dropped lightly into a chair. "But I must request that it be forgotten at once by everybody concerned."

"Then we were right! And she *was* murdered!" Cockburn came back to the meaning of the dingy man's presence in front of them. "I caught sight of her first, you know," he explained to Pointer. "I can't, seem to get the memory of it out of my mind." His voice was husky.

Pointer immediately asked for an account of the findings of the body and of last night's alarm. He asked a few fresh questions, and sat listening intently.

"And you chose the colonel's study to-night, just why?" he asked finally.

Cockburn took out an envelope, and from it two bloodied bits of cord. Evidently some of the same cord Pointer had found in the stove of the summer house.

"After the superintendent turned us down, we had one more go, at the place by the sand-pit," Bond cut in, "before we went back to town. And we came on these under the copse. Now, my father makes ropes. That cord is Indian. I happened to comment on the same stuff lying on the colonel's study mantelpiece yesterday. He said that it had come around a consignment of Bengal chutney. So when we found it near that sand-pit, and stained like that," he paused and looked up at the ceiling, "well, we thought it was well to come on down and have a look for the rest of it. The chief constable is a friend of ours. Besides, we couldn't get away all yesterday, so we decided not to lose another moment and come at night.

"But Scarlett gave the cord on his mantelpiece to di Monti," Thornton put in.

"Ah!" Cockburn sat up like a terrier that hears a rustle.

"Didn't you see him? The count wanted something to tie up the tennis net at the inn. Said he must remember to get some string. The colonel handed him a coil from the end of his mantelpiece, and di Monti drove away with it in his car."

Bond flushed to the roots of his curly hair.

"And to think that I broke into the colonel's—oh, Lord!" He buried his face in a whisky and soda.

"Di Monti! That's what we came to see about. I mean," Cockburn turned a very, grave face to Pointer, "I mean that our breaking into Stillwater House had nothing to do with any one there. Of course, we know *they're* all right. But this Italian—I never saw a crueller face. More pitiless. More hopeless to appeal to. If Miss Charteris had angered him in any way—God help her!"

Bond murmured his agreement. Thornton stared at the fire.

"What do you say, Mr. Thornton? You're the man on the spot. Do you feel certain that the inmates of Stillwater House are beyond suspicion? All of them?' Pointer asked in Brown's husky voice. He had not dropped one of the latter's characteristics throughout the interview.

Thornton shot him one of his unreadable glances as shook his head vaguely.

"What was it that made *you* go over the top?" Bond asked Thornton curiously. He could not imagine Thornton sufficiently stirred to take the initiative in anything.

"Oh, just a vague feeling that I wanted a competent judgment on the whole matter. To settle doubts once and for all. Mr. Brown here is very kindly spending the last days of his leave with me."

"Well, I wish to Heaven that we could be of some use," Cockburn said regretfully. "Isn't there anything we can do, Chief Inspector?"

"Anything?" echoed Cockburn.

Pointer thought a moment. Any light thrown on Rose Charteris's circle was all to the good. But friends of that same circle? Thornton, for one, an actual member of it? And young men who climbed into library windows?

"Are you staying for the rest of the night?" he asked.

Cockburn spoke of the Medchester Arms, but Thornton put his second spare room and a Chesterfield at the disposal of the two. His shed only held his own cars, but, as before, they could run their Buick into the colonel's garage.

"Is your garage always locked, sir?" Brown asked Thornton. "I left a notebook in your car when I came, I'm afraid."

Thornton ran his fingers into his pocket, but his expression betrayed his amusement at Scotland Yard's brilliance.

"Here's the key. Yes, I always keep it locked. Wilkins has a duplicate, if you should leave anything else behind you, and I'm out."

"But what about us?" queried the two friends. "If we can be of any use, we'll do anything."

Brown blinked at them.

"Then suppose, when the postman calls to-morrow at Stillwater House, one or other of you could be on hand and get hold of any letters that come for the colonel. I want them steamed open, the contents copied, and the letters carefully closed to show no signs of—"

"Look here, Chief Inspector, what do you take us for?" Bond broke in stiffly.

"Sweeps?" suggested Cockburn hotly.

"No. Amateur detectives," Pointer said innocently. The two men laughed ruefully.

"I see your point. Considering the prod it's just given us, I may well. So we can't be of any help? Rank outsiders, eh?" Bond was a trifle piqued.

"If you'll come out with me in the morning, and show me where that shot seemed to come from, I should be very grateful," and Pointer arranged for a meeting at eight.

"And now I think I'll get a wink of sleep." He left the three together.

"I hope he's up to the work," Bond said gloomily. "Of course one has to discount the make-up and those frightful clothes, but even so, I'm not impressed with the quality of his brains."

"You don't need brains at the Yard," Cockburn complained. "Their place seems to be generally supplied by something called 'information to hand'. With that—whatever it is—you may do quite well. Without it, you're lost."

And the meeting broke up with a vote of lack of confidence in the man who was apparently looking for the wink of sleep of which he had spoken, among the colonel's chutney cases.

There were two of them below stairs. Neither was corded now.

Next morning Pointer found the three men from the cottage very punctual.

"I was walking somewhere about here," Cockburn waved a hand towards a clump of trees. "The shot came from directly in front of me. But I'm afraid that I can't be more exact as to where I stood at the moment"

"I picked up a matchbox yesterday morning a little to the left of us." Pointer pulled one out of his pocket "Is it by any chance yours? That might settle the place where you were standing when you used it."

It was Cockburn's. He pocketed the little silver slab with thanks. "I dropped it when the shot startled me. So it came from over there." He pointed ahead of him. It was where, much farther off, lay the, sand-pit.

Now Thornton had indicated another direction in the account that he had given Pointer. He waved his hand towards it energetically. "Surely you said from over here!"

"And I thought you said this way." Bond took a turn at flapping his arms around The three looked for all the world like signallers at a first practice

Pointer was used to this sort of thing from amateurs. Bond finally came over to Cockburn's unchanging certainty as to whence the sound had reached him the night before. Thornton, however, was, or appeared to be, unconvinced. But as he had been so certain in talking to the Chief Inspector, he could not be expected to change now, if only to save his face.

CHAPTER FOUR

A FEW minutes later that same morning, Mr. Gilchrist, the Coroner for West Hertford, and incidentally the Stillwater family solicitor, rang up Colonel Scarlett. He explained that a letter had come for him from Doctor Metcalfe last night, but that he had not noticed it till now. In it he learnt, to his own boundless surprise, that the doctor refused to issue a certificate of Miss Charteris's death without a post-mortem, which painful preliminary would take place this morning, Saturday, before the inquest.

Colonel Scarlett turned away from the instrument with a gray line around his mouth. He was already pale enough under his tan. He stood for a moment in deep thought. Then he walked into the breakfast room, where Paul hastened to bring him the morning papers.

"Look here, Paul—" The colonel paused. "Shut the door. There's an infernal draught this morning. I want to speak to you. It seems the doctor isn't satisfied about the cause of Miss Rose's death. God only knows what he means by that. Now the inquest may spread into other fields, and I do not want the professor's private affairs needlessly broadcasted. You know how he would dislike that."

"Yes, sir. He would indeed."

"In his own way the professor is one of the cleverest of men, but not in all ways. Dear me, no! Not in all ways. He particularly desired that no word should get about of his having to go to Genoa. I'll tell you why. Frankness is always best. My brother-in-law is on the eve of concluding some very important and very delicate negotiations there. One breath about them, and they are off. I may mention that I, too, am financially interested in the matter, and have a very personal concern in silence on the point. Now the professor has unfortunately mentioned Genoa in a letter of his. The point is, I do not want that town referred to at the inquest, or at all. You understand? Italy, of course. He's in Italy. But not Genoa. I know he would very much resent this. You understand?"

"Yes, sir. I quite understand. Italy if need be, but Genoa not in any case," Paul summed up. The colonel drew a deep breath as he made for the library. Now for Sibella.

He had not seen his daughter this morning, or at all since the dreadful news of yesterday. He sent up word that he would like to speak to her downstairs.

He stared at her when she entered the room, and Sibella stared back at him.

Each face showed marks that had not been there before. Each eyed the other distrustfully.

"Things have taken a very unpleasant turn," the colonel spoke without looking at his daughter, "very unpleasant. There's to be an autopsy."

She stared at him without comprehending.

"You mean—on Rose?"

"For God's sake, don't act the idiot!" snapped her parent. "On who else, pray?"

"But—but—-" she passed her tongue over her lips, "that means—?"

It was his turn to stare at her.

"It means that they want to know how she died. You know what an autopsy is. They want to know what killed her."

Sibella sat speechless. She would have given a close observer the impression of buckling on some armour.

"I see," she said finally. "I wish you would tell me what you have heard about it."

"I don't know anything more than I have told you." The colonel gave her the message that had reached him over the telephone. "But the point is this, Sibella. Your uncle is in Italy; that's nothing to do with Rose's terrible accident, but all sorts of questions may be asked. The point is, I don't want Genoa mentioned."

"Genoa?"

Colonel Scarlett came close up to her.

"Understand me, Sibella," he said fiercely, almost in her ear, "not a word about that town. Not a word! Italy, yes, and any place you like, but not Genoa!"

"How can—"

Something in her father's face stopped her. He looked ghastly.

"I shan't mention it, dad," she said gently, looking very steadily at him in her turn. She left him with that to his own thoughts, and his thoughts, after rather a dark-seeming interlude, led him upstairs to Rose's sitting-room, and to Rose's desk, which he went through quickly, but carefully.

He did not stay to read the letters, which, however, he took out one by one and looked at. He was apparently searching for something that he would recognise at a glance. He stood for a second looking around him after he had closed the desk, but, unlike Sibella, very unlike Sibella, his face wore an expression of satisfaction, of so far, so good, before he turned and walked slowly down and out into the grounds.

Medchester is not likely to forget the inquest on Rose Charteris in a hurry. The proceedings opened quietly, with no hint of the thrills to come.

Thornton, very much on the alert, with the face of one who has not slept well, watched with considerable interest the man who sat beside the local police superintendent. Mr. Brown had told him that this would be Chief Inspector Pointer. The Scotland Yard man's look of energy and poise impressed the critic. Thornton decided that to start him would be one thing, to stop him quite another.

The first of the surprises came when Rose's maid deposed that she had only that morning noticed that her young mistress was wearing another dress under the knitted silk frock. What had been taken for a loose lining was the peach-coloured evening dress that she had worn on Thursday night for dinner. A few amethyst beads had tumbled out as she shook the dress to rights. The frock was very thin, low-necked, and sleeveless, and could easily pass for a petticoat slip. But the shoes were the kind that Miss Charteris always wore with the knitted dress, of stout gray buckskin with low heels. Her stockings, too, were of a gray ribbed silk that only suited the outer frock.

The maid did not know when her young mistress had left the house, but she had last seen her about ten on Thursday night. Miss Rose had then been dressed as she was when found. She had not been wearing her beads. Miss Rose had been examining some letters in her writing-desk.

"Examining? What do you mean by that?" asked the coroner.

"She had her writing-desk open, sir, and was turning them over and over, as though there were one there she couldn't find. I heard her murmur, 'Where can I have put it? What can I have done with it?' But I don't think she rightly knew what she was doing at the moment."

"What do you mean?"

"Miss Rose looked that anxious and upset, sir. She wasn't really looking at the papers at all. I've never seen her like that before."

"Like what?" asked the coroner impatiently.

"Like she was then," replied the witness helpfully. "She looked to me, Miss Rose did, as though she had had a warning." The maid dropped her voice.

"A warning?" snapped the coroner. "A warning of what?"

"Of her coming death," breathed the woman. "Oh, she looked beautiful, sir. I've never seen even her such a pitcher. But when I asked her if there was anything more as I could do, she stared at me as though she didn't understand, and said she wished she were dead."

"Eh? You asked Miss Charteris if you could do anything more for her, and she replied—what?"

"Just what I said, sir. She said to me, she said, 'I wish I were dead!'"

The legal mind gave it up.

"And you?"

"I said to her, 'Whatever is the matter, miss?' And she said to me, impatient, 'Oh, nothing—just everything!' And then I said to her, I said, 'Has anything gone wrong, miss?' And she looked at me, as she sometimes would, half-laughing, with her head thrown back, and a little to one side—oh, she looked a lovely pitcher! —'Everything, Maud, and nothing! What's the time?' I told her, 'Just gone ten,' and she says to me, 'Ten already!' Then she gave me a look as though she wanted to be alone, so I said good-night to her, and closed the door. And I never saw her alive again." The woman wiped the tears away.

"Now, going back to that phrase of Miss Charteris's about wishing that she were dead. Did she say it lightly, petulantly? You understand what I mean? Or did she say it as though she were in some great trouble?"

The maid hesitated. "Sort of impatient. Sort of frightened, too, though."

And the coroner could not shake her conviction that it had been fear which she had felt, or divined, in her young mistress, any more than he could her certainty that Rose had not been wearing her string of amethysts when she last saw her.

Mr. Gilchrist shot his lips out and pulled the papers towards him again. He glanced at Colonel Scarlett, who sat listening avidly, the air of composure gone with which he had entered the room.

"Well, well! Just the young lady's way of talking, I take it."

"Oh, no, sir! Miss Rose had had a warning. She had been frightened, underneath all her way of carrying it off. She had been frightened!"

Sensation.

"Now to pass on to other things—had the bed been slept in when you went into the room next morning?"

The question caused a stir, but the answer was explicit. It had.

Sibella and Mrs. Lane were next called. Sibella first. Their evidence was practically identical.

Sibella had not seen Rose after dinner. Rose was frequently out in the evenings, with friends, or in town at play, or concert, or meeting. As to her strange words to her maid, Sibella professed to have no key, except that apparently some little trifle had gone amiss. There was nothing really worrying her cousin. On the contrary. Rose seemed to her particularly happy and contented that last day, Thursday. Just for a second her eye met Thornton's. Just for a second they fell. As to any letter for which the maid thought that her cousin might have been looking last night, Sibella could not hazard a guess. Rose had a great many letters. She generally tore them up at once, unless they were business matters. She had her own friends, as well as her father's friends, many of whom were quite apart from the Scarlett circle. She could not explain how Rose came to be wearing Thursday's evening frock on Friday's early morning sketching expedition, even though it was under an outdoor dress.

Count di Monti was next called. Those present who expected an outbreak of Italian passion were disappointed. The Count looked as impassive as a meditating Bonze.

"You were, I think, engaged to Miss Charteris?"

"Yes. It was to be announced on the return of her father."

"I may take it that there was no, eh, hitch—of any kind?"

A rustle ran through the hall.

"In our engagement? Oh, none whatever."

As to when he had last seen Rose, di Monti replied that he had said good-bye to her at Stillwater about six. He had an important engagement in town that evening, or he would have stayed and gone on with her to a concert which was being given in Medchester. She had said that as he was not going, she did not care to go either.

There was a movement of sympathy at this announcement. But di Monti's arrogant gaze roamed the hall without softening. If it lingered for a second on one face, only a very keen observer noticed it. If Sibella felt it on her, she gave no sign.

"Can you suggest any meaning, any point to those words Miss Rose used to her maid last Thursday, night?"

Di Monti could not. But he had often heard Rose use just such expressions many times before, about the merest trifles.

As to the beads which Rose had been wearing, or was supposed to have been wearing when she met with her death, di Monti absolutely scouted the idea that they could have tempted any tramp to murder her for their sake.

He seemed, indeed, so anxious to minimise their value that Pointer looked at him curiously. Even to the pendant, he refused to allow any interest, intrinsic or sentimental, to be attached, though he acknowledged that it was a present to her from his father.

Then came the great sensation.

Doctor Metcalfe was called. He was very honest. He said at once that he had been mistaken in his first impression as to the cause of Miss Charteris's death. He had assumed, too quickly, as he now knew, that that cause was a fall into the sand-pit on to some stones. Fortunately another medical man from his aid hospital who had chanced to drop in for a casual chat had heard of the death, and had been struck by one or two of the details.

A swab taken by them both from the cut in the head showed earth, but no sand. The superficial sand first noted was only on the surface of the hair.

It was for this reason that he had withheld the death certificate, and had decided that it was his painful duty to hold an autopsy, which had taken place that morning.

He passed around a swab to the coroner which had been taken from the cut.

A low murmur of amazement swept through the hall. Pointer's eyes were on the little knot of faces seated almost in front of him. Colonel Scarlett was staring at the doctor with a look which even the Scotland Yard expert could not decipher. He showed no emotion, yet there was a something about his mouth that spoke of tension, great but controlled. Mrs. Lane might have been an ivory statue, as she leant far back in her chair. Sibella's eyes shone like green lamps. She looked, not at the doctor, but just once at di Monti, and then resolutely down at her clasped hands Pointer could almost feel the effort she was making to keep them fastened there—in safety.

The doctor realised the sensation which he had created "I deeply regret to make such a statement. Had I been able to reach you, sir, yesterday, on the 'phone, or Colonel Scarlett as the nearest relative, I would have let you know."

Superintendent Harris, very red in the face, hastily scribbled a line and passed it to the coroner.

"The police would be obliged if you would adjourn the inquest."

The coroner nodded. But he found that to stem the doctor just then would have meant carrying him bodily out of the building. He submitted, he insisted on submitting that Miss Charteris had been killed by a single blow from such a weapon as, for instance, a sharp-edged cudgel. There had been no struggle. Death had been instantaneous. There was a tear in the back of her dress where it must have caught on a branch as she fell among the trees in the copse. The force of the blow had broken her neck. Then her body had been thrown into the sandpit close at hand.

On this second examination, made in company with his learned colleague, he had found, lying beside the body on the bed at Stillwater House, some twigs and leaves from her relaxed fingers. These, too, he passed to the coroner, who was sitting without a jury.

The presence of these leaves proved, the doctor pointed out, that it was in the copse that the actual murder had taken place, for in the pit there were no trees or shrubs. And there was one thing more which the doctor could not be prevented from saying, and that was, that he was by no means sure of the time of her death. It was possible, or rather probable, that it had taken place earlier by far than he had at first assumed. Certain indications, indeed suggested considerably before, rather than after, midnight.

But this was going too far, and the coroner adjourned the inquest in the middle of the doctor's next sentence. Doctor Metcalfe's "learned colleague" tapped Pointer on the shoulder after the inquest.

"My car's outside," he said in a low tone; "come along."

Pointer came along. The doctor whizzed into a quiet street.

"Did it go to your liking?" he asked gleefully.

Pointer gave him a reproachful look.

"Letting all the cats out of the bag at one bound," he complained. "I can still hear them yodelling."

"That was Doctor Metcalfe's doing. Look here, Pointer"—Doctor Scott was one of the divisional surgeons of New Scotland Yard—"I deserve a treat for hopping down here like a bird when you whistled for me yesterday. What's the real story. What do you see behind all this, eh?"

"I see a case that you and I know to be none too uncommon," Pointer replied, looking at his boot tips."I see a case that may—likely as not—end in a 'No thoroughfare.' Where the Yard is sure of their man, but can't get evidence enough to send him—or her—for trial. You know how often that happens, and the public begin heaving rotten eggs. But you can't manufacture evidence—at least, the Yard doesn't, and you can't invent a motive—again, we don't in the force. And yet, if one has to sail out into the unknown—unguessed—-" He was talking to himself.

"Even so, you'll make port with a fine cargo," the doctor said confidently. "But I see that you don't intend to spill any beforehand. You asked me to drop you at the police station. Here we are. So long, till the next time you want me to swindle a brother medico into thinking me a Doctor Thorndyke!"

Pointer was shown into Superintendent Harris's room. The two were old friends. Pointer had served under him when he was first sent to London as a young police man.

"So there's murder to pay!" Harris said very soberly. "Thank God, you're here, Alf! Makes it seem like old times, my lad. Though I ought to call you 'sir,' of course!"

"You try it, if you think it safe!" Pointer said fiercely. For a second Harris gave his genial laugh, then his face clouded swiftly.

"Murder! Terrible word to use about our Miss Charteris. The town's been proud of her. Proud of having a great London beauty living here, and proud of her father, the professor, too. Murder!" He shook his grizzled head, and crossing to a cupboard, took out couple of glasses, a siphon, and a bottle. "Say when!"

Pointer said it before the cork was drawn.

"I don't mind telling you," Harris went on, "that when I got my breath after the doctor's evidence, and knew you were there on hand in case the Yard was asked to take over, I said to myself, 'Saved!' Yes, that's what I said. The flesh may be willing, but the spirit's a bit weak—like this in the bottle."

Pointer looked uncomfortable.

"You're pulling my leg, Harris!"

"Fact, Alf," the superintendent said solemnly. "I got along quite nicely with a tramp now and then, an gippies, and drunks of a Saturday night. And once we had a missing gal, but this isn't that sort of, thing. This'd be my ruin. I'm due to retire in a month, and I want to go out at peace with my neighbours as far as may be. I'd do my duty, of course, but it's making a hash of that same duty I can't stand, and turning my old friend upside down, only to find that the criminal was perhaps miles away all the time. Why, Alf, that cottage the Wife and I are moving into belongs to Colonel Scarlett. And then this here foreign nobleman—no, no! We'll finish this, and another like it, or at least I will, and then we'll up and along to the chief. He's down with the flu, but I slipped out and telephoned him the news during that surprise inquest. He'd be having a heart to heart talk with the Yard at this moment, and sending you S.O.S.'s by the hatful if you weren't here. I call it sheer Providence."

So Major Vaughan seemed to think, and Pointer and the superintendent were making their way out to the former's car, after a pleasant interview with the sick man, when Colonel Scarlett almost bumped into them on the top step. Superintendent Harris introduced Pointer.

"So New Scotland Yard's taking over. I'm thankful to know the case will be in such thorough hands. Though I fancy there's nothing very deep about the terrible affair. Those beads and a passing tramp, I think. Some garnet on the pendant and the snap looked just like uncut rubies to any eye but an expert's, and the setting, though silver might have been taken for platinum. However, you'll find out all about that. I only came to hear how my old friend the chief constable is getting on. I suppose you'd want to ask us all some questions up at my house, Chief Inspector? I'll telephone them to have the library ready for you, and I'll be there myself in a few minutes."

He passed into the house, and the two men drove off.

"What's the colonel's reputation hereabouts?" Pointer asked, after a short silence. Harris eyed him askance.

"Not going to start in by having trouble, with my future landlord, are you?" he asked in half real, half assume trepidation.

"He's not an easy man to read," Pointer said slowly. "We gave him a nasty jolt just now. He's anything but thankful that the Yard's taking a hand. I wonder why not?"

"He's plenty of friends," Harris ruminated. "The Scarletts have lived at Stillwater since they dispossessed the abbot up at the ruins, and took the monastery land. He's none so well off. Had to leave the Tenth Hussars because he found it too expensive. Some say he's a bit grasping. I think myself, that rent for the cottage's a bit steep, but take him all in all, he's very popular. Betting man. Good eye for a horse, and yet never lands a winner. Odd, ain't it!"

Pointer digested this, then he said briskly, "By the way, I'm in possession of a set of casts of Miss Rose shoe-prints on that short cut, and a drawing of them to scale. I'll leave them here, at the police station. If you'll take them on as your own, it'll save bother." He began to unpack his bag in the inner room.

Superintendent Harris eyed the casts ruminatingly.

"Found on the doorstep? Or blew in by chance through an open window?"

Pointer told him of Thornton's message, and his arrival, as Brown. Harris was amused.

"And the chief telling you kind as father who everybody was. You're deep, Alf! But this sets Mr. Thornton, at least, in a good light, doesn't it?" Harris had a most undetective like eagerness to see his neighbours in a good, or at least a satisfactory light.

"Humph, seems so. But possibly he was rushed by those friends of his, 'Bond and Co.,' as he calls them."

"Ah, there's that, of course They did rather take the lead. And what's that other parcel you're getting out for me?"

"This is Lady Maxwell's evening dress that she wore on Thursday at dinner at Stillwater House"

"Anything wrong with it? It looks all right to me."

Pointer gave a demonstration by artificial light.

Harris drew a deep breath as the splotches showed. "Isn't this pretty conclusive?" he asked.

"I don't know yet," Pointer said frankly, "and the rest of what I don't know about this affair I'll tell you and Inspector Rodman this evening. It'd take too long now. This Lady Maxwell is being watched, of course. But I want to speak to the inspector a moment. Ah, here he is"

Pointer had liked the keen, smart look of that police officer at the inquest He gave him his instructions in a few sentences. The frock was to be returned to its owner, and at the same time as much information as possible was to be obtained.

Pointer and Harris drove off separately.

Pointer did not hope for much from the questions at Stillwater House. That part of the work seemed to him what asking a patient to put out his tongue was to the old-fashioned doctor, something expected on both sides; a sort of preliminary canter. Not by sitting asking questions would the real bones of Rose Charteris's murder be laid bare, of that he felt quite sure. Yet a few useful items might be collected. He left that part, for the moment, to Superintendent Harris, for he had to go to town to see the head of Scotland Yard, and be formally invested with the case. But first he stopped at Mr. Gilchrist's and had a short interview with him. Then after an equally brief interview with the assistant commissioner of New Scotland Yard, he made for 17 Upper Brook Street, Professor Charteris's town address, outside of which Watts was already waiting.

They came, as two solicitor's clerks, armed with letter from Gilchrist to take away some papers of the professor's which were wanted for the adjourned inquest.

The manservant showed them up to the first floor and opened a door.

The detectives examined the professor's three room with care. Pointer came to rest before a semicircle of tobacco-shreds behind a tobacco jar.

"That wasn't done by filling a pipe. Looks as if some one had stirred that Shiraz like a Christmas pudding within the last twenty-four hours. For they're fresh." He passed on. "Letter-book of the Professor's missing unless his secretary took it with her."

Pointer turned to the book-shelves and pointed.

"Five books upside down in one batch." Watts stepped over to them. "Been lifted out in lots apparently."

Pointer clapped the boards together of a couple taken out at random. They seemed to be unusually dust free. Much more so than the furniture, or the carpet, would have suggested. He rang the bell.

"Look here. Has the professor's secretary been in these rooms lately? A book is missing that we were sent to fetch."

The man shook his head.

"She left before the professor. Some ten days ago, that was."

"But some one was in here lately. Yesterday or the day before?"

The man raised a mildly surprised eyebrow.

"Sharp that! You're right A young person did come to do some repairing on one of the professor's rugs They're his own, and quite valuable, I understand."

"Who sent her?"

"She came from Liberty's, I think she said. Anyway she brought me a visiting card of the professor's, with instructions to let her mend the carpet in front of the sitting-room hearth, which I did. I didn't stay in the room, of course, but I was in the hall when she went out. She had nothing in her hand but the little sewing-bag she brought."

"What was she like?"

"Seemed the usual sort of sewing woman to me. Middle-aged, stout party. Not the kind to notice much. Dark-skinned, very."

"And the hour? Mr. Gilchrist'll want to know all about this."

"She came shortly after eight. Most unusual time, but being a foreigner—"

"And she left—about when?"

"Close on nine. I was just carrying in breakfast to a very punctual gentleman."

"Got the card she brought?"

The man said that she had kept that.

"Well, we'll have another look. It doesn't sound as though she could have taken anything," Pointer finally. He looked at Watts as the door closed. "That settles the tobacco, I fancy."

"Was the point of any importance, sir?" Watts asked.

"I think so. That spilt tobacco looks as though the woman had been hunting for something which she thought might have been deliberately hidden in these rooms. Not merely for something which might have been in professor's possession. And now let's go through correspondence. I want, first of all, anything that will have arrived within the last few weeks that looks important or interesting. Next, I want anything that may give a clue to his whereabouts. Italy is a bit large, and a post-mark isn't much to go by."

They found nothing definite. Pointer made up a packet of "possibly wanteds," and dropping Watts at the Yard, returned to Medchester.

He drove back deep in thought. He had already a very fair idea of how and when the murder was committed. He had something more than a suspicion as to one man in Rose's circle. But the accomplices? For there seemed to be accomplices. This search of the professor's rooms had taken place at an hour when the man to whom Pointer thought that the clues led most directly was not in town. It might, of course, be unconnected with it. Professor

Charteris's correspondence had shown world-wide interests. He believed himself to be in possession of at least one fortune-making discovery.

Pointer slowed down a while as he reflected.

If the motive behind the murder of the beautiful young creature, whom he had seen, lying ready to have the coffin lid closed, was connected with jealousy or with money, then the investigations would easily enough be able to prove as much, and would be able to prove nothing else. Where motives were concerned, Pointer always left the obvious on one side at first. You did not have to be afraid that motives would bolt for some earth before it could be stopped. And if the motive were not obvious in this case, to fit the man whom Pointer believed guilty, it would be a difficult one to find.

Pointer thought of that room that he had just left. Supposing the search there, and the murder at Stillwater to be connected, what was the object that had been hunted for in the Professor's rooms? It was something that could be hidden in a book as well as in a jar. A piece of paper probably. Possibly a letter. But why should it have been thought to be hidden?

Those words which Rose had been murmuring as she turned over her letters last night, were they connected with this hunt? "Where can I have put it? What have I done with it?"

The daughter killed. The father's rooms searched as soon as possible after it.

Pointer had noticed the Airedale kept at the house in town. A night attack of the position would have had to reckon with him. And he looked a ready reckoner.

None of Professor Charteris's letters were to be found in Rose's rooms or in Colonel Scarlett's study. Had they been taken? Stolen? And their loss not yet noticed? Did some one think that among them might be found what was sought for?

If that hunt of the Professor's rooms were not chance timed, it suggested urgency. That suggested—

Pointer thought of the empty, long, envelope which had found beneath the tea-table that had been in use yesterday. It came from her father. "Brown" had had a chat with the postman. It was the last letter that Rose had received from the Professor. Father and daughter seemed linked by this search in town.

When Pointer arrived at Stillwater House he found the police inquiries in full swing. Superintendent Harris had finished with the servants, and the colonel, and was just about to ask Mrs. Lane to come to the library.

Harris had learnt no new facts, but he told Pointer that the colonel took full responsibility for Mrs. Lane. He had assured Harris that he had had a personal recommendation of the very highest with her, from the lady whom she had been a companion for some years, as well as a life-long friend. The lady was the late Mrs. Seymour, widow of a former Bishop of Zanzibar.

Pointer had watched both Mrs. Lane and Sibella Scarlett very closely at the inquest. One of them must have played a part in the strange drama of Thursday night. One, or both. He had been struck by the fact that each told a story so like the other's. That the younger, like the elder woman, had taken up an attitude of absolute stillness and taciturnity, volunteering nothing, and striding all answers to the barely essential; that the elder woman, like the younger, would not dot an *i* or cross a *t* until she had made quite sure to what words they belong. Yet the two were essentially different characters. One would have expected them to react differently.

Pointer pigeon-holed both under the heading, "Capable of Anything." But the "Anything" of Mrs. Lane would he thought, only be what she herself had decided on, after careful weighing of all the consequences. Once she had made up her mind, he would expect her to go on unflinchingly to the end. A dangerous type in connection, with a crime.

Sibella's "Anything" would be of a different calibre.

Literally anything to which she was moved. Anything to which her strange personality might incline. If Mrs. Lane could be dangerous because of her energy, coolness, and courage, Sibella might be still more so by virtue of her incalculability, and the smouldering fires which he felt sure were deep within her.

Mrs. Lane looked very composed as she sat facing him. She answered all questions with more readiness than she had shown at the inquest. But Pointer purposely kept to the same round.

Rose had not lingered after the dinner, which, on account of the concert, had been at half-past seven. Mrs. Lane had not seen her since she passed the drawing-room and declined coffee.

As to where she had spent the evening, the lady suggested that doubtless Rose had spent it in her own room, as she often did. The maid had seen her in the gray frock, Pointer threw in lightly. Upon which Mrs. Lane suggested that Rose might have changed for an evening stroll in the grounds or down to the village.

Sibella was next asked to come into the big, comfortable room. She had nothing fresh to add apparently, to what she had said at the inquest.

Pointer asked her finally whether Rose Charteris had heard from her father lately.

Sibella said that her cousin had received a registered letter from him, from Italy, only on Thursday. It had come while they were at the tea-table.

Could she describe it at all?

Long and narrow. Red sealing-wax. Inside was a note for Rose, and another enclosed letter.

Could she say what became of it?

Rose read the note, put it back in its envelope, an laid it on top of some weeklies under the tea-table.

And the enclosure. Could she describe that?

It was another longish envelope, sealed with black sealing wax, and with a name written on it. This Rose doubled in half, and stuffed into the silver chain bag on her lap. Sibella thought that both the writing and the name on this enclosed letter were those of Professor Charteris himself, though she could not be sure.

She went on to explain that while away on his travel her uncle would occasionally send any very private note or memoranda back to himself in sealed, addressed envelopes. He generally enclosed these to his secretary in town, but sometimes to Rose at Stillwater. As a rule the accompanying note would merely ask that the envelop be laid in a certain drawer in his desk, at either place where they would accumulate till his return. But some times later directions would request that the enclosure be sent on to some given address.

Rose was very careful of her father's correspondence. If neither the enclosed letter, nor the note to herself had been seen since her death, she had probably destroyed the one—Rose rarely kept letters—and had dealt with the enclosure as suggested. Sibella described the first as being a half sheet of white paper with some hotel heading a the top.

Pointer had gone piece by piece on Friday morning through the paper baskets and dust bins of Stillwater House, on the plea of having torn up some valuable instructions. He had the envelope, but he had found no trace of any such letter to Rose, anymore than of its enclosure. He thought that Sibella, however, was absolutely frank about the whole occurrence, whereas Mrs. Lane, when recalled and questioned, though she confirmed the other's account, showed a meticulous care to answer only what she was asked that suggested caution.

Paul, too, had very much the same to say. But the colonel professed absolute ignorance of the whole matter.

Sibella had hardly left the three police officials when di Monti was announced.

Superintendent Harris glanced at his watch.

"He's to the minute. He tapped me on the shoulder coming out of the courthouse, and asked for a word. So I gave him an appointment for here and now."

Di Monti looked very striking as he strode into the English room with its soft colouring, and stood in its cool spring light, he, a creature of a fiercer sun and of far darker shadows.

His hair, with the waved, floating top locks of a Fascist shone like black satin, springing up from his rather sloping forehead in an impetuous push. His eyes, with the heavy lids, clear-cut like those of a Holbein drawing, were as impenetrably black as ever. Of that shade that never, lightens, never changes The harsh lips were a trifle tense, the heavy jaw well to the fore. He carried himself, as always, with a steel-spring erectness. When he sat, he sat as though on wires.

"*Complementi, Signori!* I have come to speak to you about something which, unimportant before, is now of great importance. I think the maid was right. I know she was. I feel sure my engaged had something on her mind, especially the day before yesterday. Her last day." He closed on a tone of deep sorrow.

"Indeed, sir!" Pointer was all attention. So were the others.

"She asked me if it were not possible for me to be with, her on that evening. That last evening! I asked her if it was to go to the concert with her. She made me an odd reply. She said—the words are, as nearly as I can remember them, but the meaning is absolutely accurate—No. There is another place I am going to to-night where I should have liked you to be with me.' I took it lightly, 'A dance, eh?' She was fond of dancing, so am I. But she only said, 'As you are not coming it does not matter where it is.' I thought she was—piqued—I think you say—and I talked of something else. But now I see there was another explanation." He bit his lip and sighed "I tried to get her to say more, but my intended—" Di Monti, as always, had been talking with his hands as much as with his tongue. They now finished the sentence for him with a gesture that said, "You know how hard it was to make Rose speak when she did not want to." And they said it quite easily.

"Who do you think she was afraid of?"

"I have no faintest idea."

"There was some talk," Pointer went on, "you must excuse me if I pain you, there was some talk of a previous admirer—of a Mr. Bellairs."

Di Monti shrugged his shoulders. "I cannot say what I do not know. But the maid was right. I am sure that Miss Charteris was going to some definite place, possibly to meet some definite person, of whom she was in fear." He seemed unable to add more.

When he was gone, Pointer went up with Harris to Rose's studio, an empty room above her bedroom.

"Wonder where her sketches are? According to all the evidence, she was often out with her painting outfit. I want to see the result of so much industry. It looks as though that one drawing we have at the station is the only thing there is to show for the many sunset hours that Miss Charteris was supposed to've been working on the ruins. Ah, here's a sketch book! But only portraits. This one of the count is distinctly good, eh?"

Pointer was turning over the leaves as he spoke. "Suppose we take it with us and have a look at the ruins. I went yesterday as Brown, and learnt that Miss Charteris was often there mornings and evenings, including late on Thursday. At least, so a shepherd said. Know anything of the old fellow?"

"He's worked for Farmer Mason for forty years. Excellent character."

The scene by the abbey ruins that closed one end of the common was charming. Over the bright green turf gray and white sheep moved slowly along, browsing as they came. Above them, as though the earth were but changed reflection from on high, gray and white cloud swept steadily onward over another bright field, but deep blue this time, and vast and airy.

The shepherd, brown and wizened as a prune, touched his hat to Harris and looked keenly, at Pointer.

The superintendent opened briskly.

"Heard of the inquest?"

"Ay, master, I heard there wur to be one."

"Are you quite sure that you saw Miss Charteris Thursday evening, here?"

"I be. About an hour after sundown. Coming after nine, it wur."

"What was she doing?"

"Walking about. Taking notes of the moon on stones, like."

"You know that it's now thought that she was murdered?" Pointer spoke for the first time. As he had guessed, the man had not yet heard the real news of the day.

"Murdered! That young lamb! Missie murdered. Master, you"—his voice shook—"you fair 'maze me."

"The police are going to know about everyone who had any connection with the young lady. What about yourself? You've been a bit free with your money lately, I hear. Bought some fruit trees for your cottage, treated friends at the inn, and so on."

Pointer had made good use of yesterday afternoon. The shepherd looked at him with his clear old eyes. "Police yourself, master? High up on the roll-call likely?"

He nodded as Harris mentioned Pointer's rank. Then his mind went off to the more important facts.

"Murdered!" he repeated to himself. "Missie! Ay, now I wonder," he stood marking circles on the grass with his stick, "I do that!"

There was a little pause.

"I spoke naught but the truth when I said missie wur here night afore last, Thursday night. She wur here ten and she wur here afore that, but not so often as I may have led people to think, and never of a mornin'. She told me that she didn't care for drawing herself, but that her father he wur main set on it. So she slips me a shilling, or a crown even, now and again, to say to any askers that she come night a'ter night, and mornin' a'ter mornin'."

"How long would she stay?" Harris asked

"Long enough to hand me a bit of baccy or a summat, not longer."

"And then?"

"She'd go on by the short cut as she came by, on into the town."

"You never saw her go back this way?"

The shepherd shook his head. "Never. But come dark I fastens the sheep up in their hurdles, leaves Bob in charge, and I goes down for a bite and a sup before coming back for the night and all around ten."

"And how often was she out here?"

"She started coming a fortnight ago last Tuesday, and she comed twice that week, once the week after, and ivery even this last week from Monday to Thursday"

No questioning could shake him as to his certainty on these numbers.

"And you never saw anybody with her?"

"Never. But night afore last—Thursday—a gentleman come up after she wore gone by, and glances this way and that, looking for some un like, but he says naught"

"Did he go on, too, by the short cut into Medchester?"

"He come from theer, and went on towards Green Tree Farm."

That was also the direction of Stillwater House

Pointer produced the sketch book taken from Rose's studio.

"Is there any face among these drawings that reminds you of that gentleman?"

The shepherd turned over the pages with a chuckle, Though he shook his head at the trees.

"The branches of a noak, wi' the trunk of a birch! Eh, but she wore in a hurry, wore missie. You can't do naught wi' trees in a hurry. Longer than men they live, and they don't understand it. Time means naught to them. They don't understand—" He stopped. "Here he be." He laid a wrinkled finger on di Monti's portrait. "At least, if this baint he, 'tis none of t' others." This wind-up was feeble, but the old man would not commit himself more definitely.

"I think it's he, master, but I seed un but the once. It mightn't be he at all."

"You may have a chance to see the man himself before long. How did he strike you? You've a good eye for a man, I dare say."

Pointer offered the other some tobacco. The shepherd filled his clay pipe thoughtfully.

"Carried his head like a bellwether, he did. Set his feet down wi' a 'I lead you'm follow' sound to un. Ay," the old shepherd said from a cloud of smoke and reverie, "he wore a finely clad gentleman, to be sure, but he had a look to his face that night that made me think horns, and hoofs, and a tail, would a been his proper wear. Ay, master, it wore a look to chill you worse nor a Jannivary norther. And hearing what you've told me on today—" He broke off, and smoked another interval of thought away. "He wor the only man Bob was ever afeared on."

"Bob?."

"My mate. My dog. Bob he barked and growled when the gentleman come striding in among the sheep, for it wore latish, but he turns and says summat to Bob in his foreign tongue that fair humbled him."

"Foreign tongue, you say. Was he a foreigner, then?"

The shepherd ran a slow, bright eye over his questioners.

"Masing how the pollus has to learn from others," I mused.

Pointer and Harris laughed.

"Well, was he?"

"Ay, misters. The build on un would a told that. Ye don't get bones, slender and strong, like that wi' us. Nor an eye cut that shape. 'Tis the eye's cut that tells foreign blood in man or sheep."

"What country did he belong to, do you think?"

"Frenchy, I shouldn't wonder, though more like Eye-talian."

"He didn't speak to you?"

"No, though he wore half-minded to do it. Ay, and more than speak to one. He gives me a look from those black eyes of his as though he would 'a liked to've flayed the skin off me bones to make me tell him summat I wanted to know. But he thought better o't. He can bide his time, can that young gentleman, and 'tis more than thick fleece would be necessary to keep him from getting his teeth into ye, if he wore so minded."

CHAPTER FIVE

POINTER left Harris talking to the shepherd and walked on. The first house he came to was set back behind some cedars, but it had two gates opening on to the common, and would have been in full view of the ruins were it not for a deep bend in the road and some tall trees. An obliging postman had told him already that it was Mr. Bellairs's studio.

He swung the gate open and looked around him. There was no one about. The windows, of the bungalow-like building were all shuttered. Close to the front steps was a patch of grease and oil. A car must have stood there a couple of days ago. The path was too narrow for its wheels to mark the gravel; The knocker next interested the caller. Some one had nearly wrenched it off. And long ago. Pointer opened the door with one of his own keys.

The studio itself was a black and white and gold affair, superbly lit from behind a gilt cornice.

In front of one of the four fireplaces a black rug made an oasis, on which gilt Bergère chairs with thick black satin cushions stood around a gilt table.

Pointer walked the black and white marble squares of floor carefully, looking them over inch by inch.

He heard steps outside. Superintendent Harris had followed him, and was breathless with shocked amazement at this infringement of a fellow-Briton's castle.

"I'm glad the inspector isn't with us. You big-wigs of the Yard are the limit!" He looked fearfully about him. "Not a search warrant between the pair of us!"

Pointer swept a flake of black sealing-wax on to a sheet of paper and examined it. It matched the other dots that he had found in Rose's chain bag and in the empty registered envelope beneath the tea-table.

Then he began examining the built-in cupboards. In one was a black and gold Spanish tray set with gleaming amber glass. There were peaches, and strawberries, and a few macaroons. A small decanter with some Château Yquem, a beautiful crystal jug, evidently intended for water, and a couple of glasses, finished the preparations

"I don't call that much of a spread," Harris said "Not for a young lady, I don't. Just a bite for himself, I fancy. Nothing's been eaten, I see."

Pointer thought that the tray showed a very good knowledge of Rose Charteris's tastes. She never touched wine, she never ate cake, and the fruit was perfect. But he continued his search without speaking.

"Looking for anything in particular?"'Harris asked.

"Miss Charteris's portrait."

"Eh?" Harris almost dropped the tray.

"Well, a studio suggests a painting. So does an R.A," Pointer went on casually. "Suppose she was here to have her portrait painted, that might explain that pretty, frock under the knitted dress, and yet the fact that she didn't bother about shoes and stockings to match. It's the only explanation that I can see. I rather expect to find the picture damaged," he went on, half to himself.

It certainly was. Some one had hacked at it till it hung from the stretcher in ribbons, and then stuffed the whole behind a black velvet screen.

Rose's face in particular had been cut and cut again. There was something cruel about the way that the damage been done. It suggested a ferocious pleasure. But nothing could undo the fact that it was a three-quarter size painting of Miss Charteris.

In her pale peach silk frock with a knot of pink and the camellias on one shoulder tied with silver, and another gleam of silver at one hip, she sat in a gilt armchair, her white shoulders coming up like a tea rose from gold shadows around her. One hand toyed with a line of deep purple amethysts that ran around her neck on to her knee. The men gazed long at it. Bellairs caught something of a Rose whom even the superintendent had never seen. The young face was turned up, a wistful, eager, inquiring gaze, and the effect, considering the darkness even then about to close around that head, was tragic.

Harris's eyes were dim as he moved away.

"It doesn't seem possible," Pointer said at length, "that the man who painted this had anything to do with the murder of the girl there on that canvas. No, it doesn't seem possible."

"Mr. Bellairs gave my boy Arty French lessons, and helped him to get his first place in town." The superintendent spoke as though that clinched the certainty of the young man's innocence.

"My boy Arty" lay with many another father's only son in one of those corners of France that are for ever England, but to the superintendent he still lived on.

"As for the picture, painted by Bellairs right enough, but signed by—" Pointer began wrapping the torn picture in paper.

"Signed?" asked the literal Harris.

"Someone learns of these meetings," Pointer went on, "and gets them to open that front door at last. Then the canvas is chopped up. Now I wonder who would be likely to do all that?" He looked at Harris with a smile.

"Sort of thing one might expect of the count" Harris began to think that he, too, might have distinguished himself in the detective line.

Pointer was off again, continuing his search of the room. He stopped before one of the windows by the side door. The pulley arrangement was out of order. Some one had not waited to find out which acorn, the black or the gold, would open the heavy velvet curtains, but had jerked them apart, and the cords almost off the eyelets. He looked at the sill and then at the other window-sills. Only one showed those newly-made scratchings.

Stooping, he picked up an amethyst bead, and an opened link of silver chain. He examined the catch of the casement window.

"Looks as if she caught her chain of beads on that as she jumped out of the window—probably at the time that the Count was performing his fantasia on the front door. I wonder how she made her way home?" Pointer mused.

"I particularly questioned Maud about Miss Rose's shoes when she saw her at ten, as you told me," Harris put in. "She says they were quite clean."

"That means some one must have taken her home in a car. There were no taxis going begging Thursday night in Medchester, because of the concert. And, by the way, Harris, I wish you'd ask about, and find out, who really saw Miss Scarlett or Mrs. Lane there, and whether at the beginning, middle, or end of the entertainment. Try Doctor Metcalfe."

Harris's eyes bulged his question.

"Oh, just as a matter of routine. Just to check off all statements."

Harris made a note of it.

"It wouldn't be Miss Scarlett, in any case, who drove her cousin home," he assured the other. "She never drives at night. Too timid. Mrs. Lane now, she likes a bit of a risk all right."

Pointer thought of the garden mould on Sibella's shoe-buckles. But he went on with his work, testing each piece of furniture by laying hold of the back, and shaking it vigorously. When he did this to the table, a leg promptly parted company.

Harris, with a householder's feeling for another's property, would have stooped with an exclamation, but Pointer grasped his arm.

"Hold hard a minute. Your finger-prints aren't wanted, old chap" Pointer lifted the leg as though it were a blazing faggot, and looked carefully at the break. It had been wrenched off the table, and very recently. He tested it for finger-prints and smiled a little as he looked at them.

"By the look of it, some one swung this around his head like a club. Now let's see." He opened his notebook. "They're Count di Monti's," he said after using a magnifying glass for some very careful minutes.

"When did you get his?"

"This afternoon he took a glass of soda water. Remember? I took care of that glass afterwards. So now we stand like this. We think Miss Charteris was here because of her frocks, the portrait, the fruit tray, and the marks on the window. We know di Monti was here, and in a fury because of these prints. The other finger-prints sprinkled all about so freely will doubtless turn out to be those of Bellairs himself. And now I'm done here."

At Medchester police station they found that Inspector Rodman had carried out Pointer's instructions very successfully.

Lady Maxwell had been informed that a navy evening frock of hers had been found among some stolen property which the police had just recovered.

The lady was both surprised and impressed by the speed with which it had been traced to her. Rodman had merely told her that "the force has its own ways, madam," with some inward amusement as to exactly what those ways had been.

He wanted to know whether it had been as crumpled as now when last seen.

Lady Maxwell thought that it had been shamefully treated by the thieves. The maid thought that the ill-treatment had taken place at Stillwater House. Between the two, of them, Rodman, listening avidly, and putting a few questions now and then, had managed to get a clear account.

The frock was quite new. Lady Maxwell had worn it for the first time at dinner at Stillwater House on Thursday and torn it. As the frock had cost some thousands of francs, simple though it looked, she had gladly accepted Mrs. Lane's offer to send it for her next morning to a woman in Medchester who did beautiful "invisible mending."

After dinner, when she went to her rooms, her maid had folded it up and laid it on the hall table for Mrs. Lane to see to in the morning. And when the terrible accident to Miss Charteris decided her mistress to hurry away, the maid found it still on the table, but tightly rolled up in paper, and very crushed.

Mrs. Lane, had come up herself a little later, and offered to still have it mended in Medchester. She had pressed Lady Maxwell to accept her offer, but that lady finally decided to take it to town with her.

Its loss from the hotel had been discovered at once, but it was believed that by some oversight it must have been taken to the cleaners.

Rodman's explanation, such as it was, evidently cut short a very promising triangular duel between mistress, and maid, and cleaner.

"So we now know that the frock might have been slipped on by any of the women in Stillwater House that night," Rodman muttered.

Pointer nodded. "Just so."

He proceeded to give the two police-officers a straight, condensed account of what he had found yesterday morning at the summer house down by the lake.

Harris said afterwards that if he hadn't had the presence of mind to catch hold of his jaw it would have fallen off altogether.

Even Rodman gaped.

"So those beads that were found by the sand-pit must have tumbled out of Miss Charteris's frock when they lifted her body off the truck."

Barns remembered the two brought him.

"Now," Pointer finished, "we want to find out three things of almost equal importance.

"First, who was the man of the summer house. He was not of what I call the Stillwater circle. That is, he wasn't the colonel, nor Mr. Thornton, nor Mr. Bellairs nor Count di Monti, nor Mr. Bond, nor Mr. Cockburn, nor any of the menservants. I've seen all their fingerprints by now."

He went on to speak of the probable connection between the stranger and the letter received by the colonel on Wednesday noon.

"It was delivered by the chauffeur of a Sir Henry Carew.

"Who's he?"

"Neighbour of the colonel's. Late of, the same regiment. Tons of money."

"Married?" asked Pointer.

"Grandfather," Harris said triumphantly, in a tone that nipped any romantic suppositions in the bud.

"Any sons?"

"One. Fell at Givenchy."

"Then very probably he sent the colonel a warning."

"Ah, he would do that!" Harris quite approved of this idea.

"According to Paul, the colonel dined with him on Wednesday in town, and spent the evening with him, getting back about half-past twelve."

"They're often together," Harris threw in "Sir Henry, for one thing, owns a horse at this moment that the colonel's going to back for all he's worth, I hear. I'm rather inclined myself to—"

Pointer brought the talk back to the matter in hand, and ran over the possible suppositions about the unknown man who had lain on the bed of the summer house, very much as he had done to O'Connor, but in a tabulated, abbreviated form.

"That's the first point. The second we want to find out is, who was the man who pushed the carrier to the sand-pit. Thirdly, we want to trace out the woman who walked beside the man. She probably wore the stained blue dress. So much for the main facts. As to the motive for the murder—there's the idea of jealousy. We have two men and two women belonging to Miss Charteris's own circle that might have something to say to that. Bellairs and the count, Mrs. Lane and Miss Scarlett.

"The count, you remember, said that not only had he a perfect alibi for all Thursday evening and night from eight on, but that he was going to bring down two friends, a Prince Cornaro and a Mr. del Greco, a relation of the Italian Ambassador, to confirm it. We know there was a meeting at which he spoke at eleven, but if he was late he could have reached it after Miss Charteris was killed. However, if his alibi's as good as he says, he's out of it—seemingly.

"As for Mr. Bellairs, of course, in the ordinary way, we should ask for an explanation at once about that studio of his. But he's staying at Windsor Castle until Tuesday, painting a portrait of the Queen for the coming World's Conference of Women. But now, suppose the motive isn't jealousy, or anything in that line. Suppose Miss Rose's death was to some one's advantage—"

"Ah, but it wasn't!" put in Harris almost gleefully. "Not advantage enough to the Stillwater lot. Miss Sibella gets that Italian legacy, if it's ever paid, and that's all the profit there is. Her money don't come to the colonel till after her father's death. I've been talking to Mr. Gilchrist."

"I suppose the count's too wealthy to feel the pinch of letting the property go?" Inspector Rodman puzzled aloud, "but, of course, now there's only one girl to marry."

Harris turned on him quizzically.

"Look here, he's an Italian, not a Mormon."

"What I mean, sir, is this. That Italian property went to Miss Charteris, and, after her death, to Miss Scarlett, and then back to the di Monti. Now Miss Charteris's gone, if the count marries Miss Scarlett, it takes it back into the family at once, as it were?"

"I thought it went to Miss Scarlett permanent to will away," Harris said after a pause. "Let's look at the papers. I laid a note of her money affairs in with 'em."

He opened the safe and took out a parcel, untied it, and then started.

"Why, they're gone! These newspapers have been put in instead."

"When were they out of your keeping?" Pointer asked equably.

"The chief asked to see them, so I sent Briggs up there, yesterday about seven. The major sent them back again about nine. Mr. Thornton returned them. He'd been dining there."

"Who else was at Major Vaughan's at dinner, do you know?"

"Only the colonel, Briggs said."

'You may be sure that any one even remotely connected with the case would look in in the course of the evening," Pointer said a little grimly.

"I know the count did for a fact. But, Alf, the major wouldn't show these papers to outsiders—"

"But he might leave them in some downstairs room, tied up, labelled, and ready to be sent back."

Rodman nodded. He thought that the chief constable might very easily have done that.

"But," Harris tried to keep his head above water, "they were only letters, except that note I shoved in, only Miss Rose's letters—".

"Just so," Pointer said briskly. "Letters. Possibly some one thought that that missing enclosure the professor sent his daughter, and which no one seems able to trace, might be there too."

"You thought that flake of sealing-wax on the table at the studio meant it had been there. Perhaps she had handed it over to some one, Mr. Bellairs, say."

"Possibly. I've written to him to ask for a full account of how he spent Thursday night, from eight onwards. But that flake was on a little table by the door, you know, not on the central table. It looks to me more as though the black-sealed envelope had been merely laid down on the small table to be out of the way."

"Pity one can't just ask the professor what the letter, and second, inside envelope, is all about," Harris said.

"The colonel is inserting an advertisement in all the Italian, French, and Balkan newspapers addressed to his brother-in-law, and asking him to return immediately. That ought to reach him soon, wherever he is." And with that, Pointer left his two helpers and began to look through the reports that had been sent down by a motor cyclist from Scotland Yard.

He learnt that no hospital had taken in any case on Thursday night that could possibly be connected with the man he wanted. Private nursing-homes were being investigated, but they would take time, as all inquiries were to be so carefully made. A list was furnished the Chief Inspector of all the doctors and surgeons who attended the French hospital in Soho. One of these, Pointer noted, had a nursing-home in a smart part of the West end. He was Sir Martin Martineau. In accordance with his instructions, very special inquiries had been made there, but they had led to nothing.

Pointer filed the notes and went out for a stroll. The stroll took him to Doctor Metcalfe's. But that young man's flood of gossip had nothing in it which threw any new light on the facts of the case, and Pointer decided finally that perhaps sleep was not a mere luxury, even in the beginning of a case, and, following Harris's example, was soon himself tucked up in a room of the superintendent's. For Brown had taken his departure from Red Gates before the inquest.

Next morning he was early up at Stillwater House for a chat with Paul, who liked him.

"Nothing has been changed, I suppose?" Pointer asked, following him into the deserted dining-room

"No, sir. Funeral's at three," Paul said sadly. "Hasn't been a funeral of anybody under sixty from this house since I've been in service here. And me having been born on the estate can be relied on for facts. And to think of its being our Miss Rose now. It still don't seem real sometimes."

"Ladies going?" asked Pointer.

Paul said they were.

"With whom is Mrs. Lane driving?" Pointer asked again.

"With Miss Sibella. At least—well—that had been so arranged, but they've had a little—ahem, ladies will be ladies," Paul finished obscurely.

"Trouble, eh?" Pointer offered him a cigar. "Mrs. Lane looks to me as if she had a bit of a temper."

Paul eyed him in mild amazement.

"Then I should try glasses, sir," he said finally. "Mrs. Lane's as gentle a creature as ever stepped. Now, Miss Sibella—"

"What was the trouble between the ladies about?"

"I don't rightly know myself. It took place at dinner last night. The colonel started talking about the concert. You would not be aware of that, sir, but there was a concert in Medchester on the Thursday night, the last night our Miss Rose was alive."

"Was there indeed?" came from Pointer.

"They were all joining in friendly like, when all at once you could hear sort of daggers in the ladies' voices. Don't ask me what it was about. Talking of the concert, they were, as I said. Mrs. Lane only said that she thought she had heard more of the music than Miss Sibella, or something like that, when our young lady gets up, and says she isn't accustomed to have her word doubted, 'not even by Mrs. Seymour's late companion,' she says, with a nasty little laugh, and I could hardly get to the door in time, before she sailed through."

"Humph, and then?"

"The colonel, he looked—well, you know how a man feels when the women about him get to nagging each other —he looked just like that. And after a minute he said, 'I'm afraid poor Sibella's nerves are upset by this terrible affair.' Mrs. Lane she sits there, trying to keep the tears back, I thought, till she suddenly jumps up, and says low, but boiling over as it were, 'And so are mine!' And with that she leaves the colonel, too. The colonel he says, 'Good God! It's past bearing!' And then he went to his study."

Pointer filled in the gaps as he walked away. So Mrs. Lane and Sibella were not on the best of terms.

As he passed Red Gates he heard voices in the little arbour. Pushing open the gate, he caught sight of Thornton talking to Cockburn, who had come with Bond for the funeral.

"Look here! Should one, or should one not, tell all that one suspects in a case of this kind, as well as all that one knows? Terrible to bring suspicion on the wrong person." Cockburn's voice was hesitating.

"Worse to let the right person escape!" came from Bond, in the balcony above them.

"I like to be sure I'm right before I go ahead," murmured Cockburn doubtfully.

"And I like to be sure I'm wrong, before I stop," Bond. retorted firmly.

"I think," Thornton's voice came thoughtfully, "I think I should feel it my duty to tell everything, even though it incriminated my nearest and dearest."

Pointer sincerely trusted that Mr. Thornton was speaking the truth. But he did not feel sure.

"You would, eh?" Cockburn seemed to have some difficulty in accepting the ruling.

"You're a thorough chap, Thornton. That's what I like about you," Bond said approvingly. But Cockburn seemed wrestling with doubts.

"That's easily said," he muttered around his pipe stem, "but take a man, an innocent man, as innocent as you, or I, of Miss Charteris's murder, and let him do something suspicious. I don't quite see—" His voice fell off.

Thornton repeated firmly that he would tell everything, and let the man clear himself.

"Excellently put, sir." Pointer stepped out into the tiny pergola. Thornton seemed to realise, that his emphasis-might have given away the topic, so he said lightly,

"Oh, I'm only quoting from a friend's play I'm reading."

"That's what the hero says, I suppose," Cockburn grumbled.

"Or perhaps what the villain says to throw others off the track," Pointer suggested suavely, looking at Thornton. Had he, or had he not, lent that car of his last Thursday night?

"Suppose it's just an onlooker's speech. Just a puzzled onlooker's," Thornton parried.

"Puzzled because what he knows won't square with what he hears?" Pointer asked.

The eyes of the two men met and locked.

"Look here, Co., we're in the way." Bond jumped up.

"Oh, I don't think that I'm going to be arrested yet." Thornton gave his sardonic smile. "Have a chair and a cigar, Chief Inspector?"

Pointer took the first, and produced his briar. "You were saying, Mr. Cockburn—"

"Oh, just fancies—generalities," Cockburn spoke a little shyly. "It's about last Thursday. I felt something was in the air down here at Stillwater, and I've just been wondering whether it could have anything to do with a story, I heard last night. There's a girl I know in town, who knows Bellairs jolly well. She thinks he means to marry, her. Perhaps he does."

"Perhaps he doesn't," Bond put in sceptically.

"She says, this girl I'm speaking of, that Bellairs saw quite a good deal of Miss Charteris lately. She's convinced that he was down here at his studio last Thursday night, though she has no proof. Of course, this may only be her jealous imaginings, but on Thursday, I thought—" Cockburn broke off vaguely.

"You thought?" Pointer prompted, after a little wait.

"Well, supposing, the colonel and di Monti had got wind of the same story? Di Monti played a single with Miss Charteris after tea, and I never saw such serves, nor such returns—to a girl. By jove, he as good as tried to bang her with the ball more than once"

"Oh, come now!" Bond gave a laugh of sheer incredulity.

"Fact! Miss Scarlett, who was looking on, too, made some comment about his playing so hard, and he got himself in hand a bit after that. But the man was in a murderous temper. Absolutely murderous. And," Cockburn went on doggedly, "you, too, noticed the look on the colonel's face when we heard that shot on Thursday?"

He had turned again to Thornton, who nodded shortly "Well, there isn't any one who carries a revolver around here but the count. A Facistt is always armed, he told us once. I'm convinced that the colonel half-feared the truth then. And what about those blood-stained bits of cord we tried to match in the colonel's study when you caught us, Chief Inspector? It was the cord that the colonel had given di Monti, though we didn't know that then."

The four men sat awhile in silence.

"Is di Monti being watched?" Bond asked suddenly.

"My dear Bond, we're all being watched!" Thornton snapped out in a tone which suddenly charged the atmosphere with menace. Murder had been done. The murderer was still at large. Something grim and horrible showed its vague outline. The monstrous deed seemed to loom nearer.

Pointer shook his head.

"I'm sorry to bring you all down to humdrum earth, but don't think you have any idea how expensive the watching of three people would be. I'm afraid that only the possible criminal gets as far as that."

"Supposing there isn't a criminal?" Thornton said abruptly, and as always with him, Pointer had the impression that his speech had been looked over, inspected, before he allowed it out. "Suppose there has been no crime?" He was watching the chief inspector as he spoke.

"Suppose what, instead, then?" Pointer asked curiously.

I hardly know—an accident, for instance, and some attempt to cover it up?"

Pointer, had asked himself that question very seriously at first, but he had thought even then that the efforts to cover up all traces of the death having taken place at the summer house were too intense. Those steps along that short-cut, behind the dead girl's body, straightening her bier, while wearing her shoes! Would any woman do such a thing unless the need were of the most extreme urgency? Apart from everything else, he thought not. If either of the women were Mrs. Lane, or Sibella Scarlett, he was sure not. That it was one of them, the disarrangement of Rose Charteris's bed seemed to prove conclusively. Only these two, barring the servants, would have easy access to Rose's room, would think of the sketching box.

"That's an interesting theory," he said. "Could you enlarge on it at all, sir?"

No. Thornton said that he had no data, but that all along he had had a feeling that some most unfortunate combination of circumstances had made Miss Charteris's death look as though a crime had been committed, when possibly it was only a blunder.

"Bond and Co." seemed to find much food for thought in the novel theory. Pointer went off, saying that he must think it over. Perhaps Mr. Thornton would think it over, too, and let him know if anything bearing out his idea occurred to him.

He himself took up an inconspicuous position near Stillwater's front door. Lady Maxwell was the first to arrive for the funeral. She was shown into the drawing-room, and Pointer decided that the Virginia creeper beside it needed more attention than it had had from him. He was busy examining the trellis when Sibella entered the room. For a while the talk was a very one-sided affair. Pointer got the impression that Sibella did not like her visitor any too well. Or else she was so wrapped in her own dark thoughts that it was only with difficulty that she could rouse herself to take any interest in what the other was saying. One such momentary flicker came when the name of a Miss Winter was mentioned.

"Miss Winter?" Sibella said, as though miles away. "Oh, yes, of course, Mrs. Seymour's cousin."

"Yes, the head mistress of Biswell. She and Mr. Seymour practically lived together. She's abroad, unfortunately, just now. But I wired her at once, as soon as I saw the statement in the papers, and she wired back that she had never heard the name of Lane, and that her cousin never had a companion."

"Surely we don't need to discuss this now? There might be a truce to-day? All such things seem so petty." Sibella spoke very low.

"But in view of Rose's having been murdered, Sib, darling, every moment may be of value. The woman may try to run away. You don't know who she is. Your father is such a good sort that he would never suspect anything wrong. Rose never liked her."

"I know, but—" Sibella seemed to have no strength to waste in argument. "Oh, well, let us get it over it then. What is it you want to do?"

"I don't want anything," Lady Maxwell spoke with some acerbity, "but I think the police should be told at once that the reference is false—" The door into the hall was standing open. The colonel appeared with telegram in his hand.

"Bellairs says he can't—" He stopped at sight of the woman talking to his daughter. He tried to back noiselessly away, but Lady Maxwell called him. Apparently the colonel did not hear her, for the door of the study shut very swiftly, but not before the watcher outside saw the look of alarm that was on it. The visitor, with a murmured word of apology or explanation, rose and went after him.

Sibella paid no heed. She sat with her forehead leaning on her hand, her eyes closed.

A minute later and Mrs. Lane came in. She was very pale, with purple shadows around her eyes. Coming across to the girl, she put her arm around the slender shoulders.

"Sibella, my dear, I thought you would be here alone. I want to say—" Her, voice was very gentle, but Sibella jumped to her feet, her long, black gloves falling to the floor.

"Oh! They're bringing her—IT—down the stairs! Talk to me! Talk to me! For God's sake don't let me hear the sound of those heavy steps! Don't!"

She grasped Mrs. Lane's arm, trembling violently. Mrs. Lane, too, looked as though she were all but fainting. Pointer thought that only a very unusual will kept her upright on her feet. Her face was green white. Her breath came in little gasps. In silence the two women inside the room, and Pointer outside, heard the heavy tramp and scuffle as the top of the stairs were turned.

Sibella fell back into her chair.

"Rose! Rose, who always ran down them!" She was almost writhing as she put her fingers into her ears. Mrs. Lane hid her face in her hands.

There came a sudden, loud peremptory knock at the door.

It was the coffin, one corner of which struck it in turning.

Sibella's head and shoulders plunged forward. She was in a dead faint, and Mrs. Lane looked as though one straw more would break her.

Lady Maxwell returned. There were tears in her eyes. She had met the men at their task. The lady-housekeeper waited till she bent over Sibella. Then she felt for the door-knob as though unable to see it.

Di Monti almost collided with her as he stepped in hastily. He was obviously, giving the undertaker's men more room. The strange thing was that he stepped in with a look of fierce satisfaction on his face. It vanished as he helped Lady Maxwell lay the girl on the sofa.

"All the better if she doesn't hear them carry the coffin out of doors. Though it's really quite absurd. Giving way like this. It isn't as if they had been fond of each other. But Sib always was one to let her feelings run off With her. Now she's coming to." Lady Maxwell spoke as one who had scant sympathy with weakness.

"You are mistaken, Lady Maxwell," di Monti said in his most formal manner, "I happen to know that Miss Rose was very fond of Miss Sibella indeed. These last days especially."

"I shouldn't overdo it, if I were you," was the lady's caustic and rather surprising reply.

Di Monti looked as though he had been struck. His eyes flashed, his face crimsoned. His upstanding top-locks quivered. But he only bowed, and at that moment Pointer had to move away from the window, for Paul was looking for him.

Pointer's mind as he drove in the funeral cortege was with the two women whom he had watched in such a convulsion of feeling.

Each felt herself guilty. Was it only in some measure, or in full measure? A good deal would depend on temperament. But even allowing for the most highly strung nerves—and both Sibella and Mrs. Lane possessed that doubtful blessing, there was more here than they would explain. Some knowledge, some fact, some deed, lay behind such emotion. Of that Pointer was sure.

The afternoon of Rose Charteris's funeral was a marvel of song and bloom and scent. It was the May of the poets, of bud-swollen branches and filmy green leaves. The pink of the crab apple trees around the old churchyard showed up in spaced beauty against the wild cherries. The blackthorns reached their snowy arms, beginning to look a little ragged, from out the beautiful young green of their cousins, the hawthorns, whose blossoms were only a promise, a closely-kept secret, as yet.

The pale-green bud clusters of the hollies were just tinging into white, but a cloud of their blue butterflies—symbol and warning—swept past the mourners' faces like a delicate smoke wreath, on the first flight of their lives. A thrush sang a wonderful song as they lowered the body of Rose into the earth to which it was to return.

The service affected the men officially engaged in the hunt very keenly. There was not one who did not swear to himself a vow—by that bole in the ground, by that oblong box—to do his utmost to see that the murderer paid.

After Colonel Scarlett had dropped the first earth on to the coffin, di Monti stepped forward. From his handful came a rattle that made the clergyman peer over his prayer-book. Some stones must have got picked up as well. Di Monti did not seem to have heard them, as, with bent head, he stood beside Scarlett, a picture of mourning.

CHAPTER SIX

POINTER had a short talk with Lady Maxwell after the funeral, but he learnt nothing fresh. She repeated her doubts about Mrs. Lane, and the fact that the colonel, when she had felt it her painful duty to speak to him on the point just now, had said that his lady housekeeper was too efficient to lose, and that if there were any mistake, it was his. He must have confused two Mrs. Seymours.

The object of the lady's suspicions was sitting very quietly in the arm-chair into which she had sunk on her return from church.

After a long time spent in thought, she walked downstairs and into the study. The colonel, too, was sitting staring into space.

On seeing her he rose abruptly, and with a look of caution went to the door and shut it again to make sure that it was caught.

"Does she suspect anything? Lady Maxwell, I mean?" he whispered "Paul's downstairs. Those damned police are off the premises for once. Does she know anything?" he repeated irritably.

"Nothing, I think, except that I was never a companion to a Bishop's widow."

For a second Scarlett stared at her, as though she had spoken in some foreign tongue.

"Oh!" he said at last, "you mean your reference? Well, I had, to say something when the police sprang the question on me. But was that—"

She interrupted him. "I think it would be as well if I were to go to town. I don't see else—there's danger," she said in a low voice.

"Danger of having communications cut off," he finished. "I was just thinking the same when you came in. Have you thought of where to go?"

"You have a furnished house at Victoria standing empty till June. I'll go there as a sort of caretaker." She raised her hand. "Don't let's talk any more about it to-day. I feel as though," she was at the door before he had guessed her intention, "I want to be alone, for a while."

She was gone. The colonel mixed himself a stiff drink.

Pointer found Cockburn's car waiting for him at the police station. It had been waiting some time.

"Bond had to get back to town. He went by train, but I wanted to see you about something. You know that shot I heard, or thought I heard, last Thursday night?" Cockburn began briskly.

Pointer nodded.

"Well, Count di Monti's tyre burst coming back from the funeral. I heard the sound again at that moment. It wasn't a shot after all, but one of his tyres I heard go *phut*. They're a patent, reinforced, balloon type, of a very curious make."

"You're quite sure of this?"

"I'm prepared to swear to it. Such a sound might travel far on a quiet evening just before a storm. Anyway, that's the noise we heard and mistook for a shot." Cockburn's voice was quite definite.

Pointer turned over his latest addition to the puzzle for a minute.

"You see," he explained—Cockburn was talking to him in his own sitting-room, "the trouble is that Count di Monti has a very good alibi for the hours from eight on Thursday till Friday morning. Prince Cornaro and a Signor del Greco are prepared to swear that he was in their company from dinner till the meeting of Italian Fascisti, which took place at eleven, and afterwards till ten the next morning, or a little after. They're both very definite and very positive. The head waiter at Frasati's bears out the dinner hour as eight. The count most certainly spoke at the meeting. For the rest of the time we have to rely on the honour of the two gentlemen."

Cockburn nodded in his turn. He was listening very seriously. "I quite understand all that. But can't the alibi be tested?"

"I don't mind saying that it's so good it's suspicious."

"That's what I think. Now, Mr. Thornton, it seems, knows a Cavaliere Rossi, the London correspondent, for the best Italian papers. An anti-Fascist. He might be able to tell us something about di Monti and Thursday night."

Pointer heartily commended this idea.

Armed with a letter, and preceded by a telephone message from Thornton to the Cavaliere, Cockburn sped up to the Italian's club.

Rossi turned out to be a tall, good-looking young man with a merry, dark eye. He burnt Thornton's little note in the wood fire.

"Have a cocktail of my family Vermouth while we talk. This corner is absolutely safe from eavesdroppers and, what is more difficult to secure in England, and much more important, from draughts. Now, what do you want me to tell you about di Monti?"

"Oh, all sorts of things. First of all, what is his position here?"

"Slippery. If the Ambassador likes, he can disown him. If he likes, he can throw his mantle over him, and then you won't be able to touch him."

"I can hardly imagine a war over that chap! But which way would his Excellency's preferences run?" Rossi bent forward in mock intensity.

"It depends on how much there is to throw his cloak over. A little heap of political trouble or a great mound of it. It would stretch in the one case, but not in the other. At least, that is how things seem to stand. Di Monti is on a mission, straight from our 'Musoon.' Sent to organise the Italian Fascisti in London. The anti-Communists, that is—."

Cockburn glanced meditatively at his glass.

"The *pro-'Italia uber alles,'* eh?" he asked quietly. Rossi shrugged his shoulders, with a laugh at the mixture of tongues.

"Perhaps! After all, every country sings that song. 'Britannia Rules the Waves' sounds so very like it to some ears, my friend. But to continue—the mission is a sort of test. Cangrande did splendidly with d'Annunzio's *Arditi* in Fiume."

Cockburn made a face.

"That is as may be, but he did well. Then came that Corfu incident. He was partly responsible for the way that was carried out. So he got into semi-disgrace. Now, as it happens, the dream of his life has always been our colonies. Tripoli, and then this Oltrajuba. He wants to be sent out with a free hand to organise the latter. He may get it—if there is no trouble, no hint of disgrace. But he will not get it if he is mixed up publicly in this story. And it is being decided in the Inner Council at Rome even now."

"Tell me, Cavaliere, do you think the man capable of murder?"

"Are we not all capable of murder? I am."

"No," Cockburn said with conviction. "That is one of our catch phrases, that 'Every man is capable of murder.' In reality, few people are. And here it's a question of a young and frightfully, lovely girl. Not one man in a million would have been willing to harm her."

"I know. I've seen her more than once. Madonna, she was beautiful!"

"Do you think the Count capable of murdering her?" persisted Cockburn.

Rossi looked uncomfortable.

"Jealousy is a fearful poison," he confessed.. "I think we of the south feel it more than you can. With us it is something that can change us altogether until it is past. How can I say he would not fall, where so many men have fallen?"

"Look here, did you see him yourself at the meeting on Thursday?"

"I did. He took the chair from eleven till twelve."

"Well, then, was he late?" Cockburn felt sure that all was not as it should be with that alibi. He was convinced that di Monti was in the events of Thursday night for something.

"Not to speak of. Perhaps half an hour, more or less. You know with us Italians—" The hands finished the. sentence, gracefully.

"Did he seem as usual at the meeting?" Cockburn probed. He had discussed with Pointer the best questions to ask.

Rossi thought a while, running his slender hands through his hair.

"In no way—no. He is never a magnetic speaker, but he is reliable and very much in earnest. Last Thursday I thought he seemed rather duller than usual."

"Duller!" Cockburn had not expected this.

"Well, then, put it that his thoughts were somewhere else. He had a colour in his face, and a red light in his eyes that I had never seen in him before."

Cockburn sipped his Vermouth.

"You don't like di Monti?" he asked.

Rossi shook his head.

"I don't. But I've told you only the truth, none the less," he added with a slight smile.

"May I ask you why you don't like him?"

Rossi shrugged.

"Why don't I like him? There is something—what shall I say—sinister?—in the man that repels me. Then, too, his name has been mixed up at home with some very savage punitive expeditions, and you know what that means, when the Fascisti—"

Rossi checked himself here.

"I've told you all I know of the man," he finished.

"Thanks ever. I wish some of your facts had been more discreditable," Cockburn said in a low voice, and

Rossi chuckled. "Now, a last favour. Just let me have the address of the friend who took di Monti to his rooms, will you? The name was del Greco."

Rossi was able to give it him, and Cockburn put in an hour's work learning, by a few, very shrewdly-placed questions, from a couple of maids in the flat below, that the rooms upstairs had been empty till after midnight on Thursday.

He felt quite pleased with himself as he walked away, though Pointer could have told him that servants' testimony against a man of di Monti's position was not a sure move.

Pointer meanwhile was up in town, too. He had decided to pay the count's rooms in the Albany a visit himself. Watts had gone over them in vain, but the Chief Inspector thought that he might find some neglected trifle.

The rooms showed more books than Pointer had expected. Besides the inevitable bust of Dante, the Italian tri-colour, and a well-thumbed Carducci, there were books on agriculture, grammars of Tuareg and Arabic dialects, pamphlets on army training, and a host of similar works The only letters were business letters, except a few from his own family in Italy.

At the back of the boot-cupboard he unearthed a little posy of flowers. Some one had set the boots down on the top of the delicate blossoms. Pointer picked them up with a dim sense of cruelty. The touch told him that they were artificial, but they were beautifully copied from nature. A little bunch of pink and white camellias tied with silver ribbon—the shoulder-knot that Rose had been wearing in Bellairs's portrait of her. They had been flung with such force to the back of the cupboard that their stems were doubled up. The petals were worse yet. It looked to him, it certainly looked to him, as though a boot-heel had crunched on them. Accident or intention?

Pointer thought a trifle grimly of the patent anguish with which Count di Monti had spoken only yesterday, before himself and the two police-officers, of his dead fiancée's feeling of fear.

He closed the door and descended the stairs. He was due at the commissioner's shortly. At the entrance di Monti passed him. The Italian stopped at sight of the detective-officer, and a cold smile flickered across his face. A smile with no suggestion of mirth in it.

"A visit to me?"

"Another time will do as well. I am due now at New Scotland Yard," Pointer replied civilly.

Di Monti stood for a second looking at the other without speaking, and Pointer suddenly smelt danger, and very close beside him.

It was a mad idea that he could be attacked in broad daylight, but he knew it to be a fact. He turned away with a nod, and walked slowly on out of the door past the big gray car. The driver, di Monti's man, watched him sleepily.

Pointer, thought that he, too, resembled a beast of prey with forest laws and forest passions. He drove on to the Yard with a feeling that things were about to take some definite turn. That smile of di Monti's, like a snake it had crossed that hard face, it meant something. He felt certain that the count had taken some decision at that moment. What one?

Back at the police station, he learnt that neither Harris nor Rodman had been able to find any one who had seen either Mrs. Lane or Miss Scarlett at the beginning of the concert last Thursday, though at the very end Sibella had slipped in, and Mrs. Lane had taken her seat about the middle of the entertainment.

"Just so." Pointer handed Harris back the report to file away. "They were off on two different missions. Now, Miss Sibella's evening shoes were pretty well covered with garden mould when I saw them on Friday. I think we may take it that she was the one who helped Miss Rose home from the studio in that little two-seater both use."

"I shouldn't wonder," Harris said with alacrity. "Shows that she realised how nasty the count might be, for, as I say, she bars night driving."

"I shouldn't wonder," Pointer quoted with a smile "And now, here's the latest find"

He laid a sheet of notepaper in front of the superintendent. Harris picked it up.

"Never saw such a fist in all my life! Whose is it?"

"The Professor's. It's the letter that Miss Charteris got on Thursday, the one that accompanied the enclosed black-sealed envelope. It's in Italian. Here's what he says."

He laid down another slip Harris read in English:

"B0LZAN0 HOTEL LAURIN

"My DEAR DAUGHTER, I am sending you an enclosure with this, addressed to myself, which please keep by you pending future directions. I may want it destroyed. I may not. The weather here is very cold. I wish I had taken your advice and brought my warmer underwear. As you thought, it was quite chilly at Genoa.

"Your affectionate father,

"HENRY CHARTERIS."

"Bit of a sell, eh?" said the disappointed Harris. "And why Italian? His writing would have been enough of a safeguard, I should have thought."

The date was the Monday before Rose was murdered

"Lady Maxwell told me that the professor often talked and wrote both to his daughter and to his niece in Italian so as to keep it up. I found this letter tucked between the pages of a new Italian dictionary in Mrs. Lane's bedroom."

"Hidden?"

"Or laid away in safe keeping. There's nothing much in the letter itself, except that it seems to point to the importance of the accompanying enclosure, which was, as we were told, addressed to the professor himself. The odd thing is, why was this half-sheet taken? Why did Mrs. Lane buy that Italian dictionary late on Thursday at

Jephson's in the High Road? Why was she, or they, so anxious to learn what was in the letter? And Genoa," Pointer paused a moment to fill his pipe, "Genoa! That's not the way the colonel told us three separate times that the professor was going into Italy. If you look at your report, you'll see he says that his brother-in-law was going through Italy by way of Modena-Turin-Milan-Venice. His very insistence struck me as odd. Now, here the professor refers to having been in Genoa, and that not as though it had been an afterthought"

Pointer stared at the note a little longer.

"I shouldn't be surprised if Mrs. Lane came so late to the concert because she was in some quiet nook, railway station or bun shop, translating this It would take her some time The professor's handwriting ought to be forbidden by law. I thought the letter was in cuneiform at first."

"Instead of being in Medchester. I see." Harris nodded solemnly. "Of course, Mrs. Lane's a newcomer down here." His tone indicated resignation to any blows from that quarter. "You think she's in it, then?"

"'It was always the Case to all the men engaged on "It."

" 'Fraid so. I think she's the woman who walked in Miss Charteris's shoes on that path to the sand-pit late that same night." Pointer spoke very gravely. "She has a short-stepping gait. Not like Miss Scarlett's stride. And her weight and size of foot would fit the marks."

"Lady Maxwell wears sixes or sevens," Harris said ungallantly. "I measured her footsteps."

The door opened, and Rodman saluted.

"Mrs. Lane's just left for town, sir. The servants say that she told them that the colonel had asked her to look after a furnished house of his some time ago, and that she only waited till the funeral was over before taking up her new duties. Miss Scarlett's going shortly, to stay with Lady Carew at their Devon place. The colonel's remaining on."

Rodman went back to his observation post at Stillwater House.

"With Lady Carew! There you are Alf!" Harris said triumphantly. "You wondered, why Sir Henry wasn't at the funeral. I told you he'd gone to Sledmere. The colonel himself dropped that to me. Now you see that there's no ill-feeling."

"Sir Henry left on Friday afternoon very suddenly for Yorkshire after having backed out nearly a week before at the last moment," Pointer observed.

"Well, what, of it?"

Pointer eyed Harris's indignant face with a twinkle.

"Search me! as the Americans say, and if at the same time you could find the answer to why Sir Henry Carew does not seem to've been notified of Miss Charteris's death, I should be obliged."

"How do you make that out—about his not having been told?"

"I can't be sure, but I came across a list of names to which notices were to be sent that had been given Mrs. Lane. It was a long one. His wasn't on it. One of my men is in the Army and Navy Club, where the two generally hang out, and he says that, according to one of the waiters, Carew learnt it by chance late in the afternoon from a mutual acquaintance. The waiter says Sir Henry had a cab called within the hour and just caught his train."

Pointer glanced at the last note on Harris's pad of the afternoon. Mr. Cockburn had telephoned the result of his efforts to crack the count's alibi. The Chief Inspector looked pleased.

"Good! We'll get him to find out more about the count for us."

Next morning, the morning after the funeral, Pointer received a very austere reply from Mr. Bellairs at Windsor Castle.

The artist stated that he was at a loss to understand the communication which he had just received. He had been indisposed on Thursday evening, and had kept to his rooms, even cancelling a dance engagement. He had not been in Medchester for some time, a fortnight or more, he thought.

Pointer raised a reflective eyebrow, and filed the letter. Then he went to Stillwater House to take a few soundings.

In the lounge sat Sibella, a note open on her knee. Pointer put on a pair of very special glasses. Their action was that of short-range field-glasses. Stepping noiselessly nearer, he read over her shoulder, in di Monti's sharp, black characters:-

"*Egregia Signorina.*"

The letter was in Italian. Translated it ran:

"I shall be on the grass tennis-courts at twelve to-day. Would you be so kind as, to meet me there?

"With the most perfect esteem and the most exquisite respect.

"CANGRANDE GIULIO di M0NTI."

Sibella shivered, as though chilly.

Pointer would have liked to witness the interview, but he was due in town to give some evidence in an International forgery case which was being tried.

Harris telephoned him an account of the meeting during the lunch interval, and Pointer decided from its brevity that it had been used to settle the time of another appointment. Harris had not been able to hear anything. But he said that only the briefest of sentences on the count's part, and even less on Miss Scarlett's side, had passed.

Pointer was detained. The Bank of England was involved, and he saw that he must confide to Harris and Rodman the watching of events, and trust for the best.

Sibella kept to her rooms all the afternoon. Her father was up in town for the night, closely watched.

One of Pointer's best man from New Scotland Yard was shadowing the count. Rodman, who was proving himself quite good, was ready to take up the chase if

Sibella stirred. Her car, Rose's car it had been, was left turned in the garage. The inspector had noted the full tank.

At eight a door creaked. Down the stairs stole Sibella, wrapped in a motoring cloak, with a dark veil wound closely around cap and face, leaving only a mica slit for her eyes. She looked like a rather bulky mummy, but the mummy could see all right, for she made her way swiftly into the grounds.

At the first sound of her, Rodman was out of the lounge where he and Harris had installed themselves behind a couple of easy-chairs. When she reached the garage he was through the front gates, bending over his bicycle.

Hanging on behind, the inspector was driven by Sibella into town and up to a well-known Italian restaurant near Victoria station.

Here she slowed up preparatory to stopping. He fell behind, and getting off, stood with his back to her, talking to a match seller.

"The count's been in here half an hour, sir," the plain clothes man reported, "wrapped up like a conspirator. I think he feels a draught, if you ask me. He's engaged a couple of private rooms. Dinner for one was ready when he came. It's just been cleared away. Coffee for two's been upstairs three minutes. Luigi tells me there's an Aberdeen terrier of the proprietor's on guard outside the door who growls at every foot-fall."

"Did the Chief Inspector give you any further instructions?"

"Yes, sir. To follow the count afterwards. If he goes back to his flat I'm off for home, too. There's another chap watching his rooms all night."

"Good. I'll follow the lady."

It was not a long wait, an hour at most, before the two reappeared in the door. Rodman watched the Alfa Romeo glide away into the darkness. Then he attached himself again to the back of Sibella's car, and was driven home to Stillwater once more.

Close to the main gate he dropped behind. After some minutes he slipped through, stacked his bicycle behind a potting shed, and crept into the house.

Behind his arm-chair sat Harris.

"Gone up yet, sir?" whispered Rodman.

"Hasn't come in yet."

They waited a little longer. Then Rodman rose. "I'm going to the garage to see if anything's up."

Sibella's cubicle was empty. The inspector dared not switch on the light. She might be waiting outside on the drive. He crept forward foot by foot along its winding curves, the awful truth rising higher with every step.

Sibella had gone.

She must have nosed the car down the drive, lights out, and passed on into the road again through one of the two other gates

He went indoors and asked Harris in a whisper to come out.

"Did you follow her all right?" asked the superintendent.

"All wrong!" groaned Rodman, and he told of his failure.

"Too bad," sympathised the kindly Harris. "Would have happened to any one. But not to Alf," he said privately. "Alf never gets left. Never did. Wherever do you think she's gone to?" he asked aloud.

Rodman wisely refused to start a list of the towns and villages of England.

"Well, when you feel like tackling an early worm, come around to my house. I'm off for bed, as there seems nothing doing here that one man can't handle."

And Rodman certainly did not, and could not, consider himself overworked for the remainder of the night.

It was nearly six in the morning when, like music to the tired ears of the detective, came the sound of the little two-seater again. The front gates opened once more. This time Sibella left her car in the garage, and walked rapidly towards the house. By the light of early day, Rodman had traced the marks of last night quite easily. They ran as he had expected.

At the police station he found the Chief Inspector in possession of the news. Pointer greeted him with at least outward calmness, though he looked very thoughtful. Poor Rodman could hardly swallow a morsel of food.

Half-way through the meal Briggs's voice sounded outside, all eagerness.

"The report's come in from the man who's watching the count's rooms, sir. This *is* a rum go, and no mistake!"

Pointer lingered to finish his cup of tea. It must serve him at a pinch instead of a night's sleep. Harris shook his head as he led the way into the station.

"A little more of what the chief calls '*tenew*' wouldn't harm you, Briggs. You might be an old maid receiving her first proposal. Why, you're all of a twitter. Now let's learn the damage."

Harris took the receiver, and listened with a slowly opening mouth.

"You don't—not Miss—not—well, I'm blowed!" And the upholder of *tenew* dropped into a chair, then looked at Rodman.

"Some one's drunk. Either you, or me, or that chap who's just reported. Didn't you follow Miss Scarlett all the way back from the restaurant here?"

"Certainly, sir."

"Well, the Yard 'tec says she left Count di Monti's rooms at exactly ten minutes past five this morning."

Pointer, who had come into the room, stared at Harris as though the truth lay graven on the superintendent's very spine, and stretched for the receiver. Then he dropped his hand.

"I'll go myself. But what's the good? There's no need to hurry—now!"

"You talking English?" Harris asked curiously.

"I'll translate." Pointer spoke rather dryly. "Inspector Rodman followed, not Miss Scarlett, but II Primo Capitano del Fascio Arditi, Conte Cangrande Giulio di Monti commanding the 41st Legion of the II. Cohort, from the restaurant to Stillwater last night.

"You said you noticed how much better she was driving, as though she had a weight off her mind," He turned to the breathless Rodman. "The two changed rigs in restaurant, and what with those cloaks, her veiling, his goggles, besides some sort of a lift inside her shoes, they fooled you, Rodman. But that's what happened. Doubt less they chose that restaurant because it's one of the few where cars can be parked practically at the door. She went to his rooms and stayed there till he should be safely aboard a ship, friend's yacht probably. He bought a duplicate outfit of the clothes she was wearing, and left it at his flat for her, as well as a woman's rigout for himself, which latter he sends in a box to the restaurant. She rests in peace and quiet in his rooms, and changes again. At the hour agreed on, five, she comes down to Stillwater by taxi. He leaves her two-seater at some place not far off, when he's picked up by a friend's motor. There you have their little plan. Simple, eh?"

"Well, I'm glad it ain't what I first thought!" Briggs said simply.

"So 'm I!" said Harris. "Though helping a murderer, to escape! In love with him. Must be! If so, this version sounds the sort of thing Miss Sib might do. She's all the 'go' of the Scarletts in, her. But to connive at an escape!" Harris ruminated on. "She has gone and got herself into a nice fix! She can't have thought him guilty, that's sure!"

"On the contrary," Pointer almost laughed, "on the contrary! It shows that di Monti told her that he murdered Miss Charteris. Or Miss Scarlett would never have done what she did. If, by some mischance, say a fire, she had been found in his rooms! She wouldn't have run that risk unless she thought beyond a chance of a mistake both that he was guilty, and that he was in a very tight place. I rather felt that he was putting his back against the wall when I met him on the stairs of his rooms. Now what could have—I won't say frightened him, di Monti isn't a frightenable, man—but shown him that if he wanted to get away he must do so at once?"

And as though it were a play at a theatre, and those words his cue, a constable entered the room and supplied the answer.

He held out a pear-shaped, dark blue stone that glittered and sparkled as though rolled in gold dust. At the smaller end was a wreath of silver leaves with clusters of grapes in amethysts and garnets. A grape tendril served as a loop, and cut into the other end were three gold bails and the initials C.M. It was the Medici pendant.

"Where in the world did you get this from?" Superintendent Harris got out his notebook.

"From Fiery Jim, sir."

"Temper?" asked Pointer.

"Neither. He's a good sort, is poor Jim, but he can't resist a fire. Born that way. Chronic. He'd set fire to himself if there were no other way of turning out the fire brigade, and they don't like it. Neither do the farmers."

"Naturally?"

"Very naturally. So we see to it that he stays in workhouses when he's not in prison. Never for anything but incendiarism, I assure you. He's quite a favourite, when he's safe. There's no vice in Fiery Jim."

"And bow does he explain this find?"

"The shepherd put me on to him, sir. He'd noticed' him playing with it. At first the old chap took it for granted it was a piece of glass, but when he looked closer he recognised it by the description, and brought Jim here."

"Have him in."

Fiery Jim was not good at consecutive narrative. But the superintendent was capital on this, his own ground, and unwound him as I neatly as a silk spinner would a cocoon, firmly but gently drawing from him what he wanted.

Jim's many half-tales, woven together, made this:

Last Thursday night he was walking along the short cut on an errand from the Master of Medchester workhouse with a boy as guardian, when they saw a tall, dark, well-dressed man come striding out from the copse. This was just as the church clock struck ten, for it was to count the strokes that the two had stopped and turned. Jim saw that the man was a stranger, and asked for a match. The stranger didn't understand. Jim held out his hand, repeating his request. The man seemed to mistake him for a beggar. He snarled out something about an echo, and flung a stone at him. Jim's black eye was an "exhibit" to this part of the story. The stranger tore on, and Jim groped for the stone, to carry it and his tale to the Master. But he liked the way it flashed, and sparkled, and kept it as a plaything, taking it out every now and then, and watching it. Fiery Jim had no idea of values.

Harris sent him in to have "something from Mrs. Harris," after he had made quite sure that Jim could not identify the man.

"We don't need identification beyond what he heard," Pointer said at once "The echo that Jim heard spoken about was, of course, the Italian for here!'—Ecco! This only bears out what we know already, but it does explain as well why the count decided to leave so hurriedly."

"Once he knew or heard that that pendant was found he was up a tree!" Superintendent Harris agreed, locking the stone carefully away in the safe. "The chief told me that on Saturday the count had spoken of a large reward he wanted to offer for this stone, and then on Monday morning he had dropped in to say that on the whole he thought he would postpone the offer till he heard from his father."

"Just so," Pointer stared at his boot tips. "His flinging that stone at Jim here is all of a piece with his slashing Miss Charteris's portrait, with his dropping a pebble or two on her coffin, with his trampling on the flowers that she had worn in the studio, and which came off as she scrambled out of the window, I suppose, or which she took off when she flung her knitted frock on over the other. Yes, the count both wanted, and feared, to get that stone back. If he could lay his hands on it again without any risk of it leaking out how and when he had flung it away, he wanted it back in safe keeping. But as soon as he remembered that the man at whom he had dashed it in his mad fury at ten on Thursday night might bring it to the police instead of to him, he decided to let sleeping dogs lie. So that was why he insisted at the inquest and afterwards on the fact that it was of no value whatever. Not of much value, perhaps, but of considerable danger—to him!"

"I see it all now." Harris spoke as though the sight were rather pleasant, compared with some mental visions which had been vouchsafed him lately.

A telephone inquiry confirmed Pointer. Di Monti's rooms were empty. Master and man had gone, and had their luggage, conveyed piecemeal to cleaners and bootmakers by the astute valet to be re-assembled elsewhere, and packed in new valises.

Pointer had hardly rung off when his telephone tinkled again.

"Chief Inspector Pointer wanted. Mr. Gilchris speaking."

Speaking, apparently, from the context both as coroner and as the Charteris's family solicitor.

"I acted on your suggestion, and managed to reach Miss Jones, the professor's secretary, who was on a walking tour in Devon. She went up to his club last night and fetched his correspondence. The hall porter knows her, and that she is empowered by the professor himself to take charge of any letters in an emergency."

"Good!" said Pointer, for there is no place in the world more inviolable than the letter-rack of a club, and within the august portals of the Athenum, Scotland Yard's highest were lower than the youngest buttons.

"If you care to step in this morning about eleven," Mr. Gilchrist went on "she'll be here with the letters and you can have a look at them."

Pointer was prompt to the minute. He found Miss. Jones to be an intelligent, middle-aged woman, evidently devoted to her employer and his interests.

"Here is a letter which the professor has sent, addressed to himself and sealed, in another covering-envelope, also so addressed." Gilchrist handed it over to be looked at.

"He often sends me private papers in that way," Miss. Jones explained, as had Sibella before. "I put them in his desk, just as they are, till his return."

Pointer saw a long envelope, looking much the worse for wear, having evidently been folded across the middle, sealed with black wax, and addressed to Professor H. Charteris.

"Where's the envelope it came in?" he asked.

Miss Jones fished it out of the waste-paper basket.

It was addressed to the professor at his club, and had been sent from Milan on the Friday that Rose had been found murdered.

The handwriting on the outer envelope was not Professor Charteris's, but Miss Jones explained that his eyesight being weak when he had mislaid his glasses, which occurred every five minutes, he would commission the nearest-at-hand waiter, or hall-porter, to address an envelope for him.

"You have not heard from him otherwise in any way?"

She had not. Like the solicitor, she was not in the least anxious on account of the silence, though the latter was beginning to think it time that Charteris should come across the daily advertisement asking him to wire or write, if he could not come to England.

"I should like to examine this a little more closely." Pointer still held the long envelope with the black seals. "I should like to photograph it at my rooms."

"Short of opening it, you're welcome to do whatever you think fit," Gilchrist said heartily. "The rest are a couple of circulars of no importance."

Pointer, in his own rooms at the police station, tried the little fragments of black sealing-wax that he had ,found in the professor's envelope that he had fished out of Rose's chain bag and taken from the table in the studio. He found that they were not too numerous to have dropped off the seals if the letter had been carried about for some hours.

He believed, from the envelope's frayed look, that this was the same letter that had been posted to England once before, reaching Rose on Thursday at tea-time, and which had not been seen since her death. There was still a faint fragrance lingering about the flap that matched the perfume in her bag. The description tallied absolutely. He looked up the trains in Bradshaw. It was now Saturday.

Suppose some one left London by the boat train either Thursday night or even Friday morning and his Paris-Milan express was on time, then he would have an hour in Milan station in which to post the letter back again in the returning Milan-Paris express.

That looked as though some one had taken the letter by mistake, or accident, and posted it from Italy in order to make it seem as though the professor were sending it. In that case, it must be some one who knew that the professor had sent it, to his daughter in the first place, but that she was now dead.

Suppose that he, Pointer, were right, and that Rose had taken it with her in her little bag to the studio, had noticed it when there, and, taking it out, had laid it on the table by the door, in a place where she thought that she could not overlook it on leaving, had forgotten it in her hurried dash when she heard the furious Italian at the front door. Suppose that di Monti, finding Rose gone, had swooped on the proof of her presence in the room,. Pointer imagined that he might intend to keep it to confront her with. But after her murder the letter would be very incriminating evidence. Yet, however violent, di Monti was a gentleman. He might kill, but Pointer could not see him tampering with correspondence.

Pointer imagined him giving the letter to a friend. In all likelihood to a brother of the Prince Cornaro who had confirmed the count's alibi. For Scotland Yard knew that young Prince Amadeo Cornaro had left early on Friday morning for Italy. Certainly the envelope must have been returned by some one who knew of the professor's little way of sending securely fastened letters back to himself.

Pointer photographed the envelope. There were no signs of its having been tampered with in any way Or rather, to his microscopic scrutiny, it showed many little proofs that it had not been opened.

With a thin, warm knife he sliced off the seals, and then steamed open the envelope

Inside was a single sheet of paper, headed, in the professor's writing, "Memo on Refractions". Below came couple of lines of figures and equations.

Pointer photographed the paper and fastened the envelope up again exactly as it had been. When the wax was cold he returned it to Gilchrist, who put it with the professor's private papers.

CHAPTER SEVEN

DRIVING to New Scotland Yard at once, Pointer learnt that the memo was of no value, though it was connected, as he had surmised, with the manufacture of emeralds.

This was a blow. He had expected something from those algebraical formulae. What, he himself hardly knew. But something big.

He dropped in at his Bayswater rooms and found O'Connor waiting for him with lunch. Over the cheese, and a pile of the curly toast beloved of the Chief Inspector, thin, and brown, and crisp, as birch leaves in a frost, he told his friend of the latest developments.

"So the letter isn't the clue after all!"

"Why not? I seem to've been misled as to its contents. Suppose some one else was mistaken, too? Suppose I wasn't the only one who hoped for something different from what was there? A hunt after letters, or papers, runs through this case. There was the search among the professor's rooms shortly after his daughter was found dead. Then there's the theft of Miss Charteris's own letters from the chief constable's house."

"And there's the Odyssey of this enclosed letter itself. The one just sent back from Milan. Though, faith, it doesn't look the sort of thing to interest the count," mused O'Connor. "But it might some of the others. How about getting him back again, by the way?"

"It'll only be a matter of days before the Yard learns of his whereabouts, unless he intends to go permanently into hiding."

"But when you've got him," O'Connor went on, "you've still to find the motive for all the rest of that Thursday night show. The moving of the body, and what happened on those flags. D'ye think the colonel could help you to a short cut?"

"I told the superintendent that Scarlett's a difficult man to read, and so he is. At first he acted as though a weight were lifting off him. Yet every hour that passes without disclosing the criminal in a case of this kind usually gets on people's nerves. And now lately, he's just opposite. He looks to me like a man ridden by some ever-growing fear. He's all on the *qui vive* every time any one approaches him suddenly."

"Perhaps he's afraid for himself, or his daughter?"

"Neither. He never carries even a stout stick. There isn't a fire-arm handy in the house. He takes no precautions. But he does take two Italian papers since about a week ago. About the time of the murder."

"I wonder if he's in this," O'Connor speculated, "with di Monti and that Mrs. Lane. Of course, we know di Monti struck the blow, but who else was there?"

"The funny thing is," Pointer reached up for a Chinese ball-puzzle on the mantelpiece above him, "that I've a perfectly unsound idea, which I wouldn't mention to any one but you, connecting Mrs. Lane with—not di Monti nor the colonel—but with Thornton."

"How's that?"

"Difficult to explain. He's never natural when her name comes up. Either too indifferent, or changes the subject, or something—I can't put a name to it. But I've had from the first a very strong feeling that she moves him, touches him in some quite peculiar way."

"In love with her?"

"Why not be so openly? All our accounts show that he rarely talked much to her, nor she to him. Yet he kept his eyes on Mrs. Lane, and on Mrs. Lane alone, at the inquest, once the doctor began to stir things up. As she went out she looked at him. Odd look. One I haven't a label for."

"You'd expect that she and di Monti would be standing in together—"

"Then that won't be what we'll find," Pointer said dryly.

"And how's the pencil getting along?" asked the Irishman.

"It's feeling a bit lonely, but still hopeful. So far, it's only led us into *cul-de-sacs*, but as it's my best find, I mustn't decry it."

There was a long silence while the two old friends smoked on.

"Could that formula be more valuable than you think?" O'Connor asked at length.

"Our expert is quite certain. It's not possible for him to be mistaken."

"True. One never did hear of a policeman making a mistake," O'Connor murmured pensively.

"But unless the owner of the pencil turns up, I'm running over to Italy the day after to-morrow to see if I can't find Charteris."

"You are, eh?" O'Connor eyed him gravely, speculatively.

"And," Pointer returned his look, "I feel, like you, by no means certain that I shall find him."

"Looks that way to me. If his daughter was killed for anything to do with a letter which he might have written or sent. And what's the artist doing all this time?"

"Bellairs? He comes back from Windsor Castle tonight But I'm going to leave him alone for the moment He's watched, of course, but I'm trying to unwind the affair from the other end."

"And the chief constable down there. How's he getting along?" O'Connor liked to keep count of all the cast.

Pointer laughed. "I may be doing a most zealous officer a bitter injustice. But I suspect him of being exceedingly glad that he's out of it all. The colonel and his friends are all friends of Major Vaughan's, too. We'll see a marked improvement when this case is settled one way or another, I fancy. And it's going to take some stiff routine work before it's settled. It's the most extraordinary affair for one reason. You'd expect a gang of apaches to hang together, whatever the crimes, but the Stillwater crowd are all well-to-do, well-behaved, wellborn. They're not like a tenement house of starving east-enders."

"Me noble father having been Court Chamberlain, and talking as I am to the belted son of a duke," O'Connor murmured lackadaisically, "it's natural we should look on tenement-house dwellers with proper scorn."

Pointer grunted. "You know what I mean," he said impertinently. "Of all that Stillwater circle, there's not one, not one, mind you, of whom I can say with absolute certainty, 'Whoever's in it, it isn't he!'"

"Him!" retorted O'Connor, "don't be a prig, Alf. You wouldn't say 'It isn't he under any circumstances,' and you know it."

"It isn't he," Pointer repeated unmoved. Not to him had the English grammar come unprized, as a birthright. Son of a coast-guard, it was with many an hour's work that he had bought freedom in it, and he valued that ease accordingly.

"And yet all of them should be above suspicion by their positions, you'd think. But they're all in it, in the most baffling way. There's the colonel—apart from everything else, why did he cut down that blackthorn tree before any one was up on Friday morning? But his record is quite all right. Late of the 10th Hussars. No shady relations. Only son's a Commissioner in Uganda. The last *Tan ganyka Times* is full of some exploration of his around in the interior. Then there's Mr. Thornton—"

"He called you down, didn't he? Ungrateful bobby!"

"I allow him due credit, for, without his having done that, the threads of this case would have been impossible to pick up—from this end. There're always two ways of reaching any goal. But he's an odd fish. He's not straight with me. His hand, mind you, was practically forced by two young men from the Foreign Office."

"But who is he?"

"Took high honours at New College. Member of the bar. Councillor to various embassies abroad for some years. Travelled a bit in Persia. Knows everybody, and yet hasn't an intimate friend, unless it be Professor Charteris.

"Then take Mr. Cockburn and Mr. Bond. We know all about them, too. Blameless pasts, promising futures. Yet I found them breaking into the colonel's study on Friday evening."

"In order to help the case forward," put in O'Connor.

"So they say! Then the women. Mrs. Lane's, of course, the dark horse of the outfit, so far. There's only one thing I can prove for certain against her, whatever we may think, and that is that it was from her silk cloak that the piece is missing which I found in the clutch of Thornton's car. As she wore the same cloak driving in to town on Friday, and made no complaint about it, and told the maid that she had just stepped on it while getting out, I take it that she tore it herself. Then there's Lady Maxwell. It's her frock that's bloodstained, and the colonel backs off at sight of her. Then Miss Scarlett—she's too much shaken by her cousin's death. She looks like a ghost."

"You're hard to satisfy, Alf."

"I try to be."

"But who, in God's name, would shield the murderer of that lovely girl?" O'Connor asked. "You'd have thought the count would have had short shrift from every one down there. Do you think it's two sets of crimes? Jealousy that struck the blow, and then some other interest altogether? Something to do with the enclosed letter that moved the corpse and searched the bag?"

"I'd rather not say what I think just yet, but the professor has some very important affairs bubbling along, apart from the emeralds."

There was a short silence, then O'Connor paused in his work.

"That man you're trying to get hold of seems to be an extra down there? I mean, the man of the summer house. I suppose he couldn't be the professor returned unexpectedly? Perhaps saw his daughter murdered, and went for the murderer?" O'Connor asked, half-sceptical of his own fancy.

"I don't know," Pointer replied seriously, "but I do know that neither the professor nor any one else even remotely connected with what I call the Stillwater circle was the man inside the summer house bedroom. I've examined all their finger-prints most carefully."

Back at the police station Inspector Rodman met Pointer with a face officially wooden, but with a very human satisfaction betraying itself in his voice.

"Mrs. Lane's lost, too, sir. The detective from the Yard has just 'phoned to you to report as much."

"She went into one of those all-over-the-place shops, and they haven't seen her since," moaned Harris. "Lost in London!"

Pointer gave him a fleeting smile.

"Sounds like the title of a film, and you might be the bereaved parent. She's not out of reach. On the whole, its possibly as well. We were getting a bit stale. Now she thinks she's safe, and she may send some message that will let us get hold of things more important still. And who are these in bright array?"

It was Cockburn and Bond, driving up post haste. They had just learnt of the count's disappearance from his rooms in town, and were down to find out if there was still nothing that they could do.

Harris, according to the immemorial rule of the Force, assured them that all had gone according to plan The two young men looked as unbelieving as though they were hearing that time-honoured phrase in a battle report.

"I'd got quite a step along," Cockburn put in disconsolately, "I mean finding out that his alibi was rocky. Not bad that for an amateur, was it?" He looked at

Pointer for approval, and he got it very heartily. Cockburn had done quite well in finding out the shakiness of the much-vaunted alibi.

"The count isn't out of reach," Pointer assured the two friends. "Safely isolated is the way to look at it. But if either of you could find out anything about the plans of the Inner Fascist Council in Rome concerning meetings, places, and so on, we might be able to guess where next to locate him. I don't deny that in matters of this kind, the Foreign Office naturally has a great pull over the Secret Service."

They drove off quite full of how the news might possibly be obtained through a certain agent which the F. O. employed in the heart of Roman aristocracy, which is tantamount to saying in the heart of Fascist circles. That done, Pointer turned his attention to the two microphone-dictaphones which Rodman and one of Scotland Yard's flying squad brought in daily. Stillwater House telephone and the telephone of the Army and Navy Club, the only one which the colonel now used, were both connected with these useful inventions.

For at the club, one of the waiters, after a talk with Detective Inspector Watts of Scotland Yard, had decided that he was feeling run down, and that a week's breathing of the pure ozone of Brighton's picture-palaces would just suit his budding complaint.

So Watts, who, it seemed, was his brother, took his place, and was proving a most efficient locum tenens from every point of view.

All messages received by either house were repeated into the attentive ear of the Chief Inspector twice daily.

Suddenly Pointer gave an inward start. He was busy with the club records.

"Sir Henry Carew, please," asked a woman's voice, the voice of Mrs. Lane. "Will you ask him to come to the telephone for a minute?"

There was a pause. Then the voice came again.

"Sir Henry Carew? Good-morning, Sir Henry. You know who's speaking, don't you? Will you tell our friend that M. M. is quite satisfied. He thinks the horse is getting on excellently. Yes, that's all. Good-bye."

The remainder of the messages were of no importance.

"M. M.!" Pointer arranged with Harris and Rodman to "carry on," and sped up to his friend the divisional surgeon.

"Look here, Scott, I want you to get me into Sir Martin Martineau's home. You told me he was chiefly for head-trouble or accidents. Channel islander, I think you said. I've a splitting headache. Had it for days. My eyes pain me every time I turn them. When I suddenly stop walking, I see strange flashes—"

Doctor Scott hummed a tune with heartless accuracy as he walked over to his shelves. He pulled out a book.

"If I had this beggar examined by some of your unholy arts at the Yard, I should find your finger-prints on it, Pointer. You were left here for just ten minutes while I wrote out that girl's prescription, and you haven't wasted one of them."

"My name's Brown," Pointer went on, "and I had a motor smash a few days ago. It's since then my head hurts me so."

Pointer slumped back in his chair, and gave a groan. Scott turned around with a startled exclamation. "Where in the world did you pick that up? That groan, I mean?"

Pointer looked at him with a twinkle.

"I studied that for a matter of days and nights when I was in charge of a very prominent Greek gentleman who feared assassination. We had a stormy sea all the way from Portsmouth to the Pireus, and he spent every hour of it groaning. I stored them up for future need. I used to practise with him, up and down, to make sure the timbre was right. He thought the sea affected me too. But you've only heard the Channel one; you wait till I let off my Cape Matapan heartbreaker. He's a peach!"

"How long do you expect to be in that home before they turn you out as an impostor?"

"How can I be an impostor when I pay my way? I may be a neurasthenic, but only poor chaps are impostors."

"Well, how long do you expect to stay?"

"One night will do."

"Oh, of course, in that case—as a matter of fact, Sir Martin's away in Scotland, I saw in the papers, so now's your chance."

"I suppose he won't operate on me in my sleep?" Pointer was just a trifle in earnest. He had no love for surgeons.

"My dear chap, you won't get within a dozen rooms of his knife. They'll X-ray you first, find nothing the matter, and tell you so at once."

"Good. 'Phone up for me and ask for their best room. I'll take a taxi after a little preparation. May I use your bedroom?"

Pointer dressed himself in purple and fine linen, and packed an expensively-fitted bag with clothes to match. A skilful sprinkling of bleached hairs was all that he dared try, but that, and his drooping, quivering lids, and tremulous, saggy mouth, and slouching attitude made a marvellous difference.

"I hope I shall live to get there, doctor," he mumbled as Scott hailed a taxi and Pointer hobbled down the steps, "I hope so indeed!" And he gave a moan that made the driver's spine, crawl.

As for Doctor Scott, to the man's indignation, he merely, shut the door and said callously, "Oh, you'll be all right, if you pull yourself together and make an effort, Mr. Brown". He gave a signal and off Pointer started.

The doctor's telephone message had made the entering of the handsome old Georgian house quite easy. A sympathetic matron superintended his entry on the arm of a solicitous house-porter. His room was ready for him. In about an hour he would be X-rayed, and then the trouble would be easily found. Sir Martin would be back tomorrow afternoon, and possibly by the next day all would be right. Thus the matron, and Pointer nodded wearily as he sat in the lift huddled together. When it stopped, he gave one of his groans, Bay of Biscay this time, and had the satisfaction of seeing the matron nearly trip over the sill. Without a word, she had him helped to his room, and tiptoed out, saying that she would send Nurse Mason to him at once.

Pointer's eyes, deep hidden under his nearly closed lids, studied the young woman attentively. He did not often make a mistake, if the person left a clear impression on him, and Miss Mason left a very distinct one. He judged her to be both exceedingly honest, and exceedingly loyal. Most estimable qualities, as he was the first to admit, but not at all what he was in search of to-night. A few hours later Pointer was shown into the X-ray room by an orderly, and took an instant liking to his foxy face with the avaricious mouth.

"Come to my room the last thing to-night," Pointer muttered, and the man bowed with a knowing and obsequious smile, "Very good, sir."

Something in a glass for the patient, and something in his pocket for himself, was the usual outcome of this often heard remark. Once they were "cases" the thing was too risky, of course, but beforehand—why not let them have a cocktail?

So at eleven o'clock that night in slipped Mr. Keane. He saw in the light of the reading lamp a bulky something in bed, and closed the door with a gentle cough.

"I'm come, sir."

He turned with a gasp. The door was locked behind him, and Pointer faced him with a very masterful look.

"It's all right; don't be alarmed, man! I'm a private detective. I want some information on behalf of a wealthy, client who's prepared to pay for it."

"Well, this is a movie!" The man grinned. "To think those moans of yours were fakes! They'd make the fortune of a street beggar, wouldn't they! Nearly froze my blood, they did, and I've heard some in my time. But what's all this about?"

"It's about a man who was brought in here late last, Thursday night, May 1st, with some cuts on him." Pointer took out his notebook and also a five-pound note. "Know anything about such a man?"

"Is that a book-mark?" asked Keane, looking at it.

"It's a prize for a bright boy," Pointer assured him "Did any man come here that night?"

"I know that a chap came, but that's all that I do know."

"Can you get me a glimpse of him?"

"Nothing doing," the man said glumly. "Had your groans for nothing. No one is allowed near that room but her High Mightiness the Matron and her equally Grand Highness Nurse Mason. He's had an operation, by Sir Martin on Saturday, and seems to be doing well as Mr. Carlyle, that's the house doctor and assistant surgeon, only visits him night and morning. That enough for a fiver?"

Pointer shook his head and returned the note to his letter-case.

"Might run to ten shillings," he said musingly.

"And how do I know who you are? Looks a fishy job to me, if ever I saw one."

"I'm Merton, of Merton and Mertons, private detectives. There's my card; you can 'phone to my office and ask about me."

The head of the firm in question was an ex-inspector of the Yard, and Pointer had made his arrangements. Keane looked at the ten-shilling note.

"Hand it over then."

Pointer cocked his head on one side.

"Takes a bit of earning, does a ten-shilling note these hard times, my man. I might raise it to a pound if I could see into the room for a second."

"You might!" ironically repeated the other, "and what price my place? Nothing doing!"

"I might double that again if I could go over the clothes the young man wore when he came. I suppose he is a young man?"

The ten shillings changed hands.

"Can't say. How's that for honesty? I never saw him. The matron and Mr. Carlyle were waiting for the car, and got him on to the stretcher themselves. His mother helped them."

"Was that usual? The house-surgeon and the matron being on the lookout like that?"

"Not unusual, perhaps. But they've never made such a fuss before about not letting any one into the room afterwards. I happened to open the door by mistake, and that Mason snapped my nose off."

"Severe case, eh?"

"Not since the operation. There's been no call for ice bags, let alone the oxygen pump. But that stretcher was a sight! He must have all but cut an artery."

Then Keane went off for the clothes.

"Nothing doing," he said on his return "Blest if they haven't gone. To the cleaners and laundry, says the tag hanging in their place. But his shoes have gone, too! And a travelling rug, that I know came with him, isn't there. Fine and stained it was, too."

Pointer got the name of the laundry and cleaners generally patronised by the institution.

"When was the operation?"

"Tuesday morning."

The date was the first Tuesday after Rose's death. "Sister in charge of the theatre approachable?"

"I don't think!" Keane made a grimace which it took handsomer features than his to carry off successfully.

"Now, the man's mother, can you describe her?"

"Tall and slender. Veiled like one of those Eastern Harems."

"Came in a car?" Pointer asked

"She did. What's more, she drove it in. I was a bit late coming in, and I happened to slip in behind it."

"But if she was closely veiled, how did she drive?"

"Well, that's funny, now you speak of it, but I happened to be going out of the gate when she drove off—to post a letter, you know—I again happened to see her meet a big stout man around the first corner. She got out and stood talking for a minute Then he put his arms round her and kissed her, and after that he climbed into the driving seat and they drove off."

"Kissed her?" Something in his tone made Keane glance at him out of the corners of his eyes.

"You seem struck all of a heap. He kissed her as though he meant it, too. None of your hit or miss pecks."

"I thought you said she was veiled so tightly—"

"Well, what of it? He kissed one cheek, veil and all, and looked as though he would have been quite pleased to kiss the other, but she stepped on into the car."

"Did she seem to mind being kissed? Move away, I mean, or that?"

"Not a bit. She sort of half-leant her head on his shoulder, like as though she were dead tired, you know, before she bucked up and got into the car."

Pointer spread his photographs on the table.

"Can you recognise him?"

"That's him." The man picked up one of Colonel Scarlett. "That's him, right enough."

"Could you swear to him?"

"Till all's blue."

"Good. Now I want something with the patient's finger-prints on it. A tumbler, how would that do? Could you manage to get me the one he uses?"

Keane shook his head.

"No more than you could sneak the King's sceptre. He's guarded night and day."

"Guarded?"

"Well, what do you think? Of course, Sir Martin is always careful, but over this case! I tell you that chap hasn't been left alone for a half-second. He's of tremendous importance to somebody."

Pointer thought a moment

"What is Sir Martin's general fee for head operations?"

"Plain sailing ones, fifty pounds; dicky ones, a hundred. Not going to be done for the fun of the thing, are you?"

Pointer was thinking of a cheque to "Self" that the colonel had drawn on Friday as soon as the banks were open. It had been for two hundred pounds, and he had asked for it all in Bradburys.

Pointer dismissed the orderly and walked the floor, knee-deep in the detached facts of the case. They still refused to shape into that neat circle which alone means the true theory of a crime. Yet they were so numerous that he felt sure that the essential ones were here to hand, buried though they might be beneath accidentals. They could not all be tangents by rights.

As he picked them up one by one, and examined and tested each afresh, he found that there was one fact told him, and accepted by him, which, if broken, would let all the rest link in one behind the other.

Next morning he was as keen to be off as any belated burglar. The house-surgeon explained that there could be nothing organic the matter. Pointer refused the proffered arrangement with a home for nerve cases, and shambled into a taxi again, but this time with Keane's address safely in his letter-case.

Back at Doctor Scott's, Pointer changed, and, well content, drove down to Medchester.

At Red Gates he found Mr. Thornton, looking very weary of his work, and of his cottage, and of his life in general, walking up and down his balcony, an unlit pipe between his teeth.

Pointer thought of his own words about Colonel Scarlett's face after reading the letter brought him at lunch on the day before Rose was killed.

Thornton had said that his host had looked like a man who had learnt that something on which he confidently counted had gone all wrong. That description fitted Thornton's own face and manner exactly, as he stopped and nodded to the detective-officer.

"To-morrow morning at eleven, sir, would you kindly manage to make time to come to my rooms at New Scotland Yard? I want to get the people chiefly associated with Stillwater House assembled in a sort of meeting."

"Royal command? Or are startling developments expected?" Thornton asked caustically.

"At eleven, then, sir." Pointer spoke as though the other had accepted with alacrity. "Unfortunately, I can't get the women's finger-prints. Mrs. Lane's, for instance. I suppose, by the way," Pointer threw in, "that you never met her before she went to Stillwater House?"

"Never!" Thornton said the word before the other had finished his question. Yet Pointer knew from a short note that Watts had found among the colonel's papers at his club that Mrs. Lane had met Thornton before. It was a vague letter as far as dates or facts were concerned, but that was clear enough in it.

Next morning saw Colonel Scarlett, Thornton, Bellairs, Bond, and Cockburn all wedged into the inner of Pointer's three official rooms, which was all but filled by a large table.

Bellairs was a small, handsome man, with a face that Pointer would not have cared to trust.

"Close fit," Bond commented, insinuating himself lithely into the back row.

"By jove, it's a breakfast party." Cockburn bent over the centre of the table, where empty soup plates were ranged in a square. "Place-cards and all."

"Now, gentlemen," Pointer explained, "we have discovered in the sand-pit close to where Miss Charteris's body was found, the marks of a man's doubled-up fists. Such a mark as he might make if he tried to raise himself up on them—this sort of way." Pointer clenched his hands, and, leaning heavily on the table before him, raised himself out of the chair. As he had made the marks himself in the sand that morning, he knew what he wanted. "All rings must be taken off, because there is a curious mark on one—the back of the fingers in our cast where it joins the hand. As there's no room on the table, and there's mercury in the mixture, I think the rings had better go on that shelf behind there."

Watts was not a well-trained waiter, and there was some little confusion and clatter before each man had two soup plates with a thick white mixture set before him, which he had thrust his fist vigorously. Then a basin of water, soap, and piles of towels were brought in, and after a wash, rings were resumed, chairs pushed away, and the meeting was over.

"Are we innocent or guilty?" asked Thornton, getting up.

"Can't tell yet for certain, sir, but I don't see any signs of that little mark I spoke of in any of the plates." Pointer inspected them.

"D'ye mean to say you've got a list of suspects, and once you've scratched us off, you bag the remainder?" asked Bond curiously.

Pointer only made some non-committal answer.

"What about the count?" asked Bellairs.

"I expect to get his impressions myself in Italy," Pointer explained. "I hope to have an interview with him as soon as may be."

He looked at "Bond and Co.," who had forwarded him a most useful cipher cable.

Next morning the Chief Inspector was on his way to Paris and Genoa. Full instructions had been left with the superintendent and Rodman for every eventuality, but Pointer expected nothing startling or showy—until his return.

Genoa shows only its ugly back to the station, and keeps its beautiful face for the sea, its age-old friend.

Pointer wasted no time in looking about him. He made his way to an Italian hotel in the heart of the climbing town. After a wash and brush up, he went at once to the *Sotutto.*

There are many inquiry agencies in Italy, many of them reputable concerns. At the head of all for efficiency and reliability stands the one he had chosen.

Pointer's investigations were backward-reaching. He laid a portrait of Professor Charteris, and one of di Monti, and the portraits of all the people concerned in, the Stillwater case, as far as he knew them, before the manager, a pleasant, clever-faced Genoese.

"This," Pointer pencilled a mark on the back of the professor's picture, "is the man I chiefly want to learn about. Then I want to know if this man—di Monti—or any of the other men have been seen in your town. I am prepared to pay handsomely for the information. I should think the inquiry might start about three weeks to a fortnight ago. But that is only guesswork."

The manager made his notes.

"How long can you give us?"

"I need the information as soon as possible. This is a big case. Put extra men on the job. I want to be away to-night if possible."

It was possible. It is amazing what discreet track is kept on all foreigners in Italy.

When he called again in answer to a telephone message, he learnt this:

Professor Charteris had come to the Hotel Miramare on a Friday, just a week before Rose was found murdered, in company with a very tall, dark, listless-looking man, whom the hall-porter had never seen before, or since. He would judge him to be about thirty. They had breakfasted together in the professor's private sitting-room, and a good deal of low-voiced conversation had gone on between them. Coming down together afterwards, the lift had stuck fast owing to a short circuit, and they had been delayed between floors for nearly a quarter of an hour.

The lift boy had had another passenger beside the professor and the professor's companion. That was a visitor, who, like Charteris, was well known to the hotel. He had greeted the professor as an old friend, and the professor, after a pause, as the lift absolutely refused to budge, had hurriedly, and almost under his breath, introduced his companion as Mr. Sayce.

He had added that "Mr. Sayce is interested in my scheme for emeralds, so kindly forget that you've seen either of us here. Some very delicate negotiations are going on."

The lift-boy had particularly remembered the little scene, partly, because he thought that the three men were the last types which he would have connected with business or trade of any sort, and being an American, he had an eye for that well-known species of his fellow man, and partly because of the feeling that neither the professor nor, least of all, the man called Sayce were at all keen on meeting the man who had spoken to Charteris. When the latter got into the lift at the floor below the professor's, the young man had turned his back on him, until the delay had forced the three into a sort of temporary intimacy. When deposited at last on the ground floor, the younger man had had a cab called, and had driven off alone to the station. He had no luggage with him.

"The man who spoke to Professor Charteris in the lift, you have his name?"

The detective had, and his home address. He was a Professor Witherspoon, a Cambridge light, and was staying at the Villa Sole, Obermais, Meranoo.

Pointer put in some hours of strenuous work, at Genoa, tracing, tracking, comparing. Then he got the hall-porter to put him through to Professor Witherspoon.

He heard a thin, cheerful, kindly voice.

"Professor Witherspoon speaking. Who are you?"

"Sayce. You met me in the stuck lift of the Miramare a fortnight ago. I don't know if you remember—"

"Perfectly. Is the Professor with you?"

"No, it's about him I'm 'phoning. Have you heard from him since he left here, the day after we met? I've returned for an appointment, and can't learn where he is."

"How trying. He spoke of Verona, didn't he?"

"He did. But he hadn't turned up to fetch, or send for his *fermo posta* letters there. You haven't happened to hear of, or from him, then?"

"Yes. He telephoned me the next Monday from Bolzano, the branch station for Meranoo, you know, that he might just possibly drop in for a chat on Wednesday afternoon. He thought of walking over by way of the Mendel Pass. But he didn't come. He was very vague about the trip. Making it dependent on the weather, and how fit he might be feeling."

"Monday, April twenty-eighth?"

"That was the date."

"You haven't heard from him since?"

"Not a word. The weather's been very cold, even here. But wasn't he going to stay with an Italian family? I seem to remember an old Veronese name."

"Di Monti? I might try there. You can't suggest any other likely spot for a cast? The matter's most urgent, or I wouldn't have rung you up."

"I'm only sorry not to be of any help. No. I don't remember hearing our friend mention any other place. We chiefly talked of the wonderful Buru Bhudor finds, you may remember. But I think even the indefatigable Charteris would hardly have gore there."

Pointer had no idea where or what the "wonderful finds" might be.

"You could hardly call them in Italy, could you?" he fished cautiously.

"Hardly," came the smiling reply, "no, hardly."

Pointer dared probe no further, and the whereabouts of the afore-mentioned ruins remained for months a mystery to him.

The next move, then, was clearly Verona. Verona—the mere name was poetry—was Shakespeare.

Incidentally it was also the home of the di Monti. Which was more like duty.

CHAPTER EIGHT

AT Verona, that swarming little ant-heap, Pointer was wakened by the hotel porter early next morning.

A message had come from Count di Monti, to whom Pointer had telegraphed on leaving Genoa. The count, the head of the family, was not at his palazzo in the town, but out at Castello Grigio, near Rovereto.

Would the signore take the trouble to go on to the latter station, by train? It was on the direct line over the Brenner Pass into Austria, and but an hour and a half further up. The count much regretted that he was not in Verona, but he would send his car to meet the ten o'clock morning train on the chance.

Pointer told the man to say that he would come on as suggested. Then he himself telephoned to the Palazzo di Monti. The major-domo replied that the count was away at Verona at his Rovereto property, Castello Grigio.

At the station before Rovereto a young man in a chauffeur's livery looked into Pointer's compartment. Was the signore going to the Castello Grigio? Pointer said that he was. The chauffeur smiled and touched his cap. He had been sent by the count to execute a commission for him in a neighbouring village, and was to have the honour of driving the gentleman to the Castello. Saluting, he closed the door, and waited outside in the corridor till they reached Rovereto, lying like a handful of dice rolled, on to a green cloth, where he piloted Pointer through the turnstile to a fine Lancia car outside.

It was a pretty country, and soon a turn took them into a charming valley. The Castello Grigio was about an hour from Rovereto by car, Pointer had been told at the Verona hotel. At the end of that time they drew up at a huge pile. Pointer doubted whether it would be "passed" as fit for a human habitation by any council in England, but some of the grim windows, set in walls fourteen feet thick, had lace curtains to them.

The portico, which looked as though intended for a "Big Bertha" emplacement, was gay with geraniums, among which an awning umbrella gave a note of homeliness.

These things Pointer noticed, as also the fact that the man himself opened the door, and with a "*Di qua, signore, la prego,*" ushered him into a large, airy room.

One side was taken up by lace-curtained windows. Three large windows. So the curtains—they were new ones he saw now—were only in this one room. Humph. But Pointer was handicapped by not knowing Italian family-customs. All this might be customary. And again, it might not.

The man returned.

"The Signor Conti offers a thousand excuses, but he will be here in a very few minutes. He hopes the signore will take lunch with him." The man had the manners of a well-trained servant. Pointer looked about him.

The room was very sparsely furnished. But the things were beautiful. A scratch on the arm of his chair caught his eye. It was very recent, and showed rough handling. The carpet, too, was large for the room, and lay a little up on the walls. Pointer turned a corner back. The floor beneath had not been swept for generations, judging by the depth of the dust; but then, again, that might be usual in Italian country houses, where there was no mistress.

The door opened. Cangrande di Monti stepped in. He held up his hand with a charming smile.

"A truce until after lunch, my dear Chief Inspector. When you have had a talk with my father I shall be quite at your disposition. I think you will feel differently about me before long than you do now. A moment!"

He helped the man carry in a long narrow table of the kind familiar in old paintings. A beautiful lace runner lay on its polished top. It was set with old silver, and crystal thin as bubbles.

"Sorry to crowd you—*permesso*—"

Pointer stepped back hastily as the table was borne towards him He stepped back into a yawning hole, and fell with a crash that knocked the wind out of him.

"Dear, dear!" On the second di Monti's mocking face grinned down at him some twelve feet away.

"You've not hurt yourself, I hope?" An automatic glittered in his hand "Please don't move while Giuseppe searches you."

After the grating of bolts, a door in the little cellar opened. Pointer lay quite still. Giuseppe found his revolver, and then looked up.

"That is all. He has no knife but this penknife."

"Take it, too. Leave his cigars. Search him carefully for another weapon." When the cellar door was bolted again, di Monti went on, "You thought yourself, doubtless, very clever, Mr. Spy, when you followed me here. When you telephoned about my father last night, I told Bonvecchio what to say, and Giuseppe and I made ready for you. A little quick the work, perhaps, but it sufficed. We even set out some flower pots. Giuseppe did most of the cutting of that hole in the carpet. He does so dislike the police. A trait I understand. And now for a companion. I should be sorry if you were to get bored in the long, very long, hours ahead of you. Fetch the gaoler!" Di Monti turned to the man who had rejoined him. The servant was away for some minutes, during which his master apparently walked about the room, humming softly to himself.

"I thought that you might inquire if my father were really at the Castello Grigio. He is, but, you see, this does not happen to be that castello. Ah, here is the companion I promised you."

Pointer heard the clink-clank of a chain, and then there looked down at him a wolfish dog, with bristling hair and bared teeth.

"If you say one word, I shall drop him down there and set him on you." Di Monti looked as though he were half-minded to do it anyway. "A Maremma sheep dog has never a sweet disposition, and this one is peculiarly unamiable. He was to be shot. But when a little bird told me that you were coming after me, I saved him up—for you. He is not only large, but so agile! And now I must take my leave. I regret that this being, as I said, not Castello Grigio, but the Castello Vecchio, an out-of-the-way ruin, it will be a bit lonely, and also a bit hungry — but there is always Carlo."

A more ferocious expression than that on di Monti's face Pointer had never seen, unless it were the dog's.

"You are wondering how long I intend to keep you locked up here?" di Monti went on tauntingly. "Pray nod, if I am right."

Pointer did not oblige him, but di Monti thrust out his jowl and answered his own remark.

"It entirely depends on how long you—last. This is an interesting castle. You came to explore it, you fell into one of those old chambers, the one that held the lady I talked of at Stillwater House not so long ago. But I forget, that was before you came on the scene. When Giuseppe comes, in a month or so, he will at once notify the carabinieri Take up the carpet carefully, Giuseppe, I will help you carry it up to the attic again Say '*a riverderla*' to the signore, though I am afraid," di Monti turned his savage face to Pointer with a horrid smile, "I am afraid you will not see him, when next he has the felicity to see you, or what Carlo leaves of you."

Pointer heard the two men struggle with the carpet, then the door of the upper room closed. After some time the great outer entrance clanged shut, and the car hummed away down the grass-grown drive

Pointer looked at the door of his cellar. It was very old, but stout enough to last out his time if he had no weapons but his hands. Leisurely he extracted his cigar case. A thick, podgy case, looking none too well made. He touched a spot with his thumb, and lifted out a shallow tray which held the unusually flat cigars he apparently favoured. Inside was a flat glass bottle, a file not much longer than a nail-file, but of the stoutest steel, a skeleton key, and a few other interesting and equally useful oddments. Similar articles were in his left sole, but the cigar-ease was simpler. The top of his umbrella or stick held other emergency aids. The very cholera belt he wore was a roll of silk rope in a neat holder. His waistcoat buttons were not what they seemed. Pointer was always prepared. He had to be.

One of the cigars held a neat little saw, another a gimlet, still another was a handle. He made a hole in the door and pulled back the bolt with a steep loop made for the purpose. Then he began on the upper fastening. There were four in all, and had been oiled to permit of his own imprisonment. It was a tedious but very simple matter to free himself and step on out into the garden. Luckily the dog had been thoughtfully fastened into the room overhead, for he had taken a violent dislike to the Chief Inspector at first sight. Pointer climbed the handsome wrought-iron gates with a feeling that it was almost unsportsmanlike to escape so easily from what had cost so much thought and trouble to get him into.

Following the direction of the road which most of the horse-shoes faced, he soon came to a hamlet of sorts. Here he got a mount to carry him on. A little later he found a larger town with a garage, and after that all was simplicity itself.

In quite a comfortable car he drove back to Verona, where Bond and Cockburn's private information had told him that a large Fascist meeting was to be held this week. The streets were even more crowded than yesterday, and everywhere were little squads of the

Camicie Nere, the Blackshirts, their top-locks crested like so many dark-feathered cockatoos.

The Italian soldier walks his newly-acquired, or "redeemed," land as simply as Tommy Atkins, and with as little swagger. But the Fascisti are out to make an impression. They were in cheerful mood, calling across to each other little staccato cries of their own. A crowd of Fascist boy-scouts clattered along, the spindly little boys of Italy, but eager as so many terriers. Flags were floating from the houses, the gay green, white and red flashing open and shut as the wind tossed them. Even the old Arena looked alive to-day.

Pointer stopped at a wandering ice-cream vender. "What is up?"

The man laughed. "The Fash' are giving a dinner tonight to the leader of the new Majubaland exploration party. The name has just been published."

He held out a newspaper. A "soot and whitewash" travesty of Cangrande di Monti stared truculently out from the front page of the *Liberta.*

Pointer bought the paper, and stopped in a café to look at it. He laughed as he skimmed through the article below the portrait, for of all the noble natures which Italy has yet produced, di Monti seemed to be the very flower. The dinner in honour of this paragon was to take place at eight, in the old Palazzo del Consiglio, the Fascist headquarters. It was not far off five now.

Reading on Pointer saw that Cangrande's name as leader of the expedition had only been telegraphed from Rome at two-thirty.

No wonder that di Monti had been in a hurry at the Castello. One word from the Scotland Yard man, and his dream might have been dispelled for ever.

Pointer decided to see him at once.

The number of flags outside the beautiful old Consiglio Palazzo made him step in and inquire.

"Yes," some one in a black shirt assured him with pride, "Count Cangrande's here, holding a special meeting at the Veronese Fascisti. No one could intrude."

"It is no intrusion. I am from London. Come over expressly in connection with the recent stay of Count Cangrande there."

"Oh, in that case—" and bowing like a half-shut clasp-knife the man motioned him towards an attendant.

"His illustrious name?" asked the servant, hand on latch.

"I will announce myself," Pointer said loftily, and opened a door farther down.

The large room into which he stepped was crowded. He had come in just behind a long table, covered with a flag, at which sat three officers. Cangrande was the one on the right.

Pointer had not seen him in uniform before. His high black boots, his soft gray-green breeches and coat, Sam Browne belt, black shirt, showing its line at neck and wrists, and, when he turned a double row of ribbons on his breast, on one of which glittered three hard-won tiny silver stars, and the high black cap of the Fascisti, a cross between a Cossack and a Belgian cap was not becoming in itself, but its note of sombre harshness suited di Monti.

No one noticed the entry of the only figure not wearing at least a black stock, for the Fascist cry of *Eia-eia-Alala* was thundering up, each man rising and swinging out his right hand and arm in the greeting of the Roman Legions. Then the song of the Unknown Soldier, *la Canzone del Mute Ignoto*, rolled through the room, and Pointer looked about him. Every face was alight. Some were marked by little else but egotism, ruthlessness, or intolerance. But taken as a whole, a finer looking lot of young men he had never seen, nor was likely to see. They were not here to serve self-interest. In this world where money rules, they bent the knee to something higher. It was as though there swept through that crowded room a spirit from the realm of idealism and passionate selflessness. Pointer could almost hear the beating of its wings. He saw again the Thousand Heroes of Garibaldi rallying to the call. For Pointer knew the Italy of immediately after the Great War. The Chief Inspector had spoken with those who had seen men flung shrieking into their own blast furnaces at Turin amid Communist cheers. He had been present in Bologna when a partially disabled officer had had his uniform cut off him with knives that streaked the rags with his blood.

One of the men beside di Monti stepped forward.

In this meeting which was Italian, and not party—according to him—he said that he wished to mention some of the war services of the man to whom was to be entrusted the important charge of governing the newly-acquired *Oltrajuba.*

He ran over di Monti's war record. It was a fine one.

Twice after Caporetto the count had collected a mere handful of wounded men, and, calling over his shoulder the historic cry of the Great Liberator, "Here, Italians, we die!" had made a desperate stand against incredible odds at some bend in the road, some slope of the track, some point, whose selection was as much a credit to his brains as to his pluck.

Di Monti listened with eyes on his hands, which were clasped lightly on the hilt of his sword. About his mouth was a suggestion of reverie. Once only he looked up. Across to a little hunchback standing in the back row line of starred ribbons across his narrow chest, neatly in a waiter's black. The man caught the glance. Up and out shot a toil-worn hand in a salute at once friend and proud. A comrade saluting a comrade.

Di Monti's harsh mouth softened for a second. Straight back to crippled back he and this man had stood, never expecting to see more of life than clubbed rifle butts whirling in the air, and stabbing bayonets and Monti's own flashing, dripping, broken sword.

Suddenly di Monti turned and caught sight of Pointer. The Italian was singing, and he finished the line without a tremor of his strident voice.

Then he stepped back.

"A word with you in private," Pointer said quickly.

"Impossible."

"Then in public."

"Impossible. If it comes to words—one from me and you would be torn to pieces."

"Costly pieces, Count di Monti," Pointer said coldly. "I think the price would ruin your party." Pointer jaw was well to the fore. Di Monti stared at him and he stared back. The chairman turned questioningly.

"This gentleman brings me a message of congratulation from London, and some very urgent news," di Mon explained to him, "may I be excused a moment?"

They slipped out of a side door. Some one filled in the gap with a speech, some one else started *La Giovanezza*, the song of youth, the song of the Fascisti, and then more speeches.

Finally di Monti came in again. He was very pale. As for Pointer, he walked away from the hotel deep in thought. Di Monti had sworn solemnly to him that he was innocent of the murder of Rose Charteris, that he was caught in a web of circumstantial evidence possibly, but that he was not guilty. His desperate attack on Pointer's life made the assertion ring false, but the count maintained that that had been simply a way of gaining time until his own election should be ratified. He did not stoop to try to pass it off as less than it was—an attempted brutal murder, but he insisted that he had had an anonymous letter from England, warning him that Pointer was going to have him detained at once, pending an extradition order, which Scotland Yard had already applied for. Pointer had stood awhile, looking at his boot-tips.

"If I go straight to your *Duce* with the account of what happened to me this morning, where will you be?"

Di Monti was very pale. He said nothing.

"If you will give me your word of honour—I will trust it—to come to England any time within the next ten days, I shall be silent on that point. If you do not give me your word, I go to Signor Mussolini at once, and you will be arrested at once," Pointer went on.

Flight again for di Monti was out of the question. He would not try to escape from his own country, his new position. Both men knew as much.

"You mean that I am to come to England to be arrested for the murder of Miss Charteris?" di Monti asked slowly.

"That's as may be. Even so, you would have a chance of proving your innocence, a chance of an acquittal. You will have none if I go to your chief with the story of what has just happened to me at the Castello. I have witnesses who helped me to get out."

"I might have known that you wouldn't come alone!" di Monti said bitterly. He walked up and down the room for some minutes. "I must agree. I give you my word of honour as an officer and a gentleman to come if you summon me within ten days."

"Not necessarily to be arrested." Pointer did not want a suicide; and di Monti was capable of anything. "Possibly merely to help the case."

Di Monti gave him a long look, and uncovered his teeth in an incredulous smile, then, with a curt nod, he returned to the council room, and Pointer walked on downstairs.

He dismissed the young Italian from his mind for the time being. Pointer wanted to find the professor. Rose's father might hold the key to the whole involved series of events which had taken place that Thursday night at Stillwater. Di Monti said that he had not been near his family. As he was quite willing for Pointer to check that statement by a talk with his father, the Chief Inspector accepted his word.

That registered letter that Rose had received had been sent from Bolzano. To Bolzano, Pointer was therefore bound.

He telephoned to the old count. A telephone message obtained a hearing often when a caller was kept waiting. He spoke of himself over the wire as Gilchrist, Professor Charteris's family solicitor. Had the professor made any arrangement to stay with Count di Monti? A feeble voice told him that the professor had. He was to have come to Verona to the Palazzo di Monti on May first, and spend the week-end there. But he had telephoned from Genoa earlier, asking whether his visit could be put forward a week, as otherwise he must give it up. It had not been possible for the count to do this, much as he regretted the fact. There the matter had rested. The voice of the old man showed that he thought himself somewhat summarily treated, for he had had no word from his once-invited guest of explanation or apology.

Pointer caught the night train up to Bolzano. He had much to think about as the train wound up beside the Adige.

The next morning he woke to true Bolzano weather, though the year was unusually cold. May, as a rule, is hot in this wonderful little spot of Europe where north and south meet, where the grape ripens under the pine trees, where the same valley can show glacier and coral formations. Pointer liked Bolzano. Though he thought its old name of Bozen suited it better. There is something angular and wooden about the Tirol word that goes with the gables, and turrets, and arched passages of the busy town, where the swifts swoop like hounds on the scent down the main streets, dodging under the elbows of passers-by, and chasing each other like children at tag through the arcades.

The professor stopped at the Hotel Laurin.

Pointer knew by inquiries made already from England that he had arrived on the Sunday before Rose's death, alone, and had left, alone, the next day. His only luggage had been a suit-case, which he had sent to the station early on Monday morning, saying that it was to be forwarded to Meranoo.

Pointer found that it had been duly forwarded and fetched from the latter station. Either the professor, or some one else, had handed in the *scontrino* and been given the bag. But who had produced that voucher?

Pointer's first walk was to the Bolzano post-office, where he verified the registered letter sent off on the Monday before Rose's death, some twelve days ago now.

He was shown the duplicate slip, which stated:

Assegno L.—Charteris. Hotel Laurin.

Destnario—Charteris. Medchester.

The hour, Pointer learnt, must have been before noon, as at that time the clerks had been changed, and the one in whose writing the slip was made out had gone off duty for the day.

At the hotel he learnt that the professor had shown no preference either for people or for solitude. Some of his meals he had taken in the dining room, some in his own bedroom. Apparently he had acted like any ordinary traveller.

Pointer began to be more certain than ever that the murderer had made a mistake, that he had expected that registered letter's enclosure to contain—what?

What was it, what could it have been, that might have been enclosed instead of that memo, that might have been wanted by some one who thought that some important piece of news might have been sent to the daughter by the father, news so important that at all costs to the receiver, at all risks to the criminal, it must be prevented from being passed on?

Where was the professor? What had happened to him between Bolzano and his promised visit to Meranoo?

A railway line runs between the two towns, but Charteris had expressly spoken of walking over the Mendel. Where could his walk have led him that no word of his only child's murder seemed to be able to reach him? The Mendel Pass is not out of the world. It is a favourite summer resort, with most up-to-date hotels, where every well-known English newspaper would be taken.

Pointer went for a walk along the old dyke, planted with trees and shrubs, broad as the king's highway, that keeps the river in bounds.

He loved nature as only the man can who spends his life in towns. And that walk is unique. With the chanting Talfer rushing past, clear as crystal, with vineyards stretching on either hand, with feudal castles and gleaming farmhouses, and tiny white churches like, candles dotted here and there, on the slopes of the green hills of Tirol that rise on every side, while far away, as though looked at through gauze, towers the great Rosengarten range, set like a throne of the high gods against the sky.

Just now it was still hung with veils of white over its own changing purple and grays. At sunset it might show itself for a brief moment of incredible beauty, a garden of red roses blowing, tossing, blooming, only changed by the spell of King Laurin to stone, as runs the Ladine legend

Pointer stood drawing in deep breaths of the dry, pure air, hanging fresh pictures in the gallery for which he cared most, his memory gallery.

An impression of being stared at made him turn. A little man had come up behind him, and was standing examining him attentively, from his English hat to his English boots. Pointer had an odd feeling as he looked back at him. The man was unlike any other whom the Chief Inspector had ever seen, and Pointer felt that the difference was racial, not individual. He had never met a specimen of the primitive man before who still exists here and there in Europe, and he was surprised at strong sensation, half repulsion, half interest, which he felt.

The man was about five feet in height, very sturdily built, and conveying a sense of—not bad proportions but different proportions to what we call the normal. He was thickset, with next to no neck, and with odd, haunch-like hips. On his well-shaped—but still differently-shaped head, the hair grew straight, and coarse, and thick, like cocoanut fibre mat, to below the line of his low collar. He was clean-shaven, with a fawn-like face, and small eyes, brown and soft, and shifting quickly. On meeting Pointer's stare, he turned and walked away.

A gardener was sweeping the walk.

"Do you know who that little man is?"

"That's Ladiner Toni. A guide from the *Paesi Ladini.*"

"A good guide?"

"Very good. But now, of course, with the snow so late, there's little climbing to be done. He's been in Bozen a lot lately, but as a rule, other springs, one never saw him."

Sauntering down in the town proper, Pointer again noticed the little man, and also that he was deliberately following him.

The Englishman stopped in at one of the multitudinous wine rooms that are growing less of a curse to the drink-loving inhabitants under Fascist government. As he drank his glass of rough Tirol wine, a face peered around at him for a second, eyed him wistfully, and melted away. The eyes seemed to want to ask a question, and yet not dare.

The waitress knew him at once on Pointer's speaking to her.

"As a rule, he's up and away in his mountains. They're wild birds, the Ladini. But lately, two or three tourists have told me that he followed them about. I'm afraid poor Toni has found the year a bad one."

"Can you send for him? I should like to speak to him."

But Toni had melted away.

Back at the hotel Pointer could not learn whether Charteris had engaged any guide in the town or not. Bozen is a walking, not a mountaineering centre. He got the address of Ladiner Toni and his character from the Carabinieri. He lived in Sand Christina, a tiny village in the Val Gardena.

The detective officer took the motor diligence to its mouth, and set out for Toni's house. His father had been the schoolmaster. The driver knew Toni well. He, too, agreed that he had changed of late. He was in and out of Bolzano all day long, hanging around the station, or the post-office chiefly, though he would as like as not spend hours on the promenades or in the big square. He seemed to be always on the lookout for some one, the driver thought. Perhaps some one who had not paid him up.

Pointer was in the little village before he knew it, so. dark were the tiny wooden houses that they melted into the earth around them. That of the teacher's widow was like a toy gingerbread cottage.

An old woman, sitting by her spinning-wheel, looked up. She, too, was short and squat, but her brown. eyes were very bright.

"Come in. You are looking for my son?" She spoke Italian or German with equal effort. "He will be in soon."

Pointer took a stool and watched her, nimble brown fingers.

"You want a guide, perhaps, *Signo*?"

All through their talk of the weather she eyed him closely.

The door, opened, and the little man entered. At sight of him, Pointer knew that he had not had his tramp for nothing. A curious pallor came into the man's swart face. His eyes flickered backwards and forwards from Pointer to his mother.

"This gentleman wants to see you, Toni."

"Well?" he asked in German, in a throaty, husky voice. "I hear you're a good guide among the Dolomites, and I want one."

"There's no climbing when the snows are melting." A watchful, suspicious intentness was in the little man's face. He was breathing rapidly. The wheel had stopped, and the old woman, too, was staring at their guest.

"I want you to show me some of the valleys around here. The carabinieri said you were trustworthy, and that what you don't know of the Dolomites towards Cadore isn't worth knowing. I will leave the pay to you, but I want a Ladiner."

"Why?"

"Because I want to hear your legends as we walk."

The wheel turned again. A sudden flurry of spring snow was flung against the window. Pointer had first heard of the Ladine folk lore from the driver that morning. He had spoken of Toni's mother as a repository of those legends, beautiful and haunting.

"Toni, put on more wood, and I will tell you how the snow first came to us mortals."

It was like rolling back the world to King Alfred's days, Pointer thought, as the old woman span and told him wild poetry of moon princesses and gnomes and trolls.

He looked at Toni, who was carving a pipe, and thought of gnomes. But the man's face was honest. He was a good guide, the Carabinieri had said. Pointer would not admit that his work made him need it more than other men, but for a fortnight of every year the Chief Inspector went to Switzerland, and spent his days high up, climbing among ice and the snows that never melt.

Living in a white world, and yet a world all colour, sea-green crevices, sky-blue hollows, long, lilac shadows, and at dawn and sunset every tint of the rainbow to walk on. To be a good guide was, in his eyes, the highest rating that a man could have.

To refill his pipe, Pointer had to hunt for his tobacco pouch. He laid some of the contents of his pockets on the table as he did so. Prominent among them, face up, was the photograph of Professor Charteris.

There was a hissing intake of breath from Toni. The wheel stopped its purr. In the little mirror in the palm of his hand Pointer saw the woman's face. She was staring at her son in piteous uncertainty. Pointer glanced casually at Toni, who lifted a pair of frightened, irresolute eyes. The Englishman continued to speak of the storm as he replaced the objects.

"Can you put me up overnight? I only need an armchair."

He preferred it to any bed the house could have given him, though Toni offered his own pallet.

Pointer settled himself for the night after a supper which made him turn pale for days to think on. He was well wrapped up, and with his legs on a second chair, did very well. Late in the night he heard some one come down the ladder and tiptoe into the room. It could only be Toni, for his mother was next door. From beneath his lashes, Pointer saw him in the moonlight creeping forward, his face distorted with timidity and anxiety. There was nothing in his hands. Pointer guessed what he was after. With the sigh of a sleeping man, he turned in his chair, so that his coat fell open—the photograph pocket in sight.

Toni crept closer. Tiny fingers, which again gave Pointer an odd thrill of physical repulsion which his mind did not share, touched him The photo was pulled out with a difficulty that to the detective was a certificate of the little fellow's previous honesty. Then Toni tiptoed to his mother's room. The door creaked slowly open and then shut. Followed a long whispered dialogue, during which Pointer took a nap. Ladine was not one of his accomplishments.

Back crept Toni. Half-way back went the photograph, then Pointer awoke and caught his wrist.

"A thief!"

"Oh, God!" Toni cried in fright. The door opened. His mother stood on the threshold holding a lamp high above her head with trembling hands. In the heavy folds of her nightdress and cap tied under her chin, she looked like a little white statue of fear.

"What does this mean?" Pointer asked as sternly as possible, for he felt as though he were terrifying two children, "I shall have to hand you over to the Carabinieri."

"I will explain." The mother came quite close. "No, Toni, let your mother explain. Only the truth is ever right. We must take the consequences. My son was having another look at a photograph you laid on the table this evening. It is of a relative? A friend?"

"One does not carry the pictures of strangers about with one. What do you know of the man?"

Again that agonised look exchanged between mother and son.

"Let go of my Toni, who did no harm except to listen to his mother's foolish, oh, foolish words! Now, we will all sit down, and I will tell you the dreadful truth."

"Mother, you will catch cold. Let me wrap a blanket around you." Toni rolled her up like a mummy, with only the wise little face showing.

"That man in the photograph came here just two weeks ago. On a Monday. The snows were hard and firm on the mountains then, and he had been here before. He had climbed with Toni the two last years in succession for a couple of days. Well, he came here in the afternoon, walking as you did from where the diligence put him down. He intended to stop the night and set off at four next morning, for the *Val de la Saljeres*, as we call it. A place which we here of *Dla-ite* avoid. The stones of an old watercourse are there. We Ladines know the truth of it, but you of the other people tell a different tale. This man—a sort of school-master like my blessed Antoni, he said he was—"

She paused inquiringly. Pointer nodded.

"Well, he wished to go there, and then go on later over to Meranoo by the Mendel. My son was willing. He liked the man. You did like him, didn't you, Toni?" She quavered, tears in her eyes.

"I did. He understood. He never laughed at the things we know."

"They set off in the morning about four, he and Toni, and by nine they should have been up in the Saijeres valley. But before twelve my Toni came running back. Happy Heaven! How he was running!" She undid a hand to wipe her eyes, but the tears were coming too fast now for her to speak. Toni patted the roll about where her shoulder would be.

"Tell no more, mother. I will show him everything to-morrow. I cannot explain in words as you can, but I will show him everything"

"Everything?" Again the two pairs of eyes clung

Toni swallowed and nodded. He was trembling violently. Pointer, with his purely physical dislike of him, thought again that it was not as a man trembles, but as an animal shivers.

"You will be ready in the morning at four? It will be wet, but the Val Saijeres lies low. It is only, an uphill walk" Toni spoke quite resolutely.

"Good. I'll be ready. Now suppose we make your mother some tea or coffee."

But Toni poured into a saucepan some rough red wine mixed with water, dropped in a tablespoon of the black-brown honey of Tirol and some cloves, and stirred it all with a stick of cinnamon to a foamy froth This he poured into three cups. Pointer had tasted worse.

The old woman put her cup down with a shaking hand.

"It is a beautiful house, this of my husband's, but here in the valley there is only money. Happiness lies up on the hills." She left them.

Toni got up. "No, I will not speak now," he mumbled. "I am not good at talk like mother, but I will show you."

Pointer felt sure that he would be as good as his word, and fell into a sound sleep.

The old lady was astir with them next morning, heating up some of the buckwheat dumplings of their supper, and wrapping a couple in cabbage leaves for them to carry.

Toni took up his ice-axe with a strange look at its pointed tip. Then they set off by the swing of his lantern's light, and plodded on and up into a wild and stony region. True Dolomités were these, *Lis Montes Palyes*, Toni called them, and pallid and gray they were. Between this savage world the Saljeres Valley wound up, and up, with a prehistoric aqueduct at its upper end.

About eight, Toni, who had plodded along dumbly, stopped.

"We came here just like now, that man and I. Here he stopped to light his pipe, and said he would rest. I, too, sat down. On this rock here. My ice-axe I laid here. As I sat I heard a sound some way off. But this valley has so many invisible people living in it that I paid no heed. The mountain spirits do not harm me or any one in my charge. From this place a shorter way runs to the place he wanted to see, but we have had a very hard and late winter, and I was not sure whether the snow would not be too deep for him. He was not a young man. I asked him if I could climb up to that ridge there and look. If the path was open, we should be at the end of the gorge in a few minutes, but it would take me some twenty minutes to reach the rock. He said he wanted a rest, as his breathing showed. So I left my ice-axe where I had laid it beside him, and climbed that ridge you see to a little platform beyond, which you can't see. The track was deep in snow, as I thought. I was looking at it when suddenly I was told that something was wrong with the man. I ran back and I found him"—Toni began to tremble, that animal shuddering that seemed to crinkle his very skin—"I found him—around this bend. Here, on this new place. He must have moved into the sun when I had gone. But I found him—dead. Lying back with his head this way, and my ice-axe here beside him. Its point was red, and his head was red. There was a deep hole in it on top. He was quite dead. Some one had killed him with my ice-axe while I was away, and some one had robbed him of everything in his pockets, even to his handkerchief. I looked because I did not know his name. He had come two years, but there was no need of names. I rushed up that ridge there to see, but I saw nothing I shouted, but though a man over there heard me, he was a Croderes, and they never come. I was frightened—my man, my axe, and everything stolen from him—I lifted him into a cave I know of close to here. You see that stone?"

Pointer nodded with tense jaw.

"It rolls away. Behind it is a cave, dry and ice-cold. Ice-water washes around it. I put him in there, and ran home and told mother. She was as frightened as I, and it takes a lot to frighten mother"—Pointer thought of the little white-faced wisp, and smiled to himself—"and we decided to leave him there and say nothing. He is there now, and that is why I waited every day in Bolzano. I knew that some one would come looking for him. This is the rock."

Pointer helped him to get the stone away. It could be levered with the ice-axe quite easily. He stooped and entered an icy-cold hole in the rock, where, on the dry tufa, lay the body of an elderly man, frozen stiff. Pointer recognised it by the many portraits he had seen as Professor Charteris. As Ladine Toni had said, the pockets were empty. The head wound must have been made by some such instrument as the axe's point. The Chief Inspector crawled out again. Toni watched him like a half-timid, half-trusting animal.

"No one saw this affair, I suppose? No one knows of it but your mother and you?"

"A Croderès lives up there," Toni pointed. "He is a chamois-hunter. He might have seen something, but it would take a lot of money to find out."

"Why so? Surely he would speak if appealed to."

Toni shook his head helplessly.

"You mean he was there when this man was killed?" Pointer asked again.

Toni nodded several times.

"I saw him on his ledge when I looked for the short cut."

"Why won't he tell what he saw, supposing he saw the murder?" persisted the detective officer.

Toni looked haggard.

"I and my mother have plenty to live on with our big garden, but money—money enough for a Croderès—" Again he shook his head feebly.

"Can we get up to the hut of this Cro—" Pointer let the word fade away in the approved fashion of a stranger speaking an uncertain tongue.

Toni nodded after looking at the soles of Pointer's boots. They were well nailed.

"What am I to do about—*him*?"

Pointer did not commit himself. "What is a Crodere?" he asked instead.

Toni gave his little helpless wriggle.

"It is just a name we use. Some people say they belong to us, Ladines. There are not many left. They only live among the rocks, chiefly, towards Cadore."

"And are they so fond of money?"

"They are Croderès."

"So I gathered. But *why* do they love money so?"

Toni looked at him in silence, but after awhile he began to talk as they climbed the fairly easy goat path. Pointer pieced together from his disjointed confidences' the account of a race of mountain miners and bunters, who looked like ordinary men and women, and lived like them, but who were really stone men. They could feel nothing, neither love nor hate, anger nor joy, pain nor pleasure.

They are always even-tempered, he went on, and never harm any one on purpose, but a Croderès would see a child roasted alive if it happened to fall into the fire, though by merely putting out his hand he could save it. They have no hearts, no feelings, but they have clever brains, and they love money, though it can do nothing for them. A Croderès can feel neither heat nor cold.

Pointer again felt as though he were in a world unknown. Piffle, of course, but such strange, eerie piffle.

Suddenly Toni stopped. A moment more and they stood on a wide, smooth stone, evidently the entrance to a cave. A man stood inside watching them. He was about Toni's height, but broader, with longer arms. His hair was as thick, but curly. His eyes, however, were different—of a curious ice-blue, the eyes of a Siamese cat. Otherwise there was nothing odd about his tanned face. He looked rather stupid, but quite good-natured—when his eyes were downcast.

"The gentleman wants to talk to you, Seppi."

"I am inquiring about a friend of mine. He was up here in the mountains a fortnight ago yesterday. Do you happen to remember an accident of any kind on that day?"

The man looked at him placidly, turned, and went back into his cave as though to fetch something.

"He won't come out again, not unless the sun shines," Toni muttered.

"Is it permitted to enter?" Pointer asked in Italian.

"*Prego, prego*!" The man acquiesced civilly, going on with his work of clipping the ears of some chamois masks which he was mounting. The only chairs were boulders. A little fire flickered on a huge rock that served the man as table. A pot of glue stood in the centre; shears and taxidermist's knives lay on a slab beside it.

"I will pay well for reliable information."

"What will you pay?" Seppi's voice was husky and very even.

Pointer laid ten two-lire pieces in front of him, and kept his hand on them. Ice-blue eyes met gray eyes for a second.

"What age was your friend? What did he wear?"

Pointer told him.

"Yes, I saw him."

The man went on with his humming,

"Ste Ii a vardar,

El Latemar."

Pointer pushed across two of the coins.

"He was sitting on a rock in the valley," the rock man said briskly.

"Did you see anything else?" Another coin was shoved across, and so it went on, Pointer feeding the man as though he were some sort of talking automaton.

"I saw Toni go up to a ledge to see how the short cut was. I saw him shade his eyes and peer at it. I saw the old man in the valley move around a corner on to a rock in the sun. I saw another man come along the valley, pick up the ice-axe, and come crouching half around the corner. I saw Toni dislodge a stone. At its rattle the second man slipped back again around the bend. I saw that he meant to kill the old man." Seppi spoke as unconcernedly as though he had been describing army manoeuvres.

"Why didn't you shout?"

"And scare away the chamois? I was glad to see that the man intended to use an ice-axe and not a gun. He came on a second time with the axe up, and crashed it down into the head of the old man sitting with his back to him. The man fell off the boulder."

"Could you see what Toni was doing?"

"He had just reached the flat rock which would show him the short cut."

"Couldn't he see the murder?"

"Of course not. There is that crag between. See for yourself. The man raised the axe again, but evidently the other man was dead. I saw him examine him with care, or rob him. I couldn't see clearly which it was. Then he jumped up and ran behind the corner again, and on out of sight around that bend you see from here. I saw him no more."

"Could you describe him?"

The description was hopeless. Middle size, middle dark, rather young, full beard, soft hat, oldish cape over his coat. It would have fitted three-quarters of the men who had passed that way.

Pointer arranged with the man to pay him the amount of a day's chamois hunting should he need him to report the murder to the Carabinieri. The man agreed, asked for something on account, and, as he stretched out his hand, passed it accidentally through the flame. He held it there for a second, till Toni's exclamation made him look at it. With perfect unconcern he picked off the black flesh, and shoved the hand into his pocket.

"I must tie it up. It is a nuisance that I was not looking."

"Does it hurt?" Pointer asked, watching him closely. The man laughed shortly.

"Nothing can hurt me. That's the danger. You can lose an arm without noticing what's wrong, if you don't look out."

As he walked back to the cottage with Toni, Pointer was still not sure if that apparently painless burn had been acting, or the result of self-suggestion, or some sort of Yoga.

"Do nothing till you hear from me again," he told Toni.

"I want time to think things over. I may have to speak to the Carabinieri about the matter, but I shall be able so to put it that you are seen to be innocent, I think. Will you leave it to me?"

Toni shivered.

"The carabinieri—they are so quick! Always in such a hurry to act!"

"I think I shall be able to make their *maresciallo* understand, and it is the only way. The only way, Toni, believe me."

For Pointer there never was but one way—the way of the law.

Toni licked his dry lips.

"You—you think so?"

"Courage!" Pointer laid a kindly hand on his shoulder. "You have a good reputation. You are a good guide, and a good guide is not a man to lightly suspect of murder. Then there is your cold-blooded friend up there—"

"But he saw no more than I knew. I told you the man was killed by a blow from my ice-axe."

CHAPTER NINE

POINTER had plenty to think about as he took the motor coach back to Bolzano that afternoon. So the professor was dead. He had half-feared as much these many days past, Charteris had sent off that letter to his daughter on the Monday, and had been killed the next day, while she was murdered the Thursday following, the day of its arrival in England. The Professor had not been attacked in the train before he got out at Bolzano, though the first-class coaches are usually quite empty so early in the year. It would have been an easy matter to knock him on the head and fling him out, en route. Much less troublesome and dangerous than to track him to that lonely valley.

Pointer believed that the guide's life had only been saved by his having gone on to that upper point. For the murderer came doubtless prepared with a revolver or gun to account for both, if need be.

Why was the professor's life suddenly in danger, when it seemed to have been safe up till then? Rose's murder, Pointer felt sure, was connected with the letter she had received. Could he link up her father's death with it? Not unless—unless something had happened in Bolzano which he might have been supposed to describe, or send on to her. They had pillaged his body. Were they looking for something which they expected he would have on him, and which, not finding, they assumed had been sent in the letter that he had registered to his daughter in England the day before? They must have found the receipt for the letter in his note-case.

In all likelihood, a message must have been sent to England, a telegram probably, telling her murderer to be on the lookout.

But what could have happened in the quaint little town to cause such a scheme to be necessary. Money? Inheritance? Something momentous it must have been.

Pointer did not doubt Toni's honesty. "Yes," he murmured to himself, "it looks as though something very important had happened that Monday in Bolzano before twelve, before the professor sent that registered letter, and took the *postauto* on to the Grödner Tal."

Pointer made his way to the Sotto Prefectura, and roamed its passages, and blundered in and out of its rooms, with as little attention paid him as though he had been a blue-bottle. At last, by mere luck, he found an elderly, pleasant-faced Italian, who looked up, and to his oft-repeated, "*Il Sotto-Prefetto*?" replied, "I myself. To what do I owe the honour?"

Pointer laid his credentials down on the table and explained them. The Italian looked them over very carefully, then rose and bowed, glanced at the collar lying beside him, evidently decided that decorations need not be worn, and bowed again as he sat down

"I am over here to try to trace a much respected compatriot, a Professor Charteris, who we know passed through this part of the world a fortnight ago. I found his murdered body to-day."

The sub-prefect, who had been listening as one listens to foreigners, intent on letting no strangely pronounced word slip past him unrecognised, his hands pressed back to back between his knees, relaxed, to throw them out in horror.

"Murdered?"

"Murdered. Now the guide who led me to the body as soon as he heard the description of the man, was Ladiner Toni."

He told Toni's story very carefully, and the corroboration of the chamois hunter.

"They are children," the sotto-prefetto said, shaking his head, "but it has an ugly sound."

"It has, signore, but there is a private matter behind all this. His daughter was murdered on Thursday in England. He on the Tuesday morning, here in Tirol"

"Alto Adige," corrected the Italian official immediately.

"That was why Scotland Yard decided to hunt out the father—as a matter of routine," continued Pointer. Whenever he insisted on doing something in his own way, he referred to it as the Yard's doing, and himself, by inference, as the straw blown hither or thither by a higher power.

"Private affair? A vendetta?"

"We don't know. It's a very mysterious story altogether. But it would suit us to keep the fact that he has been murdered quiet for a while yet. If you could seal up that rock and leave him there—and let the matter rest awhile? It has nothing to do with Toni, that I'll stake my position on. There's an inheritance mixed up in the affair, and that may be at the bottom of the two murders. This part of the world is famous for its absence of crime—"

"Smugglers thick as flies on honey," murmured the sotto-prefetto, but he was pleased at the tribute.

"I was speaking of serious crimes, and it is only fair that the good name of Tir—the Alto Adige, should not be tarnished because of a crime undoubtedly unconnected with it. Connected quite certainly with the other affair. Now, could I see the charge-sheet for Monday morning?"

The papers were laid before him. Pointer learnt that on that Monday had taken place:

(1) A bicyclist fined for riding on a footpath.

(2) A pane of glass broken.

(3) A street accident.

It was not a hopeful-sounding list for two murders.

The broken pane of glass was in a cake shop. The criminals, two little boys. Remained the street accident.

A wealthy Bulgarian gentleman, a rose-grower of Kazanlik, had been run over by a runaway cart-horse. He had died at the hospital, or just before. His papers were all in order, and his body had been at once claimed and taken on home by his friends.

Pointer rose. This was his last hope. That gone, there remained only some chance meeting, some stray letter.

The Bulgarian had been taken to Bolzano's one hospital. Thither Pointer went and made further inquiries about this Mr. Drinoff.

The sister in charge, a quaint, tubby little person, in her ugly habit, looked up the records for him. They were very ordinary. The gentleman was dead when he got there, so be had been sent at once to the mortuary chapel. Some of his friends had arrived a little, later and claimed him, and after that—she did not know exact particulars. They had taken him back to Bulgaria eventually. If Pointer wanted dates, she could only refer him to Doctor Sanftl. He would know. He had hoped to save him at first, for the man was barely dead. What hour was this? just before dinner, about eleven, or possibly half-past. The sister's dinner was at twelve, and she had had a very sketchy one in consequence

Had a friend come with him?

Not a friend, a kindly passer-by had come in. Another Bulgarian who spoke German very well.

"Was he by any chance tall, thin, and elderly?"

"*Eben*! Tall, thin, and elderly. Some sort of a professor, judging by his scholarly face."

She was quite sure he could not be English?

Put point-blank to her like that, the sister could only say that she had taken it for granted, being a foreigner, that he was also a Bulgarian, but she had no real grounds for that belief. Doctor Sanftl would know. Doctor Sanftl had talked to the gentleman a good deal.

Could Pointer see the doctor?

He was no longer at the hospital. He had left only a week ago and was now at the Mariahilf hospital in Innsbruck, but the gentleman could write.

He could, and he could also travel, and that by the next train, Pointer thought.

Doctor Sanftl had liked him immensely, that elderly foreigner, and had asked him to come again in the afternoon, he had something he wanted to show him, but the gentleman had to go on—some excursion he wanted to make, some ruins he wanted to see, if she remembered aright.

Pointer took the next train up the wild Brenner Pass and on to Innsbrück. Next morning he drove out to the, hospital standing outside the town, all dreary and dirty in its summer gray.

"A friend of Professor Charteris, of the professor with the interesting views on chemical affinities? *Gruss Gott*!" The doctor shook hands warmly.

What could he do for the professor's friend? "Nothing, judging by your looks," he added, "though you've been worrying over something lately."

Pointer, who took all his cases very hard, was surprised at the big stout man's acumen.

Yes, he had been worrying—about the professor.

They had had no news of him since he had arrived in Bolzano. Was the doctor sure that the dead Bulgarian had been a stranger to the professor?

The doctor was quite sure.

"Where are my notes of the case—ah, I remember, they're at Bolzano."

"The sister said not."

"Which sister? Bright eyes, nose rather beaky?" Pointer-could not cope with this description in a foreign tongue, but he described her laboriously.

"*Freilich! Freilich*! That's the one. Well, she ought to know. Wonderfully accurate woman." The doctor thought hard, his hands deep in his long white overall. "I know! Of course! As the man was dead, my notes on his injuries were never asked for. I stuck them into my laboratory locker, and there they are still. I forgot to clear that out when I came on here." He suddenly flushed. "*Alle welt noch 'mal*! I do believe the man's letter-case is there, too. Oh, no money! But a couple of Bulgarian letters. I asked your friend to go over them for me in the afternoon, as he knew Bulgarian, but, as a matter of fact, we didn't need them. The man's passport and papers were at his hotel and all in perfect order." The professor could not come that afternoon, but he promised to look at them next morning. He was going out to the Grödner Tal. But he, too, forgot! Sister Fini did remind me of that locker, but I was in a bit of a rush at the last. I've the key still here," he dived into a pocket like a kit-bag, "no, not here. Here," he pulled open the table drawer, "here it is. I must send it back, and get them to send on the letter-case to its owner."

Pointer said that he was on his way back at once, and would hand the key over.

"*Famos*! That saves me a letter. Care to look over the wards?"

Pointer declined that treat, and caught the train. Sister Fini sniffed as she took the key.

"Just like him! He's a very clever doctor, but forgetful! I remember his putting down some one's name twice for the same operation. Here is the locker. The letter-case is your friend's, you say. If he left it behind him, and spoke of coming back in the afternoon, it would be just like Doctor Sanftl to drop it into his cupboard and never think of it again. It's not one he often goes to." She opened the locker. Pointer picked up at once a letter-case folded in three. Inside were a couple of business-looking letters. Otherwise it seemed empty. The letters had pictures and doubtless the name of some Bulgarian firm on both envelope and sheet. Sister Fini was pouncing on other treasure trove.

"My scissors! I knew he had them! I knew it! I only hope there was nothing of that poor dead gentleman's that got tossed in here, too" She peered around anxiously. "His friends were so sure that something had been lost or overlooked. We really had quite a scene with them. Doctor Sanftl isn't one to listen to that sort of suggestion calmly." She was peering into the cupboard. "No, there's nothing else except the doctor's own papers. They looked over the room upstairs—the room into which. the body was taken, so I think we may be sure that nothing was left. They actually thought their friend might have been robbed while in the hospital! I told them that he had not been alone for a moment. First your friend, then the doctor, and then the orderlies who carried him off."

"They asked for my friend's name and address, didn't they?" Pointer spoke as though the doctor might have told him as much.

"Yes, they were so sorry to think that they had actually passed him by on the steps. They were hurrying in, thinking of the terrible accident, and your friend was reading some directions the doctor had written down for him about the new hours when the autocar leaves for the Grödner Tal. They would so have liked to thank him for his kindness. Well, I'm relieved that all is all right now." She beamed cheerily, and showed Pointer out.

The Scotland Yard man speculated on how much time would elapse before she would have spread the news of his friend's pocket-book. If he had been able to bribe an orderly in London, so could others here.

Sister Josephine had a carrying voice. And the pocketbook might be the key, might be the reason, the long-sought motive, behind this puzzling case.

Pointer leant back against his locked door at the hotel, and took out the letters, which were in Cyrillic characters. Feeling carefully, he found an inner, secret pocket, over whose mouth a band for stamps slipped. Inside this was a very thin sheet of paper covered with what looked like a poem in faint, fine writing. It, too, was in Russian characters.

Pointer's eyes glowed. The paper was the kind used for secret messages in all countries. Very fine and very tough, capable at need of being tied to a pigeon's wing or folded into a cigarette. If he was right, he had the treasure in his steady hands—the cause of two murders.

He returned it to its inner place, for, being in Russian characters, he dared not copy it, and the ink was too faint and blue for it to photograph well. At Scotland Yard are good interpreters. He must get this home to them at once.

The registered post was too uncertain; flying machines might arouse attention. He decided to carry it home by rail and boat, home to the best brains in England to decipher, and then, and then only, he would know the motive behind the double crime.

He would have liked to divine it before he learnt it. Vaguely something of the truth was filtering in even now, but he must wait. How long would he be allowed to keep his find? As long, he thought, as some one at the hospital would take to telephone, or be had misjudged the whole affair.

He turned, and walked slowly up and down in the Piazza Walther, pretending an interest in the minstrel's statue.

Supposing, he thought, that what was wanted was merely to put out of the way, to kill the owner, or supposed owner of that paper, he would not have a chance of reaching England alive. Not one. But, as he saw it, it was the paper, not his death in itself or by itself, which they wanted.

His death might be decreed, if he had read it, like the professor's death, like Rose Charteris's death, but the possession of the paper in each case had been and would be the primary objective.

Here lay his one chance of reaching home. For the murderer was obviously not working alone. Another hand had killed the father from that which had murdered the daughter. A third person might be put on duty in his case.

Pointer went to the post-office and wired to O'Connor., "If wanting a change, join me in Bolzano. Bring Tozer."

Tozer was O'Connor's name for his automatic. Pointer turned away feeling that he had taken out a very good insurance for the paper.

His room at the Laurin was between two others. He took another for his friend, and into that upper room he himself slipped late that evening, after arranging a bolster shape in his bed. Even so, he spent the night with his doors and windows securely wedged. Nor did he go downstairs until the house was well astir. Then he glanced into his own room. The threads of finest spider-silk that lie had stretched across door and windows were broken. The dummy was not as he had left it. The clothes on the chair were not precisely as he had laid them. So the hunt was up! His blood ran swifter for the thought. There is something in the human being that enjoys a chase, even in the form of the quarry.

Pointer loafed the morning in front of the café until his answer came, "O'Connor and I arriving Friday one thirty.—Tozer."

So by noon to-morrow he would have his friend and the paper its second guardian. O'Connor must have done some rapid packing. Until his arrival, Pointer decided to take an open-air cure. Bolzano was a dream of blue skies, with the beautiful, ever-changing green of the hills around it. Plum purple, the great ridge of the Mendel range, a snowy veil still hung over the Rosengarten, all around was the broad valley of the Isarco, the river that the Talfer joins under one of the bridges. All the way to Merano stretched a sea of fruit trees coming into blossom. The little town was gay as the South and busy as the North. Pointer could have stayed on gladly for the mere beauty of it. He took his lunch, not in the hotel, but in the little garden park, off rolls and cold meat that he himself purchased in the shops. The afternoon was spent outdoors in the one smart café of the place, and was followed by dinner on similar lines to the lunch. He used neither bedroom that night, but arranged for a very late bath, and made himself comfortable in the tub with a pillow and a feather duvet smuggled from his room. The bathroom looked out on to the same side as his own room. There were two men who spent the late evening hours watching the hotel from a house opposite. About midnight he saw some sort of a sign pass, by means of a white handkerchief, to others watching in the hotel itself, doubtless in his own room. Pointer would have liked nothing better than to step in suddenly, but at present he was not Pointer, but the warden of a thing at once a possible treasure and an expected revelation, and the rope which was to hang a murderer. The bathroom handle moved very softly. Besides being locked, there was a wedge under it, and Pointer only prodded the duvet into a more comfortable mattress as he listened intently. The bathroom had had a bell, but it was out of order, so the boots had told him.

Pointer had made it worth the night-porter's while to mend it. He had tried it just before "taking his tub," and had explained to the man, a conscientious but dull-witted Tiroler, that, being a poor sleeper, he had found that nothing helped him so much on a sleepless night as a cold dip. On a bad night he would sometimes have two, or three dips. By all the signs, this was going to be a bad night. So if he, Andreas, heard him, he was not to be surprised.

"But how about a cup of coffee?" suggested the man after "studying" things over for several minutes like a true Bozener, "I keep some standing hot all night"

"Good!" said Pointer. "A cup of coffee and a bath together would be splendid. If I ring from the bathroom, just set the cup down outside."

Andreas said he would, and departed.

Pointer thought this an excellent time for that cup as he listened to the faint stirs and breathings outside. If only Andreas's step were not first cousin to a carpet-beater's thud! But at night Andreas evidently put on list shoes, for there was a sudden exclamation and a scurry from the quiet over-timers outside the door, and a scandalised "*Nanu*!" from Andreas. A tray was put hastily down, and Pointer opened the door. His bedroom was close by. He dropped pillow and "divvy" into it, and stepped back to examine the bathroom door. Like all the rooms in the hotel, it had the dangerous Continental double door, one a foot or two within the other, so that a thief need only open and close the outer door to be in a small lobby, where he can work unnoticed.

Pointer flashed his torch over the hinges. One was already half-eaten through with acid. He waited for Andreas.

"What was wrong?" Pointer asked. "Bring the coffee to my room."

Andreas shook his head with a tolerant grin.

"A bit fuddled. Gentlemen will have their joke. Two friends of yours intended to help you with your dip. They couldn't find the handle, however, and must have been trying to unbolt the hinges when I arrived."

Pointer laughed and offered him a cigar.

"Which of the lot was that?"

"I don't know their names. It's the two Fascisti who have numbers seventeen and eighteen."

"Fascisti?"

"Well, they looked it."

"Get me their names from the book, will you."

Andreas brought him back a *chit*, on which he had scrawled, "Signor Gregorio Massa and Signor Antonio Massa."

"As I thought!" Pointer beamed. "Just the fellows, to try on a joke like that. Are they in their rooms now?"

The night-porter thought that they were. He had only caught sight of the door being closed. A final tip changed hands, and Pointer was alone.

After a little interval he crept out and along the passage to the numbers given. He heard two men's voices in seventeen. Not very pleased voices either. One was very low, but every now and then one would be raised hysterically, to be instantly quieted by a sharp low word from his companion. Pointer caught one such higher pitched word. It was a name. After it came a sudden pause, a pause of consternation. Pointer could almost visualise a hand clapped over a garrulous mouth. He was no longer near the door when it was noiselessly opened, but was well away on the upper landing. Lying down at full length, he saw a tall figure, its loose top-locks falling around it like a feather duster, search the lower corridor from end to end, noiseless in its movements as a horse-fly. Then it disappeared, and the door was shut without a sound.

Pointer felt like a dog hot on a scent and suddenly pulled up. One word he had heard, one name. Well he knew now, and he realised his danger.

Friday morning was spent like its predecessor, except for a telegram to di Monti appointing next Tuesday afternoon without fail for a meeting in New Scotland Yard and by noon Pointer was shaking hands with the tall lean figure of O'Connor on the Bozen platform.

"So our long-planned walking tour is coming of last?"

"It is," Pointer agreed "We begin it by taking train for Verona in an hour. Where's your bag; this man can carry it too."

Pointer had come accompanied by one of the town luggage-carriers, so as not to chance being alone on platform or in waiting-room So far, there had been no need of this precaution, but he had not cared to omit it.

"My bag? Tozer wouldn't let me wait to pack. And how's yourself?"

Pointer breathed in his ear.

"I've a pocket-book strapped to me, with a paper inside, which we must get home to the Yard. It'll clear the air."

"You're right, she's an uncommonly pretty girl," O'Connor agreed aloud, as lighting a cigarette and whirling on one heel to throw away the match, all in one swift motion, he almost burnt the tie of a man behind. The man, a typical Fascist by his hair and tightly-buttoned black shirt and thick, cudgel-like stick which he carried, hurried on.

Pointer, opened and shut his eyes as though saying, "Even so!"

"Brother Massa," he murmured. "He's off for the ticket office. Now, you get some food inside yourself, while I take our seats in the carriage that's put on here."

"Can you manage your luggage alone?" O'Connor asked cautiously.

"Can do," Pointer reassured him. O'Connor stepped into the buffet.

The usual change had come over the platform. A moment ago all was bustle; now it was almost deserted. Pointer had told his man what seats he wanted. The porter stepped in with the suitcase. In swinging it up, it caught in the curtain and almost overpowered him, for it was very heavy. Pointer made no move to assist. He stood well out on the platform.

Suddenly something knocked his feet from under him. A bag carried by another traveller had skidded from some three yards away. The man rushed up with apologies, in his hand the rubber-covered club of the Fascisti, the Italian sandbag. Pointer dodged the club and shot out his right with all the strength of his back behind it. The man who had had the accident with the bag sagged inertly forward. Pointer was on his feet now, and directing a kick at the shins of the porter, who had leapt out of the compartment. Pointer was not sure whether he were in the affair or not, but he could not afford to take a chance. The way the man acted cleared up his doubts. Instead of a volley of abuse, and calls to his mates, he picked up his *Facchino* cap and dived under the coach, just as an official from another platform hurried up.

"*Ola! Cosa é?*"

"Apparently this man has had a fit," Pointer answered in his careful Italian. "His bag slipped from his hand and knocked me down, too."

The man bent over the silent figure. He saw the black neck scarf, the hair, thc rubber club.

"Take the man to the ambulance-room. Tell the *Commandante* about him. As for you, sir, you will be detained till he is able to tell us what happened."

"Can I telephone to your Sotto-prefetto?" asked Pointer.

A couple of Carabinieri who had strolled up said something to the station official. They evidently knew all about Pointer, for the Italian saluted at once.

"My excuses. I could not know. Nowadays one has to be careful, and he looked as though he had had a hard blow, on the point of the chin, too."

"Indeed! I took it for granted it was a fit."

"A very sensible view to take," the Italian said, with a rather dry smile as he passed on.

At Verona the two friends caught the Milan-Paris express, and settled themselves for the night in an empty first. They decided not to risk a sleeping car. Pointer was to stay awake the first part of the night, the Irishman relieving him after a rest.

Pointer was on the alert. He felt sure that further attempts would be made. He slipped back the two catches of the door opposite the corridor and wedged it with a cake of soap so that it looked shut, but would open at a touch.

"Just in case we need to slip out of the back-door in a hurry," he explained.

O'Connor nodded, and turned over, closing his eyes. The door of the corridor opened not long afterwards.

"*Favorisca, i biglietti!*" intoned a voice in the ticket-collector's usual sing-song. As usual, too, the man was accompanied by a second, who closed the door behind him.

Now Pointer had noticed a man stroll twice past the compartment at Verona. He had a bright brass eyelet shining from his black boot. When the man in the long coat and braided cap of the conductor slid open the door,

Pointer's eye was upon a similar brass eyelet in his right boot. He roused O'Connor with the danger signal of "Wake up, Tozer!" But a mistake either way would be awkward. With his left hand he slipped the tickets along the seat, the next second he caught the sham ticket-collector's wrist in a vice that sent the knife to the floor. Then they grappled. The man was a big, sinewy chap, strong as a conger eel and almost as difficult to hold. O'Connor was dealing with his companion, but he, too, was having his work cut out. Though the Englishmen did not know it, they were struggling with a couple of the most dreaded of the Naples *Maffei*, killers by trade, with lists of victims as long as their own arms. They fought like savages. Pointer's allotment always trying with his thumbs for the other's eyes, his teeth snapping at his throat. If Pointer and O'Connor were both well up in jiu-jitsu, these men had similar tricks handed down from the Moors of Sicily, and used by Neapolitan criminals for centuries. But there was one thing that the Englishman knew, and their assailants did not, and that was about the door. With a wrench, Pointer managed to slew his man around, and fling him against it. The Italian went hurtling out. O'Connor's man struggled desperately, but they heaved him after his friend. Then Pointer pulled the chain. He did not want the two men to possibly crawl away to safety.

The express did not stop, but the guard, the ticket collector—the real one—and the soldier who generally accompanies Italian expresses, rushed up to the corridor door.

"Two men came in just now, one wearing a ticket collector's cap and coat," Pointer explained "They attacked my friend and me. In our struggle the door catches must have given way. The door flew open, and the man fell on the line. I pulled the signal at once."

"The catches are in perfect order," the conductor said trying them, "and very stiff. One goes up, the other down. If the door opened, it was opened. And how could two men fall out? The affair will be inquired into thoroughly. And how about thy cap and coat?" The guard turned to the ticket collector.

That official's story was that taking them off to enjoy his supper more at his ease, he had hung them on a nail outside the compartment. He had just discovered their absence when the alarm signal was pulled.

Pointer felt sure that he could have got him twisted up in his own statements in no time, had his Italian been as his English. What he felt sure had happened was a bribe, unless the man belonged to the same organisation. The soldier was left to guard the compartment, bayonet fixed, "in case of any more accidents," as the conductor said grimly. Pointer resolutely refused to show his papers, and he and O'Connor were marched off at once on arrival at Milan to the chief of the station police's room.

When the short stop of the express was nearly over, two figures dressed in Pointer and O'Connor's travelling coats and caps got into their compartment, but as the train started they strolled down to the end and dropped off with the ease of railwaymen. Pointer had decided to wait over a train. Being a night express, their absence might not be noticed, for the officials on the train were instructed to keep their compartment locked, and the blinds drawn after the two temporary substitutes had left. As for Pointer and his friend, they spent the night in the apologetic station-master's office, which he put at their disposal, together with his dog Wolf. When they unobtrusively slipped into the buffet early next morning for a cup of coffee, and some of Milan's famous *panetone*, they were told of an accident which had happened to last night's express. It was a singular accident, too. Just after the frontier tunnel was left behind, the express ran past a goods' train between two Swiss stations. A slight shock was felt, and the whole side of a first-class coach was ripped open, as though by something suddenly protruded from the goods' train. Only one coach was damaged. It was the one in which the two Englishmen had been sitting. All the occupants in it were severely injured, one man being killed. The express was delayed at the next station, where the injured were attended to by some doctors who happened to be waiting at the station for another train.

"'Happened to be waiting,' is good," was Pointer's only comment to his friend, when they took their seats next morning in an empty carriage. They were joined by other travelers who now got in, now got out, till they were left at Lausanne with a quiet, ill-looking young man, and a doctor, his anxious, attentive companion. They were French, and judging by his talk, the younger man was a consumptive back from a "cure" in the mountains which had not cured. He fell into an uneasy slumber after the train started on again, tossing and turning. Pointer and O'Connor occupied the two middle seats. The least comfortable, but the safest. Should the window seats be taken, they had arranged to stand in the corridor.

During the war, O'Connor had come across an eye-signal language hailing from America. He and Pointer had practised it, and changed it, till they were masters of its capabilities. It was undetectable.

Pointer occasionally glanced up from the paper which he was reading, generally looking out of the window, but sometimes at O'Connor, and sometimes at his fellow-travellers. O'Connor was equally at his ease. But they were talking hard, and this is what they were saying to each other:

Pointer: "The right hand of the young man beside me seems to get more and more out of sight. Watch it."

O'Connor: "I am. His companion's feet beside me look a bit braced. How about it?"

Pointer: "When you see that right arm move forward again, give a sniff and duck. You're right. His companion next you is getting ready for a jump. I'll tackle his feet if he does."

O'Connor: "And I'll see to—"

Pointer and he ducked simultaneously. A shot rang out. The young man with a wild white face was shouting, "*Tirez! Tirez donc! Passeront pas! Passeront pas*!"

The shot would have gone through Pointer's head from ear to ear had that essential part of his body been where it was expected to be, instead of down near his boots.

It was charming to see how Pointer and O'Connor worked together. Never getting in each other's way, however cramped the space. Like the swing of a couple of navvies' hammers, what Thornton insisted on in life and in art, rhythm and harmony were never lost sight of. First, Pointer pulled the feet from under the pale young man. O'Connor did the same with the young man's companion. Pointer laid his kicking and screaming captive on top of O'Connor's, where they started pummelling each other. O'Connor sat on their chests, Pointer on their feet, while the occupants of the other compartments flocked to the door and tried to pull it open.

"Third party locked it when he stood with his back to us just now. Look out for him," Pointer warned.

But it was the genuine conductor who unlocked it with loud requests to know the meaning of this.

"*Passeront pas! Passeront pas*!" shrieked the young man, trying to get his revolver.

"Without doubt wounded in the war, and not recovered even yet!" murmured sympathetic voices in the corridor.

"Possibly," Pointer said, getting up, "but he swore in another tongue altogether when his friend kicked him in the eye just now."

"Here, don't claw down me socks like that," O'Connor protested indignantly; "where's your manners." He gave the young man a tap as he only sat the harder.

"Why this treatment?" shrieked the man used as a mattress by all the three. "I am this gentleman's medical attendant. I cannot understand —I demand explanations, and—"

"Reparations," added O'Connor under his breath. Three railway officials freed the under-dog. Pointer spoke to him reproachfully.

"But, monsieur, your patient would have shot you! My friend and I saved your life. In the mêlée it was a little difficult, I own, to distinguish friend from foe."

The younger man was led away. The elder, literally foaming at the mouth, was helped to his feet.

Pointer and O'Connor strolled into another compartment, and roared with delight as they reconstructed the scene.

When the time came for lunch, they had only two Englishwomen with them, of the usual badly-dressed, over-smiling, over-toothed kind that seems to live exclusively abroad.

"First service!" bawled the dining-car attendant. "First service!"

"Are you going?" asked one of the ladies of the other.

"I think not, dear; I've something here with me." She patted a little wicker case, and after the other had passed out, spread a napkin and took out some rolls and a thermos flask.

Pointer and O'Connor were smoking in the corridor.

The lady inside leant out and asked if one of them would be so kind as to close the window for her, she found it too hard to lift. It was a very stiff window. O'Connor entered to help her, while Pointer stood looking on, not suspicious, but watchful. The woman bent forward again and said something to the Scotland Yard man, picking up her thermos flask and a little glass as she did so.

He did not catch what she said, and leant down. As he bent, her fingers tightened around the flask which was in the hand nearest him. He had already noticed that she held it under the bottom. Her forearm muscles stiffened, too. Pointer's one hand held the strap of the door, his other jogged her elbow, the elbow nearest him. Jogged it accurately. Not so hard as to deluge her with the contents, but sufficient to let him have an idea of what the thermos held. A straw-coloured liquid spurted up, a couple of drops touching her cheek. She shrieked, and rising, would have flung the contents wildly at him. A sharp tap from O'Connor lamed her arm, and the bottle fell on the floor, the liquid running over her very stout boots. A little must have penetrated the eyelet holes, for she screamed horribly as she tried to tear off boots and stockings.

Once more their compartment became the scene of the day. People crowded into the corridor. The guard again appeared at the double, together with the ticket collector, and demanded to know what was wrong now.

The woman in the compartment had her feet bare by now, swinging them to and fro over the liquid which was smoking where it bit its way into the floor. She was moaning like some tortured animal as she dabbed frantically at her feet and cheek, all three of which were enormously swollen, and pitted with horrible-looking, white-lipped holes.

O'Connor stood by the window and Pointer held the door. She had twice tried to claw her way out.

Now he had been especially recommended in his true character to the Frenchmen by the guards of the Swiss stretch, who had received their instructions from the Milan railway officials. They knew that he was carrying important papers. There was no difficulty, therefore, as far as they were concerned. The woman was carried into some remote, inaccessible part of the tram, medical aid was fetched, and order once more reigned. It was given out that she had cut herself in some way with her thermos flask lining, and that her screams were not to be taken too seriously. The other woman would have been arrested had they been able to find her, but she was apparently not on the train.

"Changed into a young man, who would have posed as a doctor in all likelihood, and kindly done his very best for me, and for you, too. There was plenty for both of us in that flask. Then she'd have turned into a dear old lady, and been helped off by the guard himself," was Pointer's forecast of what might have been had things gone according to plan.

A tanned, pleasant-looking, gray-haired Englishman standing before his compartment a little farther down eyed them with a humorous half-smile.

"You seem to make a most efficient storm-centre, you two," he said; sauntering up to them. "I was in the train to Milan yesterday."

"It appears that I have an unfortunate likeness to some one who seems to be rather unpopular." Pointer spoke with heat, in the tone of an outraged Briton who is already composing his letter to the Press. "Member of some secret society which he's betrayed, so I'm told."

He declined the offer of a cigar, and lit his pipe. O'Connor did the same. Pointer had noticed the man, a typical army officer of the old school, travelling over the Brenner yesterday with a gunnery instructor known to him by sight, from Chatham.

"I suggest that you take refuge in my compartment till we get to Paris, if you want seats. I spend most of my time in the corridor." The man cleared off some of his belongings hospitably.

Pointer and O'Connor spent some pleasant hours chatting with him. He was on his way home from India, and had some inside information of the real currents under the surface out there.

CHAPTER TEN

AT Paris, Pointer and O'Connor were met by the former's brother, Cook's chief interpreter in the French capital. He had a group of Cook's men, who ringed the Scotland Yard officer and his companion around as he carried them off to an inner room at the station.

Here Pointer received a long cable that seemed to interest him vastly from the Yard. It wound up by stating that Mr. Thornton had gone to Paris, and was being looked after by the French police. Otherwise the "case" had marked time since the departure of its leader.

From the French police, he learnt that Thornton was still at his hotel, and had been spending blameless days in old curiosity shops and unimpeachable nights tucked up in his bed.

Pointer thought a moment. He considered that the time had come to have a look at Thornton's cards. The trouble was, that gentleman had such an aversion to laying down his hand. Pointer determined to call it without more ado. A telephone message to the hotel told him that Thornton was still up, and in the hotel lounge. Pointer entered it a few minutes later and shook hands. O'Connor, with his friends, all of them seemingly strangers to the man who had just preceded them, seated themselves some distance off. Pointer had hardly begun an, it is to be feared, inaccurate account of his wanderings when a page-boy brought him a telegram. Crushing the envelope carelessly into his pocket, Pointer read the message in a low voice, after a careful glance around to show that they were alone.

"Mrs. Lane confessed. Harris."

Thornton turned a dull lead colour.

"Feeling ill, sir?" asked, the Chief Inspector.

"This—this message—" Thornton's voice started across lips none too firm. They stiffened as it went on. "How—I thought Mrs. Lane—what does it mean?" Thornton stared at the cablegram—which Pointer and his brother had just concocted at the railway station—as though far away, in some unpleasant, uncertain place.

"It doesn't say, I see," Pointer mused aloud, "that she's confessed to the actual murder."

Thornton spun around on him with something like snarl. One would not have believed him capable of such a sound.

"Mrs. Lane—my wife—what the devil do you mean?" He looked white-hot now.

Pointer sat down again

"I see. Mrs. Lane is really Mrs. Thornton. Humph! Divorced, I presume?"

Thornton looked as though he would like to strike the bland face before him. He clenched his fist.

"Come, come, sir" Pointer changed to a pleasanter tone. "This won't help her, and she's in a tight spot, you know. But between us we ought to be able to get her out. Look here, why not explain the whole affair?"

Pointer spoke as though that bright idea had just occurred to him.

"Your marriage, for instance."

"There's nothing to explain about that" Thornton spoke wearily. "Only too usual a story, I'm afraid. An unhappy marriage—a parting—and a chance meeting again when she took the place of Colonel Scarlett's lady housekeeper. In justice to myself, I thought she was amply provided for. Her father settled a large sum on her when she married, and he died soon after, presumably a wealthy man. It was Russia's debt-repudiation that made all the difference, it seems. I never dreamt of that."

"Chance meeting?" Pointer repeated questioningly. "No, it wasn't that, Mr. Thornton. Not on her part. She knew you were at Red Gates. She came down because she knew that."

"What do you mean?"

"Just that, sir. I've seen—to be frank, we hold a letter of hers to the colonel. In it she refers to you, and says that she'll gladly come, provided that he will keep his promise, and never let you know that she knew beforehand that you were living at Red Gates."

Thornton got up, and walked quickly to a window. He stood with his back to the room.

"How can I get her out of what I've got her into?" he asked, without turning round.

"You got her into?"

"I put the matter in the hands of Scotland Yard, didn't I? I knew that she was shielding some one. I know it now. She'd shield a mad dog if it ran to her. But if so, that blow that killed Rose Charteris was struck by some terrible accident, or in some mistake—I can't explain it, but Beatrice, I mean my wife, would never shield a guilty person. There never was a woman with a dearer, cooler judgment, and a greater sense of right. To think that she ever had a part or knowledge—the mere suggestion is monstrous."

Pointer could have smiled. Beatrice Thornton had been shielding some one.

Thornton still looked out of the darkened window, and Pointer thought he heard a whispered "Beatrice" before the newly-revealed husband turned.

"Perhaps you can help her better than I can. I only seem to've drawn her deeper into things. You see, I thought that if she found herself in a tight place, she would perforce turn to me. I was at hand. She must have known that I—that—" He faced the window again, his face working. "I was a fool once. I was a poor ambitious chap once. And I won't say that her fortune counted for nothing with me, as it should have done." Thornton fought against the flood of emotion within him, but it had got past the gates, and rushed him with it "After she left me—there was no divorce. Neither of us are the kind to give the other reasons of that sort for parting I—well, I learnt as many another fool has that I cared a great deal more than I thought I did, or rather than she thought I did. I came into some money, took to art collecting, to divert my mind. But to go back to that awful Friday morning. You're the last man to believe in spiritualism, I suppose, Chief Inspector?"

"I shouldn't be the first," Pointer agreed whimsically.

"Then you do believe in—in that sort of thing?"

"I think there's a deal more to us than our bodies, than what we can feel and touch. I'm a religious man, sir. But why the question?"

"Because as I sat by Rose Charteris's body in that sand-pit early on Friday morning, I had the most extraordinary sense of urgency, of being spurred on to take some decision quickly. I felt as though it were a call for help from the girl whose body lay beside me, and for immediate help. When Bond and Co. were so keen on the police taking up the matter, the feeling had passed. I could almost think it had passed from me into them. I thought—better, not. I thought—" He paused again.

"I wonder what you did think?" Pointer still spoke pleasantly.

"Then, as now, I never doubted—my wife. Naturally! I knew, knew that she had no hand in any crime, except to help—the victim. I thought if I could talk things over with her first—but walking away from the police-station I got that message of haste again. And this time it conquered. It quite obsessed me. I felt as though Rose herself were begging me to lose no time. I can't put the sensation into words, any more than one could light or dark." There was a long pause.

"And did you lend Mrs. Lane your car, or did she get it out herself?"

Thornton drew in his breath sharply.

"You're right. Frankness is the only thing now, I see. I lent her the car. She woke me up about one on Thursday night or rather Friday morning, tapping on my bedroom window. It opens on to my balcony, too, you know. She asked me to let her have my big car at once. She asked me—" He hesitated in deep distress.

"Yes? We know the facts about the car," Pointer said very gently.

"To let her have it for a couple of hours, and to lend it without asking her any questions about it. I came down and got it out. She wouldn't let me drive it even into the lane for her, and she begged me—there were tears in her eyes, and she looked, good God!" Thornton seemed to fall into a brooding pity, "she begged me never to refer to the matter again. I promised. I got the car out and left her, and it. She even made me promise that I wouldn't watch which way the car went."

There followed a long silence.

"That's all," Thornton said under his breath. "I only hope I've done right in speaking of it."

"You've done no harm, sir, because we knew it more or less already. And that's really all, sir?"

"All. My word on that. And now you see the mingled feelings that made me ask you to look into the case. There was the sensation of being impelled to it by Miss Rose herself. There was the presence of Bond and Co. They never, let things drop. And there was—it sounds caddish, but there was also the hope that by crowding my wife into a corner, she might turn to me—in her fright."

"She didn't get frightened, more's the pity," Pointer said rather sourly. "It would have shortened things a lot if she had. You recognised her, I suppose, when she looked out at Miss Scarlett's room, when you and Doctor Metcalfe drove up on Friday morning?"

"Yes."

"She went in to speak to Miss Scarlett. She had lent her some toothache medicine and wanted it back. As Miss Scarlett was asleep, she was going out again, when she heard the car. That, at least, is what she told Maud, and I think it is the truth."

"But why—what—" In Thornton's voice was an anguish that had been racking his heart for many days now.

Pointer did not reply to it.

"What was Mrs. Thornton's maiden name, by the way?"

"Lane. She was the daughter of our minister to the Netherlands. We were married at the Hague by the Embassy Chaplain in—" He gave the date.

There was another pause, then Thornton said shyly, "That letter you found? You really mean that. Be—Mrs. Thornton—knew that I was at Red Gates?"

Pointer nodded. "That's why she took the place. It's the first time in my life that I ever betrayed to one man what I had found in the course of my investigations in another man's private papers. It's not a breach of discipline I shall care to remember. But for this once—well, in this case, I've done it." He finished with a smile, then his face grew grave again.

"What dress was Mrs. Lane, to call her by the name I've known her under for so long, what dress was she wearing?" Pointer next asked.

"I seem to remember something very dark. Blue or black."

"And what took you out so early that Friday morning?"

Thornton hesitated again. He took out his cigarette and looked at it, as though not quite certain what it was that he had been smoking. Finally he looked at the detective-officer almost as Toni had done, in mingled appeal and trouble.

"If you could have seen her face! She was all in."

He bit his own lip. "And besides, Bond and Co. had gone out, I knew. As I couldn't get asleep, I decided to take a walk."

"But where has she gone? The colonel, he tells me not to worry, but—"

"You'll meet her again very shortly. We have her address. She was a bit indiscreet over the telephone, and we traced her to some old friends. And now, patience a little longer, sir."

Pointer got up.

"I want you to be at my rooms at New Scotland Yard the day after to-morrow, that will be Tuesday, at three, without fail. Something went wrong with those casts last time. The mixture wasn't right, and we must take them all over again. But I shan't have to trouble you a third time." Pointer was quite sure about that last.

Thornton nodded. He seemed in some strangely happy mood. Pointer felt that a shock awaited him, when, on landing in Dover next day, he would be met by a telegram from the man to whom he was now talking, telling him that a mistake had been made, and that the "confession" was one of the many spurious ones that dot all murder cases. But Pointer—to atone—had ended with "Mrs. Lane's" present address.

Thornton duly departed for England by the 8.25 next day, and Pointer followed by the ten train.

He and O'Connor had an uneventful trip in the packed boat-train. They stood with a couple of "Tom's friends" on either side of them in the corridor.

At Calais they were escorted by them on to the boat, and only left when the gangway threatened to be hoisted.

Pointer and O'Connor were hailed by a cheery voice. They had caught sight of their acquaintance of the previous day, on the boat-train, but the three had mutually contented themselves with nods.

General Thompson, as he gave his name, dragged his chair up alongside theirs. They sat idly chatting together when he commented on the crowd at a particular part of the ship.

"They're for their passport cards," O'Connor explained.

The general heard for the first time that it was still necessary to get a ticket showing the passport to be in order. He groaned, and with a faint "damn" at useless red tape, he left his kitbag to keep his chair, and joined the queue on the lower deck. O'Connor strolled that way, too, after a glance at Pointer.

Left by himself, the Chief Inspector eyed the bag. He mopped his forehead, and as though in answer to a signal, as indeed it was, a tall man stood beside him. It was the ship's detective.

"Just glance at that bag, but go carefully," Pointer said.

The man went below, and reappeared almost at once.

"Can you show me the man who placed it there, sir? It's not an ordinary bag. I don't know whether it's O.K. or not. We'll let him open it."

"A friend of mine is keeping with him—just in case. Did you hear anything tick? I thought I did. May, of course, be an alarm clock."

The Chief Inspector pointed out O'Connor and the owner of the bag among the thinning crowd.

The ship's detective touched the latter on the arm.

"Sorry to trouble you, sir, but there's been a thief on board. We've caught him red-handed. That gentleman here," he indicated Pointer, "says one of the bags is one which you left on your seat. Will you kindly identify it when you've done here?"

"I strolled off," Pointer explained, "and found your bag gone when I got back. Luckily, some one saw the man making off with it."

"It was trying to pinch a bride's Paris bonnet really did for him" said the detective, with a laugh. "He might have got away with it but for that."

The man beside O'Connor gave a cheery ha, ha! and turned away to see about his passport.

"That's my bag, all right," he said, as he saw a battered kit-bag, with a newer one beside it, standing on a table in a sort of private cabin. "My initials on it. R. M. T. Here's my passport."

As the passport showed him to be Major-General Thompson, C.B., the purser handed it back with a bow, and a cold look at the detective. "That's all right, sir," he began.

"If you'll just unlock it as a matter of formality," the detective suggested, "in case of other claimants—"

"Certainly." General Thompson pulled out his keys, ran them through his fingers, and then shook his head.

"Where's that key gone to? Why, of course!" He stopped jingling them. "I left it tied to the handle, because of the Customs, you know. The chap who stole it must have bagged it."

"No keys whatever on him, sir," said the detective.

"Then he lost it, or dropped it overboard."

"Ah, he might have done that," the man agreed.

"I'll tell you what; I've got another key at home. I'll leave the bag with you, and send the key down. I'm in no hurry for it, provided I get it eventually." The general turned to go.

There was a pulse beating in the temple of his bronzed face. As soon as the door had closed behind him, the detective beckoned to another in an inner room, and working like madmen, they locked a life-buoy on to the bag, fastened both to a chain, and flung the whole very lightly far out of the special port-hole into the sea, keeping it away from the side of the boat with a long flexible steel rod which opened out swiftly.

"Mine-sweepers' gear," the detective said with a grin. "Now we'll see. I thought the general was a bit on hot plates as the talk went on."

Five minutes passed, ten were nearly over, when there was a very pretty little fountain to be seen at sea which greatly delighted those on deck, who decided it must have been a couple of porpoises off their usual beat. Those in the cabin hauled in the chain, and found a few bits of life-buoy and leather hanging to the padlock

"Very neat. Meant just for you and me," said O'Connor. "Just enough to help hitch our combined wagons to the stars, without damaging the boat. And where's the proud inventor?"

"He was shown into another cabin when he walked out of this, and by now he'll be safely secured."

But he was more. He was dead, with a tiny bottle clenched in one hand. They never knew his real name.

"Good," said the two friends, "then we can go on deck again," and they thoroughly enjoyed the beautiful approach to England. They waited till the crowd was almost off the boat. Then they shook hands with three men, one of whom was Pointer's chief, and with whom they travelled up in a special guarded car.

Safely in his own rooms at the Yard, Pointer handed over a pocket book sewn into oiled silk, and went off for a wash and brush up, feeling like a boy home from school, now that his part in safeguarding that paper was done. The paper which he believed to have cost the life of Professor Charteris, of his daughter, and of the man with the bag, as well as severe bodily injuries, so he trusted, to the two men with whom O'Connor and he had struggled in the compartment before they could get them out on to the line.

The "poem" on the thin paper was re-written within the hour by the Home Office expert. It explained the care taken to regain it. It was a paper that shook the world when it was broadcasted later. But the cipher would have been insoluble without the code-word. The Home Office had that code-word. It had cost a British life for every letter in it.

It was decided that news should be circulated at once through discreetly indiscreet channels that the Yard was in possession of a couple of Bulgarian letters and a poem which they believed contained secret intelligence bearing on Red activities in that country, but which they were unable to solve. Copies would be sent post-haste to a few thoroughly untrustworthy Russian interpreters marked on the books as in the Bolsheviks' pay. They would be asked to help. A reward would be offered.

It was about half-past two on the next day, Tuesday, when a constable opened Pointer's door at the Yard. "A lady to see you by appointment, sir."

"Show the lady in. And bring in the gentleman who's been waiting in Watts' room at the same time."

Sibella entered with a sort of rush. She looked shocking. So ill, so worn, so white. Pointer thought of some plant whose roots are perishing. It seemed to him as though all the healthy, multifold ties between a woman and the world around her had been cut through in this case, and that Sibella was dying by inches of some fungus, some mildew, of the spirit.

With all her impetuous entrance, she sank wearily into a chair. But her eyes stared at him almost as her father's might have done.

"You telephoned me that there were important developments."

"They're coming. But first I want you to answer a few questions, and to hear some facts. Ah, here's Count di Monti."

Sibella sprang up with a gasp. Di Monti, too, looked unprepared for the meeting.

"Please sit down, both of you," the Chief Inspector went on, "it may take some time, this preliminary clearing of the ground. Miss Scarlett, first of all, the information you gave Count di Monti about the meetings in the studio had nothing whatever to do with your cousin's death."

"Oh!" It was a cry of mingled anguish and relief, of horror and joy. "Oh, is that true?" Her eyes went from him to the count, and back again.

"If you were told to the contrary," Pointer went on very sternly—

"I never told you that was the reason. I don't know the reason. How can I? I had nothing to do with that death." Di Monti's voice was hard and strident as he interrupted.

Sibella turned on him. She evidently dared not trust herself to speak. She only looked.

"If this man told you anything else, Miss Scarlett," Pointer went on, "it was because it suited his purpose that you should think that you, too, in a sense, were a contributory cause—"

"In a sense!" Sibella covered her face. "Oh, it's not possible! Not possible! No one would make their worst enemy suffer what I've suffered since Rose's death. I've been down, down, down," she broke off, shuddering. "I thought that I had killed her in everything but actually striking the blow. That my hand had directed his—I mean—" she stopped herself. "Since they brought her body home I've thought that it was my doing."

She was shuddering from bead to foot.

"I want to know the whole story, Miss Scarlett. As for the count—well, that will come later."

He looked hard at di Monti, and the count's jaws tightened.

"This man has no authority to ask you a single question, Sibella." The Italian strode over to her and caught her hand in his. "If I made you suffer, I had to."

"Why?" Her eyes fastened themselves with an incredulous stare on him, as though she saw a stranger before her. "Why did you have to make me suffer? And so terribly? Why you—me?"

She did not give him time to answer. And he looked as though he would have needed time.

"What made you torture me? Torture me, soul and body? I—oh—" She flung away, as though it were a tarantula, the hand he laid on hers. "You played me! You used me as a pawn! You thought that I might speak, might betray you, if my tongue were not tied. It nearly worked the other way. I all but went to the police instead of helping you to escape. All but!" She turned to Pointer with a gesture that would have been the pride of a film actress.

"Ask whatever you want to know. I shall tell you the truth."

"*Anima mia*!" In a stride the Italian had her in his arms. He might as well have held a statue.

"I had to tell you that lie," di Monti went on, "all our future hung on my not being arrested just then, as this buffoon would have done. I knew when they got hold of the pendant which I had picked up in the studio, what was coming. My faithful Arrigo saw a policeman talking to the man to whom I had flung it, flung it as I would a clot of mud. It meant no more to me. The pendant worn by that—" he used an ugly Italian term, "I never wanted to soil my fingers with again. Don't you see, darling, that all hung on my getting away? I would never have stooped to act the mourner at her funeral but for that necessity. I—and mourn—for *her*! I knew you would not help me as you did unless you thought my life was in danger, and I must have your help—"

"I quite see the reason," Sibella said, in a hard, dry voice.

"An arrest just then, or the talk of it, would have spelled ruin. But now," he let her go as she stood unresponsive, no whit softened, "but now I can snap my fingers at the policeman here," he turned and did so, with a crack like a whip, "the post is definitely given, passed by our Inner Council."

"But you told me that you had killed Rose," Sibella repeated in a voice colourless as her face, heavy as her weary lids, lifeless as her dull black hair. "You said that you had struck harder than you meant in your anger. And so, I thought, had I! Oh, so you let me thinks had I!"

"Well, I didn't strike her, nor kill her. The man here has just told you I didn't. He said truly enough, that the studio meetings had nothing to do with the murder. That means I didn't kill her, eh? My only reason for killing her would have been because of them. *Cristo*! She deserved to die, but I did not do justice on her," di Monti snarled.

"Justice! You to talk of justice, Giulio! What justice have I had from you? When you told me that you had killed Rose, you killed something in me, too. I'm not the woman to love a murderer, but at least I could dream of what might have been if I hadn't sent you there. You've taken even my dream from me now!"

Sibella finished in a sort of forlorn whisper. Di Monti made a gesture towards her, but Pointer cut in, "And why did you tell the police that Miss Charteris was afraid of some one or some thing?" Pointer's voice was very cold and official. "She was. But of you. You knew that her fears pointed to you, and you alone. Besides, it does not necessarily follow that there was no other reason for putting her out of the way than anger or jealousy." He turned to Sibella, "Would you mind," he said gently, "telling me exactly what happened that Thursday night?"

"Sibella!" the Italian began, but Pointer, who was watching him closely, stepped between him and the girl.

"Don't forget that you're in Scotland Yard. Unless you want handcuffs on, you'll stand back, Count di Monti."

The Italian looked murderous. Just for a second he hesitated. Then, with a shrug of his shoulders, he sat down in the chair at which the Chief Inspector was pointing, and crossing his legs, lit a cigarette.

"Rose really was in love with Mr. Bellairs," Sibella. began, speaking as though she were glad to. "My father thought that he and I would have suited each other better. There had been some boy and girl affair between us, but that was all over long ago. After Count di Monti came to England, Rose hesitated between the two. Finally she decided to accept the count, but she wrote to Mr. Bellairs still. And lately they met in his studio."

"Where he was painting her portrait?" asked Pointer.

"Yes I—I thought the whole position not fair—to any of us. So I told Count di Monti on Thursday just before lunch what was going on. Then I grew wretched. I realised, when I saw his rage, what a fearful thing I had done. What an awful thing! And though I knew that neither of them loved the other, I was afraid of trouble. I knew that the count would never forgive her having played with him—he prefers to do the playing!" She shot a glance at the young man which was very reminiscent of her Italian grandmother. "I didn't go to the concert in Medchester Thursday evening. I drove on to Harry Bellairs' studio, getting there just as my cousin scrambled out of the studio window. She heard the count. At the front door. We drove home. Later, when I missed her from her room, I thought that she must have gone back for some reason. Next morning, when I heard that she was dead—oh, how could you have let me suffer what I have!" she burst out again, turning her burning eyes on di Monti.

"What time was it when you went to your cousin's room?" Pointer asked.

"When I dropped her at home it was about ten o'clock. That must have been when the maid spoke to her. I drove back to Medchester, but I didn't go to the concert till practically the end. I needed the fresh air to calm me down. When Mrs. Lane and I got back it was a little past eleven."

"And you picked up that registered letter she had left behind her—forgotten—to confront her with the proof that she had been in the studio?" Pointer asked the Italian.

Count di Monti nodded curtly. "That and the pendant, as I said in Verona." He turned to Sibella. "I would have told you the truth—-" he began, but she stopped him with a hand raised as though to ward off something distasteful, and finished his sentence in her own way.

"Had you not wanted to make use of me, of my remorse, Of my agony of mind! By a trick, you got my help, got away, and would have gone to Jubaland without a word to me—"

"*Altro! Tutt'altro*!" His face flamed. "Never! For a while—yes. I had to let you bear your burden, but you knew that whatever had happened to her she had richly deserved. She had played with me!" He trembled visibly with fury at the thought still. "But even if you mourned her, I would have made it all up to you. All, and much, much more! I would have taken you—away from all suffering—into a world all light, all gold, all fire."

He repeated the sentence in his own beautiful tongue, "*Un mundo di luce, d'oro, e di fuoco.*" His voice made each word shine and glow. He knelt before her and raised the hem of her black lace frock to his lips. He kissed it passionately. She neither swayed towards him nor away from him. Her eyes rested broodingly on that proud, bent head. On her face was a gentle, and yet a very remote look. It was as though she were hearing again a strain of music which held memories of poignant joy and love in every note, but the joy was a departed one, and the love was dead.

With a sigh she seemed to return to the present, and now there was no softness about her. He rose on the instant, feeling the change, rebuffed by it before she spoke. But he was a good fighter. He did not give up.

"Do not draw away from me! Listen to your heart. Your heart that does love me, say what you will. Let it plead for me. Love can forgive everything but lack of love."

"It does not love you," Sibella said with convincing finality. "I did love you, yes, but that was not why I helped you to escape when I thought you had killed Rose. And you know that."

She took a step towards him at last, but it was as an accuser.

"You knew that the only thing that would make me help you, was the belief that it was I—I who was guilty of throwing fuel on that jealousy of yours, that mad jealousy that burned without any love back of it only pride!"

Pointer looked at his watch.

"I'm sorry," he said, and the two started as though they had been talking on the top of Mount Everest, and had no idea that another human being could be within a mile of them, "but I must ask you to leave us now, Miss Scarlett. I wanted you to know the facts of the case—well, to know them—some of them." He pressed a bell. A constable announced that a taxi was waiting for the lady.

Sibella hesitated. She did not hold out her hand to the Chief Inspector. Suddenly she realised what all this meant, what that hand might be—in all likelihood was—about to do. It came home to her that possibly it was the last time that she, or any one else, would see Count di Monti a free man. He knew it. His cigarette end fell, bitten through, to the carpet. He had risen when she rose; and they looked at each other. Again their world dropped away from them. He made a gesture, but Sibella stopped him.

"I said good-bye to you, Giulio, when we parted before," she spoke in a low broken voice, "there is no one I love left for me to say it to now." Turning her head away with something like a shudder, she passed swiftly from the room.

Di Monti was pale enough now. Tears stood in those fierce, cold eyes. Eyes that looked as though they might have been handed down from some Etruscan tyrant of old. He blinked them away, straightened his straight back still more, smoothed a non-existent belt, and faced Pointer.

"*Ebbene*?" he snapped, "but if it was that whelp Bellairs who betrayed that I was at his studio"—he thrust his jaw forward—"I told him that I would kill him if he dared speak of my having been there, when heard that she had been found dead—"

Pointer did not trouble to answer him.

"This way, if you please. There are still a few proofs to be accumulated before the whole story is cleared up."

"And the handcuffs clicked on?" Di Monti threw back his head. "Hardly on my wrists, my good man."

"The end is very close at hand, Count di Monti," Pointer repeated quietly.

The Italian's face stiffened, as though he tightened all his muscles, but without a word he stalked through the double door into Pointer's second room, which again was almost filled by a big table with chairs set close around it.

CHAPTER ELEVEN

POINTER followed hard on di Monti's heels. Everybody summoned was present.

The Italian, after a derisive glance at Bellairs, who stared back at him like an angry cat, sat down at the place where his name lay.

Thornton alone seemed to have drunk from some fountain of youth since the previous meeting, though he shot a reproachful glance at the Chief Inspector.

As for Bond and Cockburn, they watched the proceedings with rapt attention again.

The colonel, looking ten years older, sat a little to one side, almost by himself. It was to him that Pointer first spoke.

"While the inspector is getting the mixture just right, I should like a word with you, sir. Kindly step this way." Pointer's tone was very frigid. Superintendent Harris and Inspector Rodman stared inscrutably at the inkstand before them. There had been something very official in Pointer's manner.

"By jove!" Bond muttered under his breath.

"Just so!" Cockburn replied. Di Monti bit his lip. Bellairs started to speak, then checked himself. Thornton took off his glasses and rubbed his eyes. Pointer led his captive—for Scarlett was practically that—into the farthest room.

"Now, sir, we may not know yet who killed Miss Rose, but we do know who did not. Among those who did *not* kill her, is your son, the commissioner. Mr. Reginald Scarlett had no more to do with his cousin's death than I."

Colonel Scarlett went red, then white, then a blotched red again. His features twitched.

"I suggest a whisky and soda," Pointer continued cheerily, placing them before the colonel, "while you're helping yourself, sir, I'll get to business. First of all, I'll tell you what we know, and then I'll ask a little further information. If I'm wrong on any point, please correct me as we go along."

The colonel sat silent, breathing fast.

"Your son, the Commissioner of Uganda, had a motor accident nearly three months ago now. That accident, coming on top of a bad head wound got in the war, brought on epileptic seizures. The Government, anxious to keep him if possible, sent him home secretly on sick leave, while he was given out as exploring around Tanganyika. I may say, that false report threw us off the track completely for a while. It was thought safer to leave you out of it, so Professor Charteris went to meet your son at Marseilles, putting his journey forward a couple of weeks. He travelled on with him to Genoa, where the commissioner was to undergo a sun cure at a helium establishment outside the town. He went there under his middle name of Sayce, and once, when an introduction was absolutely necessary, the professor introduced him by that name. The commissioner found that the sun cure, at Hotel Quisisana made him worse. He left suddenly on the Tuesday of the week in which his cousin was found dead. The doctors at Quisisana wired to a friend of yours in town, Sir Henry Carew, who was evidently in your confidence."

"All but at the end," the colonel said huskily.

"Sir Henry got the cable Wednesday, and sent the message down to you in a letter by his car. The Genoese doctors cabled—we had a copy, which is now destroyed—that they feared lest the young man who had left them before his cure had hardly begun, should develop homicidal tendencies."

The colonel nodded. He could not trust himself to speak of that awful cable even yet.

"He had told me that he didn't write to you. I talked with him yesterday in the nursing home, which he leaves to-morrow, as fit as ever. He says he felt too miserable to write to any one. I take it that you, here at home, were on the alert?"

"We took turns, Carew and I, watching for him at night. That was how I could play bridge on Thursday. Sir Henry was patrolling all the roads around Stillwater House till midnight. Then I took over. On the Wednesday we had reversed the hours."

"Yes, I thought that was about it." Pointer nodded to himself. "The commissioner got out at Barnet station on Thursday about ten; he was not recognised or noticed, and walked to Stillwater, hoping that the exercise would do him good. He must have got in unnoticed."

The colonel nodded. "If my son came across by Green Tree Farm, he would have been able to slip in through the orchard."

"He made for the summer house," Pointer went on, "and lay down in one of the bedrooms there, after finding that you were not in your study. There he fell asleep. What sound it was that woke him, he says he doesn't know, but it brought him up all standing, with a feeling that there was something wrong. And something wrong there was! It must have been his cousin's body that he heard striking the flags below his window."

The colonel drew in his breath with a hiss.

"He heard no cry," Pointer went on quickly, for the other was labouring under an almost intolerable strain, "but only the sound of steps running down from the top of the look-out."

"Thank God!" murmured the soldier, covering his face with his hands for a moment. "But then—however, that's for later. He heard no cry, you say? Thank God for that, too!"

"It was an instantaneous death, if ever there was one," Pointer assured him. "Your son opened his window, but the sky was overcast. He saw something rush past, below, bent double like a wild animal. And a wild, savage animal it was, true enough. He would have gone out to investigate, but just then came the sound of all your voices, as you went out after that shot."

"And I still don't understand that shot!" burst out Scarlett.

"Patience just a bit longer, sir. Being so ill, and weary after his walk, the commissioner lay down and fell asleep again at once. When he awoke the second time, it was half-past twelve. He remembered the steps running down the outside stairs, and the sudden rush past below. Curiosity, mingled with an odd sense of unease, he says, made him go out on to the flags. He stumbled headlong over Miss Charteris's body lying in a little pool of blood from the wound in her head where it had struck the edge of a flower-pot. That frightful shock brought on an attack. I confess when I think of some of the fancies those broken flower-pots gave rise to in my mind—"

Pointer shook his head. Then he went on, "You found him, colonel? How?"

"I heard him. Heard the noise he made. Don't ask me to describe the scene. I rushed into the dining-room for brandy. I wasn't sure that nothing could be done for Rose. That'll tell you how rattled I was! Mrs. Lane was awake and downstairs. She came to see if she could help. God bless that woman. I can't begin to tell what she was to me that night. It wasn't only what she did, but how she did it. She tried to bring Rose round, but by that time I had got my second wind. I knew a broken neck for what it was. Not only was Rose dead, but she had been dead a couple of hours or so when I found her—"

"What time?"

"Midnight almost exactly. I lifted Reggie into the summer house. He was unconscious, but I tied him up, in case he should come around before I had settled what to do."

"What did you tie him with?"

Scarlett had to think a moment.

"I went to my study for some rope I had there, but I had given it to the count. I had more of the same kind downstairs, however."

"Around some cases of Indian chutney?"

Scarlett nodded. He looked surprised.

"Then we put my poor niece's hat that we got from her bedroom on her head, as though she had been out, and added her sketching box. I cut away a strip of green paint on the back of her dress, and teased the place to make it look as though torn. Then," he gnawed his moustache for a moment, "then we rolled the poor girl up in my travelling rug, tied it top and bottom with the rest of the cord, lifted it on to a sort of carrier that happened. to be standing on the flags, and Mrs. Lane put on Rose's shoes and walked down to the sand-pit behind me. Anything was better than having what we thought the truth suspected. Anything!"

"What dress did Mrs. Lane wear?"

"She had on a light dressing-gown when I saw her first. She changed it for something dark lying on the hall table—I don't know what, nor whose. She thought the stains wouldn't show on it. By the way, *I* wheeled Rose to the sand-pit. *I* suggested the place. Mrs. Lane did nothing but carry out my suggestions. Nothing whatever, Chief Inspector."

"Why did she take that fearful risk? I can see why you, sir, thinking your son had killed his cousin in a seizure, took it, but Mrs. Lane?"

The colonel did not reply for a moment. "Is this confidential?"

"About Mrs. Lane? Absolutely!"

"It will surprise you to learn that Mrs. Lane is really Mrs. Thornton. Her father was an old Eton chum of mine. She left Thornton for some woman's whim of his having married her for her money. I came on her later as a half-starved waitress in a bun-shop. Mrs. Lane is a proud woman. Thornton had been poor in those days and she rich. Now the position was reversed, she would have starved, or gone out altogether, rather than turn to him. But when I offered her the post of my lady-housekeeper she took it. I hoped it might bring them together again. For a time I thought it was no good, but I heard to-day from him that they're off for a year's cruise together next week. Mrs. Lane, to call her by her name in my house, has that rarest gift on earth—a grateful heart. She felt that she owed me something for giving her a post where she could keep in touch with her husband, and try to get him back. Not that I ever saw her try."

"I know," broke in Pointer, with his eye on the clock behind the other, "I thought that gratitude must be the key. Well, sir, you lifted the body on to the truck, and wheeled it to the sand-pit. Mrs. Lane walking behind, and helping to steer. You backed it under the trees of the copse, and carried the body down by the back shelving way, and left it in the pit?"

The colonel breathed hard

"God forgive me, yes. Horrible! But it seemed necessary. Mrs. Lane knelt and said a prayer before we left. Then we walked back by the main road. I wheeled the carrier to close behind the garage. Mrs. Lane crumpled up Rose's bed. Then we took my son, and the rug we had used for Rose, away in Thornton's big car, which Mrs. Lane got him to lend her without asking the reason. My own was too difficult to get out, with Wilkins sleeping overhead, and too noisy. Mrs. Lane blurred over the tracks we made in the lane in a little two-seater afterwards. We drove to a Doctor Bodley, who had suggested the Genoa sun cure and knew the whole story. He rang up Sir Martin Martineau's home, and arranged matters so that nothing should leak out. My boy's whole future was at stake. At least, we thought nothing had leaked out, but—"

"It didn't *leak* out! We only learnt what we know as the result of quite a bit of—eh—routine work," Pointer assured him.

"He had an operation, " the colonel continued. "The surgeons found a splinter of steel from that old shell wound pressing on the brain. The motor accident had only aggravated it. He's as right as rain now, with no more chance of any trouble of that kind. But you know all this. You know the whole story. According to you, I shan't have to break his heart by telling him that he—" suddenly Colonel Scarlett's eyes fairly seemed to turn to glass. "There's no mistake?" he asked in a croaking, harsh voice. "There isn't a catch somewhere? You *know* Reggie is innocent?"

Pointer nodded,. "I do, sir."

The colonel relaxed again. He sank back into his chair and drew a couple if deep breaths. That had been an awful moment just now, when he had wondered if this were a police trap.

"But who was the murder? Who was it? Of course I know it was no tramp—but, for God's sake, who did it? Not—not the count?"

Pointer did not reply.

"And afterwards, sir?"

"We got back before any one was up, and spent the time making sure, as we thought, that no traces had been left. As early as I dared, I cut down the branches of the tree below the outlook where my poor niece had gone crashing through. They were badly broken. I gave out that I had had an accident with the ladder, but that no one was to do anything to the place until further orders."

There was a short silence.

"The difficulty will be," Pointer said slowly, and studying his boot-tips as though they might have a word to say on the subject, too, "the difficulty will be, how to keep all this part of it out of the trial. I don't mind telling you that the criminal is going to arrested shortly. But about this moving of the body from the summer house—the chief commissioner thinks with me that we had better deny all knowledge of that. It's up to the murderer to prove who did shift the dead girl. It won't alter the verdict one way or another. I think I can go bail, that, without the help of Scotland Yard, no one will be able to get at the truth. So silence on your part, sir, is the best thing."

The colonel agreed forcefully.

"And now, sir, I'm sorry to tell you that Professor Charteris has met with an accident while in the Dolomites. The exact explanation comes into my fuller report, but I think you should know at once that you brother-in-law is dead."

The colonel was deeply shocked. He had had a hard time lately, and he was very fond of the professor.

"Climbing accident, I suppose," he muttered after some minutes. "and there, too—when he didn't turn up. I wondered if my poor son—that cable of the Genoese doctors terrified me, Pointer, as I've never been terrified before. You do hear of such things when it's a question of homicidal mania. That was why I had some Italian papers sent to me—to learn if—if—he stopped—"

"You took the letter of the professor's to his daughter that accompanied the enclosure, didn't you, sir?" Pointer prompted again.

"Yes. It was in Italian. I was nervy that nothing should leak out about Genoa. The professor has—had—the kindest heart in the world, but he was a dreadful chap to let things slip out. And Rose had a way of leaving her letters around. The word Genoa hit me in the eye. And I took it till I could have some one skim through it, and tell me if it were safe. I meant to get Sir Henry to just run it through for me, but he wasn't in. Then Mrs. Lane suggested that she could do it. She bought a dictionary in Medchester and worked it out on Thursday night in a restaurant near by. She only slipped into the concert hall at the very end. Of course, we intended to return the letter to my niece at once that was why the hurry—if there was nothing about my son in it. But next morning—I'm afraid I don't know what's become of that letter. Mrs. Lane doesn't remember what she did with it either—"

"And Miss Charteris's papers—you didn't take them, I suppose?"

"Take them? Surely the police took them. I went through them first, I confess, to see if any of my son's letters were there. He was a bit in love with my niece. That's why I pressed for the di Monti engagement before Reggie should come home on sick leave, before matters got so bad with his head that he had to go to that 'cure'. I didn't want a marriage between them. Cousins. Apart from—well, many things. I knew Bellairs wasn't a marrying man. But one thing did strike me, Pointer. There wasn't a line of her father's among her papers. I had put all his letters to me in my safe in the city when I went up to town that Friday, just in case of any reference to my son, but what became of his to her. I can't imagine."

Pointer could. He knew. He rose to his feet now.

"And Lady Maxwell? Why did you act the day of the funeral as though you—well—were disturbed by her presence?"

Colonel Scarlett flushed.

"Between ourselves, if a woman could marry a man against his will, I should be a re-married man. See?"

Pointer saw.

"Also I wasn't sure that she had heard or seen nothing that Thursday night."

"And Miss Scarlett, does she know?"

"Trust a mere girl with facts that could ruin her brother's whole future? My dear fellow, Sibella couldn't keep a secret to save her life! My only terror was lest she should guess, or had guessed, something of the truth. I was afraid she had. I suppose I can't ask how in the world you found it all out?"

"Just routine work, sir. I went wildly astray about those broken flower pots at first. You would have done much better to've confided in us from the start, though I will acknowledge that in this case the position was difficult for you."

"Difficult? It was damnable. But I still don't see how you got on to my son's presence in Europe, when the Nairobi papers reported his progress week by week around Mombassa."

"It was something I heard in town, after I got on the track of a man having been taken to the nursing home."

And the colonel never knew that it was the kiss that he had given Mrs. Lane which had first opened Pointer's eyes to the true, the only possible explanation.

A man does not kiss a woman with whom he is not in love, and Pointer was certain that there neither was, nor ever had been, any love between the colonel and his lady-housekeeper, because a man whom one, or both, has badly injured is safely in a nursing home. Gratitude alone, he thought, could explain that little scene. A sudden burst of gratitude for loyal help. Scarlett had no male relatives but his son. Granted it could be that son, which it apparently could not be, then all became coherent. The operation suggested brain trouble. That suggested some epileptic-like seizure, which explained the singular way the plants were broken, the lashing of arms and legs on the stone flags. Pointer attacked the apparent proof of the commissioner's presence in Uganda. Found he could pierce it, and had the facts worried out for him while he was in Italy. He had read the report in Paris. Now the last lap was in sight Pointer's heart beat quicker as he entered the middle room. The business of taking the imprints of each man's fists was done exactly as on the first day, except that there was no accident this time. The typewriters of the constables in the outer room drowned all possibility of talking, until Pointer sent out word, asking them to defer, their activities until later in the day. The two commissioners came in as they were finishing.

"They look excellently taken. How soon can you pour in the plaster?" the Assistant Commissioner asked. "This ought to help forward the case."

"It will settle it, sir," Pointer said quietly.

The Chief Commissioner affected surprise. As for the men, who were just preparing to leave, they started as though each had been shot.

"Yes, sir" Pointer repeated, "this will end the case."

"Suppose you tell us just how we stand at present," suggested the Commissioner. "Let's all sit down again and hear it."

Every one sat.

Watts, too, took a seat, after putting the plates on one side. He chose a chair in the centre of the doorway, and quietly locked the door. He had a civilian assistant this time, who bore the not uncommon name of O'Connor.

"The details'll come out later, sir," Pointer began, "but as we are at present, this is how the case runs. Miss Charteris had an engagement that Thursday evening with Mr. Bellairs in his studio. He was painting her portrait. Count di Monti had learnt of her visits, and arrived on the scene. Miss Charteris had been fetched by a friend, but the count and Mr. Bellairs quarrelled over her."

Both men looked as though they would like to break in, but Pointer's impassive, eye held them, while he passed on.

"The count, as an additional proof of her presence, took away a letter that Miss Charteris had left behind her by accident. It was the enclosure that her father had sent her in her letter of the afternoon. When Count di Monti learnt of the 'accident', as it was called, to her, he at once handed this letter to a friend's brother who was starting that same Friday morning for Italy. It was posted back from Milan to the professor's club. Miss Charteris missed it at once when she returned to her room, and went to the top of the summer house to speak to you about it, Mr. Bellairs. She had asked you to meet her there as soon as you could come. Evidently ten was the hour one or other of you set. I take it she had asked you to let her know how things had gone between you and Count di Monti. She was sure you would quarrel. You decided not to go."

A chuckle came from di Monti.

"I decided for him."

"Had you gone," Pointer still spoke to the artist, "you might have postponed, but you would not have changed the end. The murderer caught sight of her standing alone under the light of the electric lantern up above. He thought that she was there to hand on the enclosure. He switched off the light, ran up the stairs, possibly made some comment about the lamp being out of order, and then as she leant back, perhaps to look at it, an arm was thrust under her knees, and she was flung full force backwards on to the flags below, breaking her neck as she struck them, and cutting her head on a flower pot."

There was one collective gasp from the room.

"As far as we know, she didn't even cry out. Had she done so, and had it been heard, he would have been the first to shout for help, we may be sure, and rush down to see if anything could be done for her. But he would have taken her silver chain bag just the same. Either from the top, where she had dropped it, or from beside her—"

"The bag?" Scarlett said in a dazed voice

"The bag which had held the enclosed letter. Miss Charteris was murdered for the sake of something which, her father was believed, quite erroneously, to have sent her. And now I am sorry to say I have to tell you about another death. Professor Charteris was murdered, too. He was killed in Northern Italy, for the same reason that cost his daughter her life By sheer accident he was present when a so-called Bulgarian traveller was killed. But the man was not a Bulgarian. He was Neumann, the great secret leader of the Soviet spy system. On him was a paper in cipher giving the names of all the chief Bolshevik agents in Europe. As a matter of fact, the professor never saw that paper, or knew of its existence. But the men with Neumann knew that he had helped their friend into the hospital, saw him reading a similar slip of paper on the hospital steps, followed him, and killed him in a lonely valley, where they could rifle his pockets. In his letter-case they found the receipt for a registered letter sent off immediately after his visit to the hospital."

So still was the room that the ticking of the watch which each man wore could be heard.

"But to go back to Miss Charteris's murderer. He had received news that a paper had been sent her which must at all costs be intercepted, and at once. If she had read it, she, too, was to be killed. The professor, being one of the finest cipher readers in the world, might very likely have written her the real names which were hidden in that apparent Russian poem. I think the murderer asked her about that letter before he flung her over. Miss Charteris, very much upset by the evening's events, as we know from her maid, forgot, I think, that she had taken it out, and spoke of it as still there. In any case, he jumped to the conclusion that it was there, and that she had read it. Now, he has the bag, the girl is dead, but he has no letter. He feels sure, however, from what she had said, that nothing had been done with it. It will be in her room, and he must get it later. He notices, for the first time, that when he stooped far over the rail to watch her fall, he smeared green paint on the inside of each hand. Not enough to show when close, perhaps, but enough to have some very awkward questions asked, should her body be discovered at once, as it may be. When we saw the smudges left by the two hand-grips on that painted rail," Pointer identified himself with Harris and Rodman by a glance, "we realised that the murderer must have had some way of getting the marks off. Water wouldn't touch them, nor would mere wiping do. He could neither take the time to thoroughly clean his hands then, nor chance its not being noticed. He had to return immediately and go on with the game, or risk comment. Yes," in answer to the distended eyes fixed on him, "the murder was committed by 'dummy' in the few minutes during which a hand was being played at bridge that Thursday evening. That was why that shot was trumped up, and a false alarm given—"

And then the Assistant Commissioner jumped. He stumbled over some one's legs, the table was between him and his object, but he grappled fiercely for a second. But with a laugh which was like a neigh, Cockburn got the hand with the ring he wore to his mouth, and bit off the small black pearl. It cracked like a glass phial between his teeth.

"Too late, Pelham, and there's no power on earth can stop or alter the stuff I've taken. Surely you never thought you could hang me!"

The Assistant Commissioner took it hard. His face worked silently. As for Pointer, he had sprung to his feet, too, with Harris and Rodman. The Chief Inspector rapped out an oath as the apparent pearl crunched, and that was something no one there had ever heard him do before. Now he sat down with the bitter look of a man who sees the best part of what he has worked for torn from him.

He made a visible effort to be calm, however, and turned to Cockburn.

"I must caution you that anything—"

Cockburn rocked in ghastly merriment. "My good fellow, you don't understand. What do you suppose I had in this little pearl of mine? This mourning ring I've taken to wearing lately? Something for a headache? In an hour from now, to the minute, I shall fall asleep, and nothing you can do or try to do, will prevent me from drifting painlessly into oblivion. That being so, I'm quite ready to oblige with any information—"

"I caution you that it may be used against you."

"You do, oh most excellent policeman!" mocked Cockburn.

Suddenly Bond came to life. With a slack jaw and a whitening face he had been staring as if numbed by what had happened.

"Those Polish papers," he suddenly turned on the man beside him, "I ought to've guessed when I caught you with them! Give me his keys somebody; I wouldn't touch him with a barge-pole, and his confederates may have them already in their hands."

Snatching the keys from Watts, Bond fairly raced from the room. Watts relocked the door behind him.

"Dear me," Cockburn yawned, "Bond always is impetuous. And now, Pointer, would you like me to help you out? I'm afraid the cipher—"

"It was read at the Yard an hour after I got it safely home. But we knew it was you very early in the case. Who but you raised that cry of a rifle shot and spoke of poachers. Then changed it to a revolver shot when Miss Charteris's death was no longer looked on as an accideneny. Then once more, to twist the case still again to serve ends, as you thought, you changed it to the sound of burst tyre from Count di Monti's car. That sally-out all together gave you the chance you needed that night. This chance of cleaning your hands with petrol at the garage after rubbing them well into the earth, and on all the grass of the hedge banks. Even if a smear remained, it would be set down to the hunt in the dark. The leaves in Miss Charteris's hand showed that she was killed before it came on to rain. That fitted the time all right when you were in the garden. You egged Mr. Bond on to break into Stillwater House with you on the plea of looking for more of that cord which you had seen given to the count. What you wanted were Professor Charteris's letters. All of them. You had let yourself into Miss Rose's empty rooms that same Thursday night after you murdered her, and taken all the papers you could find which were in the Professor's writing. But the paper you thought he had sent her, the enclosure you had seen pulled out at the tea table, wasn't among them. So you had that tool of the

Bolsheviks, Rebecca Apfelbaum, hunt for it in the Professor's rooms next morning on the chance that Miss Charteris had run up to town with it on Thursday evening after dinner. You got all her papers next evening, to make trebly sure, when you stepped in for a chat with the chief constable after dinner—to ask how he was getting on."

Cockburn turned on him. "So you set me on to ferreting out about di Monti's alibi being rotten, while you knew the truth all the time? I wish I'd guessed that—then." There was a sudden glint in the shallow, shifting colour of Cockburn's eyes like a mad dog's.

"It kept you from suspecting that we did know the truth," Pointer answered coldly.

"I spoofed you that night at Stillwater, anyway," Cockburn jeered, "whatever you may have found out later."

"Not a bit. I should have suspected you by that alone, if I hadn't done so already, from what Mr. Thornton told me of the alarm that no one else heard. Within an hour I had that little oil can of yours from the tools in your car. It held just the same oil as that with which Miss Charteris's door had been treated. Some Russian blend, I suppose. Anyway, we can't match it in England. Your bedroom door at Red Gates and her doors alone show it. A bad break that. You meant to kill her in her room that night—strangle her, I think—if no earlier chance came.

"And as for that matchbox, which would let you seem to prove where you hadn't been standing, when you strolled around the grounds as dummy—you dropped that Friday morning while walking about after breakfast with Mr. Thornton and Mr. Bond. It fell bottom side up. I found it quite dry, though the pattern on it would have held the slightest drop of rain. It was obviously dropped after that downpour, and when you knew about the sandpit. By bad luck, too, it had fallen on a starling's tracks made that morning earlier when he had been hunting for breakfast. Oh, we've been watching you for some time, but it was the lack of motive that we wanted to get hold of, and any possible accomplices. You had none. And as to the motive—that was supplied by finding your name on the cipher list as the British agent for distribution of Bolshevik funds. We've been hunting that agent for years. There's nothing this man can tell us, sir."

Pointer turned to the Assistant Commissioner. Cockburn broke in sharply.

"Not so fast, please. How am I supposed to have moved the body, of Miss Charteris from the summer house? Forgive my curiosity, but as I shall not be able to learn the truth of that interesting, and I confess baffling, fact at the trial—-"

Pointer looked bored.

"You had your arrangements made, I take it."

"I?" Cockburn stiffened. "I've just told you that knew nothing about it, and would like to hear the explanation. It was the count's doing, I'll swear, though why—"

"That's not the question," Pointer went on carelessly. "It's the motive for the crime that concerns us, not why she was moved when dead."

He turned again to the Commissioner for a moment, then back again to Cockburn.

"As I say, sir, we have the motive now. It was just sheer greed. Wanting more money. The love of secret power. Mr. Bond was getting into your debt. In time you intended to wring a very full payment out of him. I think he may be thankful indeed we caught you before that. As to your hostility to Count di Monti—that, course, is due to the count's anti-Communist activities. You sent him, however, a warning letter that I was coming to Italy to arrest him, in the hope that something would happen to me. You thought it might be as well to choke off the C.I.D. for a time."

"I was right. You have blundered on the truth," Cockburn said arrogantly. His gentle, pleasant mask was off now. It could no longer serve him.

"The only blunder in this story was the needless, useless murder down at Stillwater. I hope you realise that truth now. Had Miss Charteris not been killed, that letter-case with the incriminating letter in it would have been sent back to Sofia by the doctor, or the sister-in-charge, unread, unguessed at even."

"Miss Charteris misled me by her manner when I spoke to her in the summer house," Cockburn said sombrely. "She misled me completely, or this blunder, as you call it, would never have happened. I certainly have cause to regret it. But she spoke so wildly. I do not consider myself dull-witted, but I had to decide quickly for the best. I made sure she had received the de-coded list and had read it. So unfortunately—"

Pointer nodded. to Harris, who clicked on the handcuffs with a quite unprofessional gleam of pleasure in his eyes. Cockburn glared around the room.

"So you won't spare me this last indignity? You want me to die in your beastly irons? But I've tricked you. In an hour I'm away from all this."

Harris propelled him, none too gently, to the door. They heard Cockburn's snarled injunction to him to keep his hands off a gentleman as it closed.

Di Monti was the first to throw off the spell, and rose to his feet.

"Do I understand that the game that has been played with me is now over?" he asked very politely. His voice was ice over a volcano.

"This wasn't some idea of getting even with you, Count di Monti. It was vitally necessary that Mr. Cockburn shouldn't suspect we suspected him. At the F. O. could have laid his hands on any passport he liked. He was shadowed closely from the first by Inspector Watts, and relays of men from private investigation bureaus. And what about attempted murder?" Pointer spoke temperately but with inward warmth. "Think yourself lucky to have got off with no worse than a warning."

"Lucky!" Di Monti tossed him the word back contemptuously. "Lucky! In death, as in life, she brought me bad luck."

"You deserve a stiff term of imprisonment, Count di Monti," Pointer began tying up some papers before him "but though I'm a policeman, and say it, I think every man's punishment lies waiting for him, whether he get by law or not."

It was almost as though Pointer could read the near future, could see a blazing plane crash, could watch the charred body of the airman lifted out on to hot Tunisian sand, and know it for what it was—di Monti's.

Without another glance at the room, the Italian stalked out. O'Connor closed the door behind him.

The Assistant Commissioner had paid no heed to the little scene.

"Yes, Cockburn's tricked us," he muttered in anguish after the others, still silent under the spell of what they had heard, had gone.

"He's done us, right enough, at the end. He'll die a nice, quiet death before the hour's over. Why the devil didn't you keep your feet under you, Pointer? It's not like you, of all men!"

"It's not as bad as you think, sir," Pointer interrupted tranquilly. "We noticed that Mr. Cockburn began wearing a ring just after Miss Charteris's death, so naturally, as a matter of routine, we had it examined that first time the casts of the hands were taken."

He did not explain that that was the sole reason for that performance. Even superiors need not know everything until the last day.

"The room was so tight, that the rings were put on that ledge behind there. A sliding panel had been cut in the back, and to-day, while the typewriters in the outer room clicked like hall-stones on a tin roof, the pearl that we had made was substituted for the other. Mr. Cockburn swallowed a small black ball of properly prepared flavoured soap enclosed in glass. When he discovers the truth, I shouldn't wonder if there was quite a storm scene."

And there was.

THE END

Other Resurrected Press Books in *The Chief Inspector Pointer Mystery* Series

Death of John Tait
Murder at the Nook
Mystery at the Rectory
Scarecrow
The Case of the Two Pearl Necklaces
The Charteris Mystery
The Eames-Erskine Case
The Footsteps that Stopped
The Clifford Affair
The Cluny Problem
The Craig Poisoning Mystery
The Net Around Joan Ingilby
The Tall House Mystery
The Wedding-Chest Mystery
The Westwood Mystery
Tragedy at Beechcroft

Mysteries by Anne Austin

Murder at Bridge

When an afternoon bridge party attended by some of Hamilton's leading citizens ends with the hostess being murdered in her boudoir, Special Investigator Dundee of the District Attorney's office is called in. But one of the attendees is guilty? There are plenty of suspects: the victim's former lover, her current suitor, the retired judge who is being blackmailed, the victim's maid who had been horribly disfigured accidentally by the murdered woman, or any of the women who's husbands had flirted with the victim. Or was she murdered by an outsider whose motive had nothing to do with the town of Hamilton. Find the answer in . . . **Murder at Bridge**

One Drop of Blood

When Dr. Koenig, head of Mayfield Sanitarium is murdered, the District Attorney's Special Investigator, "Bonnie" Dundee must go undercover to find the killer. Were any of the inmates of the asylum insane enough to have committed the crime? Or, was it one of the staff, motivated by jealousy? And what was is the secret in the murdered man's past. Find the answer in . . . **One Drop of Blood**

AVAILABLE FROM RESURRECTED PRESS!

THE EDWARDIAN DETECTIVES
LITERARY SLEUTHS OF THE EDWARDIAN ERA

The exploits of the great Victorian Detectives, Poe's C. Auguste Dupin, Gaboriau's Lecoq, and most famously, Arthur Conan Doyle's Sherlock Holmes, are well known. But what of those fictional detectives that came after, those of the Edwardian Age? The period between the death of Queen Victoria and the First World War had been called the Golden Age of the detective short story, but how familiar is the modern reader with the sleuths of this era? And such an extraordinary group they were, including in their numbers an unassuming English priest, a blind man, a master of disguises, a lecturer in medical jurisprudence, a noble woman working for Scotland Yard, and a savant so brilliant he was known as "The Thinking Machine."

To introduce readers to these detectives, Resurrected Press has assembled a collection of stories featuring these and other remarkable sleuths in The Edwardian Detectives.

- The Case of Laker, Absconded by Arthur Morrison
- The Fenchurch Street Mystery by Baroness Orczy
- The Crime of the French Café by Nick Carter
- The Man with Nailed Shoes by R Austin Freeman
- The Blue Cross by G. K. Chesterton
- The Case of the Pocket Diary Found in the Snow by Augusta Groner
- The Ninescore Mystery by Baroness Orczy
- The Riddle of the Ninth Finger by Thomas W. Hanshew
- The Knight's Cross Signal Problem by Ernest Bramah

- The Problem of Cell 13 by Jacques Futrelle
- The Conundrum of the Golf Links by Percy James Brebner
- The Silkworms of Florence by Clifford Ashdown
- The Gateway of the Monster by William Hope Hodgson
- The Affair at the Semiramis Hotel by A. E. W. Mason
- The Affair of the Avalanche Bicycle & Tyre Co., LTD by Arthur Morrison

RESURRECTED PRESS CLASSIC MYSTERY CATALOGUE

Journeys into Mystery
Travel and Mystery in a More Elegant Time

The Edwardian Detectives
Literary Sleuths of the Edwardian Era

Gems of Mystery
Lost Jewels from a More Elegant Age

E. C. Bentley
Trent's Last Case: The Woman in Black

Ernest Bramah
Max Carrados Resurrected:
The Detective Stories of Max Carrados

Agatha Christie
The Secret Adversary
The Mysterious Affair at Styles

Octavus Roy Cohen
Midnight

Freeman Wills Croft
The Ponson Case
The Pit Prop Syndicate

J. S. Fletcher
The Herapath Property
The Rayner-Slade Amalgamation
The Chestermarke Instinct
The Paradise Mystery
Dead Men's Money

The Middle of Things
Ravensdene Court
Scarhaven Keep
The Orange-Yellow Diamond
The Middle Temple Murder
The Tallyrand Maxim
The Borough Treasurer
In the Mayor's Parlour
The Saftey Pin

R. Austin Freeman

The Mystery of 31 New Inn from the Dr. Thorndyke Series
John Thorndyke's Cases from the Dr. Thorndyke Series
The Red Thumb Mark from The Dr. Thorndyke Series
The Eye of Osiris from The Dr. Thorndyke Series
A Silent Witness from the Dr. John Thorndyke Series
The Cat's Eye from the Dr. John Thorndyke Series
Helen Vardon's Confession: A Dr. John Thorndyke Story
As a Thief in the Night: A Dr. John Thorndyke Story
Mr. Pottermack's Oversight: A Dr. John Thorndyke Story
Dr. Thorndyke Intervenes: A Dr. John Thorndyke Story
The Singing Bone: The Adventures of Dr. Thorndyke
The Stoneware Monkey: A Dr. John Thorndyke Story
The Great Portrait Mystery, and Other Stories: A Collection of Dr. John Thorndyke and Other Stories
The Penrose Mystery: A Dr. John Thorndyke Story
The Uttermost Farthing: A Savant's Vendetta

Arthur Griffiths

The Passenger From Calais
The Rome Express

Fergus Hume
The Mystery of a Hansom Cab
The Green Mummy
The Silent House
The Secret Passage

Edgar Jepson
The Loudwater Mystery

A. E. W. Mason
At the Villa Rose

A. A. Milne
The Red House Mystery
Baroness Emma Orczy
The Old Man in the Corner

Edgar Allan Poe
The Detective Stories of Edgar Allan Poe

Arthur J. Rees
The Hampstead Mystery
The Shrieking Pit
The Hand In The Dark
The Moon Rock
The Mystery of the Downs

Mary Roberts Rinehart
Sight Unseen and The Confession

Dorothy L. Sayers
Whose Body?

Sir William Magnay
The Hunt Ball Mystery

Mabel and Paul Thorne
The Sheridan Road Mystery

Louis Tracy
The Strange Case of Mortimer Fenley
The Albert Gate Mystery
The Bartlett Mystery
The Postmaster's Daughter
The House of Peril
The Sandling Case: What Would You Have Done?
Charles Edmonds Walk
The Paternoster Ruby

John R. Watson
The Mystery of the Downs
The Hampstead Mystery

Edgar Wallace
The Daffodil Mystery
The Crimson Circle

Carolyn Wells
Vicky Van
The Man Who Fell Through the Earth
In the Onyx Lobby
Raspberry Jam
The Clue
The Room with the Tassels
The Vanishing of Betty Varian
The Mystery Girl
The White Alley
The Curved Blades
Anybody but Anne
The Bride of a Moment
Faulkner's Folly
The Diamond Pin
The Gold Bag
The Mystery of the Sycamore
The Come Backy

Raoul Whitfield
Death in a Bowl

And much more!
Visit ResurrectedPress.com
for our complete catalogue

About Resurrected Press

A division of Intrepid Ink, LLC, Resurrected Press is dedicated to bringing high quality, vintage books back into publication. See our entire catalogue and find out more at www.ResurrectedPress.com.

About Intrepid Ink, LLC

Intrepid Ink, LLC provides full publishing services to authors of fiction and non-fiction books, eBooks and websites. From editing to formatting, from publishing to marketing, Intrepid Ink gets your creative works into the hands of the people who want to read them. Find out more at www.IntrepidInk.com.

CPSIA information can be obtained at www.ICGtesting.com
Printed in the USA
BVOW06s2339100815

412729BV00016B/69/P

9 781937 022815